"**Ms. Merritt pens a well-crafted romance solid in snappy repartee and entertaining characters.**"
—*Romantic Times Magazine*

* * * *

After closing the door, Blythe leaned weakly against it. When they'd been lovers Brent had often told her how beautiful her eyes were. He'd been complimentary about so many things—her legs, her laugh, her intelligence. He had been her first lover, and he'd been so wonderfully kind and patient with her.

Abruptly she moved from the door, telling herself she shouldn't be thinking of those things.

After all, they could never be more than the most casual of acquaintances again. Remembering their romantic past was out of the question.

But how could she forget?

Dear Reader,

It's the most festive time of the year! And Special Edition is celebrating with six sparkling romances for you to treasure all season long.

Those MORGAN'S MERCENARIES are back by popular demand with bestselling author Lindsay McKenna's brand-new series, MORGAN'S MERCENARIES: THE HUNTERS. Book one, *Heart of the Hunter,* features the first of four fearless brothers who are on a collision course with love—and danger. And in January, the drama and adventure continues with Lindsay's provocative Silhouette Single Title release, *Morgan's Mercenaries:Heart of the Jaguar.*

Popular author Penny Richards brings you a poignant THAT'S MY BABY! story for December. In *Their Child,* a ranching heiress and a rugged rancher are married for the sake of *their* little girl, but their platonic arrangement finally blossoms into a passionate love. Also this month, the riveting PRESCRIPTION: MARRIAGE medical miniseries continues with an unlikely romance between a mousy nurse and the man of her secret dreams in *Dr. Devastating* by Christine Rimmer. And don't miss Sherryl Woods's 40th Silhouette novel, *Natural Born Lawman,* a tale about two willful opposites attracting—the latest in her AND BABY MAKES THREE: THE NEXT GENERATION miniseries.

Just in time for the holidays, award-winning author Marie Ferrarella delivers a *Wife in the Mail*—a heartwarming story about a gruff widower who falls for his brother's jilted mail-order bride. And long-buried family secrets are finally revealed in *The Secret Daughter* by Jackie Merritt, the last book in THE BENNING LEGACY crossline miniseries.

I hope you enjoy all our romance novels this month. All of us at Silhouette Books wish you a wonderful holiday season!

Sincerely,
Karen Taylor Richman
Senior Editor

Please address questions and book requests to:
Silhouette Reader Service
U.S.: 3010 Walden Ave., P.O. Box 1325, Buffalo, NY 14269
Canadian: P.O. Box 609, Fort Erie, Ont. L2A 5X3

JACKIE MERRITT

THE SECRET DAUGHTER

SPECIAL EDITION®

Published by Silhouette Books
America's Publisher of Contemporary Romance

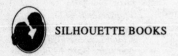

SILHOUETTE BOOKS

ISBN 0-373-24218-2

THE SECRET DAUGHTER

Printed in U.S.A.

JACKIE MERRITT

and her husband live in the Southwest. An accountant for many years, Jackie has happily traded numbers for words. Next to family, books are her greatest joy. She started writing in 1987, and her efforts paid off in 1988 with the publication of her first novel. When she's not writing or enjoying a good book, Jackie dabbles in watercolor painting and likes playing the piano in her spare time.

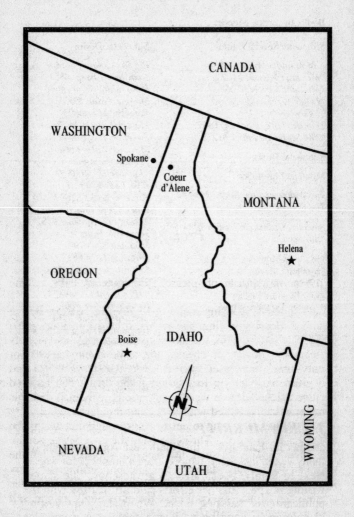

Prologue

"No…no…please, oh, please! Don't take my baby. Let me see it, *please!*"

The plaintive, pleading sound of her own voice woke Blythe Benning. Heart pounding, she sat up, drinking in great gulps of air. The same dream, she thought with a terrible melancholy as tears fell down her cheeks, the same dream again. For twenty-three years, ever since she was twenty years old and had given her baby up for adoption, the dream had haunted her. Occasionally there were long periods without it, but this summer it had occurred with agonizing regularity.

No, she was not going to put herself through that again! she thought almost angrily. Throwing back the covers, she got up. She pulled on a robe, stuck her feet into slippers and left the bedroom to go downstairs to the kitchen, turning on every light she came to on her way. The kitchen lights were the brightest of all, and she could feel the quivering within herself start to dissipate in that pleasant room.

Drawing a deep breath to attain further calm, she ran water into the teakettle and placed it on the stove to heat. She would brew a pot of herbal tea, drink it slowly and pray for blessed forgetfulness. Sometimes the home remedy worked. It was one-thirty, she saw from the clock on the wall, and perhaps in an hour or so she would be able to return to bed and fall asleep again.

But that ritual had always worked best in her own home in Connecticut. Now she was in the house she'd grown up in, her parents' home—both of whom were deceased. And while waiting for the water in the teakettle to come to a boil, Blythe wondered if living here this summer wasn't the reason that the dream had become so persistent.

That conjecture stirred memories from last January. Myra Benning, Blythe's mother, had passed away, and her three daughters had gathered in this house to grieve. It had been years since the three of them, Tamara, Sierra and Blythe, had seen each other. The Benning family was unusual, inasmuch as ten years separated each sister from her siblings. Blythe was the oldest, forty-three, Sierra was thirty-three and Tamara was the youngest, twenty-three.

As could only be the case, the funeral had been an unhappy time for all of them. But putting their mutual grief aside, Blythe had realized that she hardly knew her two younger sisters. She had also realized that Sierra and Tamara felt the same reserve she did. Their conversations had been stilted, there had been very little sense of relationship and it had been obvious that all three women had felt that their common ground had died with their mother. They'd lost their father years before and now there was no connection at all between them. At least Myra had kept them informed, through letters and phone calls, of each other's lives. Because of that, Blythe had known about Tamara living in Texas and holding an impressive position in a large firm, and that Sierra was married to a lawyer and living in San Francisco.

But they had shared no confidences in January, which, once her sisters had left to return to their own homes, had struck Blythe as unnatural and distressingly sad. They'd had their mother's estate to contend with, of course, and after several discussions about it, Blythe had offered to obtain a leave of absence from the private school in Connecticut where she taught. She would remain in Coeur d'Alene, Idaho, and see to selling the Benning house and its contents.

Tamara and Sierra had agreed, with thanks, at once. The sisters had divided some of their mother's personal possessions, and had decided to delay a division of the remaining estate until everything was sold. They'd been sure the house would sell quickly.

"Don't count on it," several different Realtors had told Blythe when she'd contacted them right after her sisters' departure. In varying ways, they had said, "You have a splendid, well-kept home in one of Coeur d'Alene's elegant older neighborhoods, but it's old-fashioned by today's standards. It's probably going to take one very special buyer to come along, someone who relates age with charm, and no one can predict when that might happen."

Blythe had not been able to visualize herself twiddling her thumbs in Coeur d'Alene for an unknown period of time. At least in Connecticut she stayed busy with her classes. Work was her saving grace, her panacea, and slightly panicky over the idea of living in her parents' home with very little to keep her occupied, she had contacted her sisters and explained that she was leaving the house in the hands of a competent Realtor and returning to Connecticut. In June, when school closed for the summer, she'd come back to Coeur d'Alene, hoping ardently to get things settled there once and for all. It was now August, and she was beginning to worry that the house might never sell.

One very good thing had occurred during the past eight months, however; she had become closer to her sisters. They spoke on the phone, and she knew that Tamara had married a man named Sam Sherard, lived on a ranch in Texas and had given birth to triplets a month ago. During their last phone conversation, Tamara had sounded ecstatically happy.

Sierra had survived an awful ordeal this summer. She had divorced her unfaithful husband in San Francisco before setting out on a long car trip, then had a terrible car accident in

Montana that had caused her to lose her memory briefly. Happily, she was now married to a cattle rancher, Clint Barrow.

Thinking back on Tamara's triplets, Blythe's eyes became teary. She had sent exquisite gifts for the babies, and Tamara had sent her a dozen snapshots, which Blythe had studied until she had collapsed into a chair to cry her heart out. She had never even seen *her* baby. She didn't know if her child was a boy or a girl, she had no idea where he or she was and she probably never would.

Of course, her child was an adult now, but in those heartbreaking dreams that struck without mercy, her son or daughter was always an infant. An unseen infant that she could hear crying, and no matter how she begged, no one would bring the baby to her, or even talk to her about it.

The kettle whistled and, heaving a forlorn sigh, Blythe got up and prepared the tea. With a cup in hand, she returned to the table and resumed her seat. Sipping hot tea, she thought about the start of the fall school term being only a few weeks away, and worried about leaving the house still unsold and returning to Connecticut again.

"Oh, well," she murmured with a sigh, and reached for the teapot to refill her cup. Perhaps she should notify the administrator of her school in Connecticut that she would not be there for the fall semester and just let it go at that. Surely the house would sell before the winter semester began.

A feeling of abject loneliness struck her without warning. Suddenly the dream was upon her again. Worse than the loneliness were the memories of being nineteen and pregnant and not knowing which way to turn.

Although Blythe knew in her soul that she shouldn't be doing this when her spirits were sinking lower by the second, she got up, hurried to her bedroom and returned to the kitchen with her wallet. From it she withdrew three snapshots. The first one she studied was of her father. Harry Benning had been a doctor of medicine and a kindly, mild-mannered man. He had practiced in Coeur d'Alene and had become a highly respected member of the community. His old patient records were still in a room in the basement, filling a dozen file cabinets. Getting rid of those records was a chore Blythe had put off, as she wasn't quite sure how to go about it. In fact, during the months she'd been here this summer she had peered into the cluttered room one time and then quickly closed the door again. It would have to be taken care of, of course; she couldn't leave that room as it was for a new owner to contend with.

She set down her father's picture and picked up the one of her mother. Blythe had always thought this particular snapshot of Myra Benning portrayed her iron will better than any of the multitude of others in the family photo albums. A hundred memories of her mother bombarded Blythe; she could not think unkindly of her, but neither could she doubt which parent had worn the trousers in the Benning family.

Blythe laid the picture next to the one of her father and then reached for the third one.

Her breath caught in her throat, as it always did whenever she permitted herself to look at it. It was a photo of a handsome young man with a broad smile and tired eyes—the father of the baby she'd never held in her arms. He had dark, almost black hair and blue eyes, and she had loved him so much that instead of going to him when she'd discovered her pregnancy during her first year of college, she had come home to cry on her mother's shoulder, naively positive that Myra would come up with an idea that would make everything all right. Brent had been working two jobs to pay for his education, and Blythe hadn't wanted to add to his financial burden without some sort of suggestion as to how they would continue college and support a marriage and their child. Myra would know, she'd believed in her heart. Mother would know.

"Who is the father?" Myra asked, speaking sharply, expressing her disappointment and disapproval by her tone of voice. *"Or do you know?"*

Blythe would never forget that moment for as long as she lived. She had fallen back a few steps, weakened by shock, as though her mother had physically struck her.

The older Blythe got, the more astounded she became that she had let her mother take total charge of the situation. *"A baby is no way to begin a marriage! And how do you know that boy would marry you in the first place? I'm going to discuss this with your father, but I already know what you must do.''*

Blythe placed Brent's picture next to those of her parents. They were the people she had loved most during that period of her life. Brent had never been told why she had suddenly decided to transfer to a college in California. She had phoned him with the news, and he'd tried, halfheartedly, to talk her out of it. Maybe he'd been too exhausted or too caught up in his own problems to try harder. But his exhaustion and self-concern had been no worse than what she'd done. She had allowed her parents to locate a home for unwed mothers in a little town in Utah, she had signed papers giving up her child before it was born and she had consigned herself to a life of misery.

No, Brent's sins were minor compared to hers. If he had tried contacting her at the college in California, he would have naturally reached a dead end, and if he had tried phoning or writing to her Coeur d'Alene address, no one had ever told her about it.

She had never seen or talked to him again.

At three o'clock Blythe stumbled back to bed, then lay awake until dawn. Rarely did she permit herself to remember everything so acutely, because the aftermath was so painful. She knew she would feel like hell tomorrow and maybe even the day after. Besides, bouts of what she'd done to herself tonight made her feel terribly bitter toward her parents, and how in heaven's name would bitterness help now? The whole awful thing was her own fault, anyhow. She'd been nineteen years old, way past childhood, and she could have solved her dilemma either with Brent's help or on her own.

Perhaps that was the most painful thing of all—that instead of dealing with her problem like an adult, she had run home to her parents. And she'd known, she'd *always* known, how concerned her mother had been with propriety, or the appearance thereof.

"Your father is a man of importance in this town, and I will never permit his daughters to shame the Benning name."

It was Blythe's last thought before she finally fell into an exhausted, troubled sleep. Outside, the morning sun shone brightly; inside the Benning home, all was silent.

Brent spent his first day in Coeur d'Alene walking and studying the property for the new hotel and shopping complex he'd been hired to design. The developers had requested something tasteful, functional, environmentally compliant and visually striking. Brent had no doubt that he could produce such a design; he had every confidence in his architectural skills, and, in fact, had made a name for himself in the field.

Finding himself in Coeur d'Alene was a bit startling, however, and he couldn't help reliving some old memories as he eyed the land from every angle and direction. Those particular memories hadn't been disturbing in a good many years, but he still had to ask himself why Blythe Benning, the first love of his life, had left him flat the way she had. Of course, he probably wouldn't even be thinking about Blythe today if he wasn't in her hometown, he reasoned, and he certainly harbored no hopes of running into her. For one thing, he couldn't believe she would be living in Coeur d'Alene after all these years, but if, by some twist of fate, she was, what difference would it make to him?

"None," he said under his breath as he stooped down to visually measure the gradual slope of the property. "None at all." Straightening, he wrote in his notebook, "Check survey for estimated landfill." Thoughts of Blythe completely fled from his mind as architectural possibilities filled it.

He hung around for another hour, speculating, thinking and making notes, then returned to the motel room he'd rented late last night, and sat down at his computer. Switching it on, he was instantly absorbed in his work.

He went to bed at eleven that night, tired and yawning. But sleep didn't immediately take him, and his mind wandered. He was going to be in Coeur d'Alene for at least a year, possibly longer, depending on the project's progress. He never left a development of this size before completion. It would, he was certain, be another feather in his cap. He wasn't a braggart by any means, but he was privately very proud of his rise to success. He'd started with nothing but a hard-earned college degree, and today was a moderately wealthy man; he believed he had a right to feel proud of his accomplishments.

There *was* something he didn't like about his chosen career, however. He was rarely in Seattle, the place he considered home base and where he owned a house, and he hated motel rooms. Apartments were almost as bad, he'd come to feel after some bad experiences with noisy neighbors in apartment complexes. During several long-term projects he'd found a decent house to rent, but then a flash of inspiration had struck him in California two years ago, and instead of renting a house, he'd bought one. When his project was finished he'd sold the house for a nice little profit, and it occurred to him now, while lying in bed and staring at the ceiling, that he could probably do the same thing in Coeur d'Alene. One thing was certain, he was not going to spend a year in a motel room.

Deciding that he would take the time to talk to a real estate agent tomorrow or the next day, he turned on his side, closed his eyes and fell asleep.

Chapter One

"Brent, I'm certain we'll have no trouble at all in finding exactly the sort of home you're looking for," real estate agent Bill Harkens said with a broad smile. "Let's talk a little and narrow down your preferences. What price range should we be considering?"

Brent was seated across Harkens's desk. The real estate office contained numerous offices and cubicles. Other agents were busy with clients, talking on the phone or working with stacks of papers. Brent felt comfortable with his choice of Realtors, as Lowery's North Idaho Realty appeared to be a productive, active firm.

He smiled back at Bill Harkens. "More important to me than price, Bill, is resale value."

"Really? You're not looking for long-term housing then. Well, let's chat a bit. What about size? How many bedrooms do you need?"

"There's just myself, so two bedrooms should be enough."

"No family?"

"No," Brent said quietly, as a dull ache began in his gut.

He'd had a family once, a wife and a four-year-old daughter, both of whom had been killed in a car accident ten years ago. He could think of Debbie and tiny Lori now without agony, but just barely, and he didn't like reminders of that terrible tragedy.

But he understood Bill's reason for asking questions. "No family," he repeated soberly.

"I see," Bill said matter-of-factly. "Brent, are you new to Coeur d'Alene? I hope you'll excuse so many questions, but right now there's so much on the market to choose from, it helps to know a client's specific requirements."

"I understand. Okay, here are the facts. I'm an architect, working on a sizable project here in Coeur d'Alene. I'm sure you've heard about the Sunrise Hotel and Shopping Center. I know the newspaper has run several articles about it."

Bill sat up straighter. "Yes, I certainly have heard about it. People around here are especially excited about the shopping center. Do the developers have some big-name department stores coming in? That's what Coeur d'Alene really needs."

Brent grinned. "Sorry, Bill, but I'm not at liberty to discuss the developers' business. I'm sure it will all be detailed in the newspaper when they're ready to publicize their plans."

"I understand. Apparently you're going to oversee the project."

"Only as far as my architectural design goes. I should be in town for about a year."

"So you're looking for a house that you can sell at the end of that year." Bill frowned slightly. "Brent, I like to be totally honest and up-front with my clients. Right now the area is a bit overbuilt and there are some great buys out there. What no one can foresee—and I can't guarantee—is a change in the market, so that whatever you buy now will sell quickly a year from now."

"I'm not looking for guarantees, Bill. I understand that investing in real estate can be risky."

"In that case let's find you a home. Come on, let's take a ride." Bill gathered up some papers from his desk and got to his feet. Brent rose, too, and together they left the office and got in Bill's car.

That was the beginning of Brent juggling his work with house hunting. He saw so many houses that his head spun. He'd thought that finding the right house would be a relatively simple task, but it wasn't. Bill Harkens remained cheerful throughout, but after the third day Brent was beginning to feel impatient.

Actually, it was a process of elimination. All Brent had to do to eliminate some areas was to ride through them. ''No, this won't do,'' he would state emphatically as Bill drove through a particular subdivision or neighborhood, and the agent would turn around and head for another.

And, to his own annoyance, Brent kept finding himself changing his mind. ''Maybe I'd like living on one of the golf courses,'' he would tell Bill one day, only to decide the next that he'd rather be near the lake. At one point he asked the agent if all his clients were so difficult to please. Bill had merely chuckled and said, ''Most of them, yes. Don't worry about it, Brent. I'm used to it.''

At night Brent would fall into bed in his motel room exhausted. But he never immediately fell asleep, because his mind, of its own accord, kept going over the houses he'd viewed that day, along with the progress of the plans for the Sunrise project he was developing on his computer.

There was one other thing that had started eating at him. Without rhyme or reason he'd been doing a lot of thinking about Blythe Benning, which he blamed entirely on his being in her hometown. Regardless, she was in his thoughts far too often. Their college romance had happened a long time ago and had lasted only a few months. What he strove very hard to remember was *why* it had lasted only a few months. He recalled receiving a phone call from Blythe, during which she had told him that she was transferring from Washington State University to a college in California. He remembered being stunned by her news, and asking her why she had made such a startling decision. He remembered a rather choppy conversation, with him attempting to talk her out of the transfer and her trying to explain without really explaining anything. Then she'd told him she was calling from Coeur d'Alene, so no, she couldn't meet with him in person to talk about it. Her decision had been final, apparently, and he never had known what had brought it about.

Of course, later on he had wondered if she'd changed schools to abruptly end their relationship, a possibility that angered him. If she had wanted to break up with him she hadn't needed to go to such an extreme. All she would have had to do was to say, "Brent, I'm not in love with you anymore and I don't want to see you again."

And yet, recalling Blythe's sweet and gentle nature, he wasn't able to picture her in that scenario. She had not been an overly courageous young woman, he remembered. He'd never heard her utter an unkind word to or about anyone, and maybe talking to him on the phone had been the best she'd been able to do. He'd known, or had believed with all his heart, that she had loved him as much as he'd loved her. To have her simply walk out of his life the way she'd done had been a terrible blow to his pride, and he didn't understand it yet to this day. Obviously he never would.

Well, there wasn't much chance of him accidentally running into Blythe in Coeur d'Alene, he thought again with a rather poignant sigh. For one thing, it wasn't a small town anymore, but a thriving, busy city with almost as much traffic on the main thoroughfares as there was on Seattle's congested streets.

He could look in the phone book for the Benning name, he realized, but why should he put himself through that? He'd never met her family—he barely remembered that she had a family. Blythe had undoubtedly married some lucky guy and taken his last name, and odds were probably a million to one against her living anywhere in the vicinity.

He would not attempt to look her up. It was mere coincidence that he was even in Coeur d'Alene, and he would leave it at that.

And then a really sad thought brought his already nostalgic mood to a new low: he'd never had much luck with women. He had loved only two. The first had deliberately and mysteriously walked out of his life, and the second, the woman he'd married, had died along with their child. He had not had another serious relationship in his entire life, nor, he realized with sudden painful clarity, was he hoping for one.

It was just the way he was.

It was on their fourth day of house hunting that Bill said, "Brent, I'd bet you'd enjoy seeing some of Coeur d'Alene's older homes. I've got one area near the lake in mind that's really first-class. As an architect, you would appreciate the style of those homes, I know."

"Sure, why not?" Brent agreed. He'd already made up his mind that if he didn't see something he liked today he would give up on buying a house and ask Bill to find him one he could rent. He simply did not have the time to waste on any more house hunting.

Bill made a left turn. "There's one for sale, and it's a grand old house. It shows like a new one because the owners have kept it in perfect condition. There's a large, beautifully land-scaped yard with attractive fencing, and the interior of the house has high ceilings and incredible woodwork, three fire-places and a country kitchen."

It sounded good to Brent. "Let's take a look at it."

Bill turned onto a street that ran in a southerly direction, toward the lake. "The house has a lockbox, so even if the owner isn't home we can go in," he told Brent.

As they entered the fine old neighborhood, Brent sat up straighter. Every house was large and strikingly attractive. It was a quiet area, he realized, very much like the one he lived in in Seattle, with beautiful mature trees and absolutely no clutter of any kind.

"I like the neighborhood," he stated.

"That's a start," Bill said with a laugh. He pulled into the wide, empty driveway of an imposing, two-story white house with black trim. "This is it."

Brent studied the front of the house, and its stately elegance impressed the architect in him. "I like it. Let's go inside."

They got out and Bill said, "I'll ring the doorbell. If no one's here I'll open the lockbox and use the key."

Brent hung back to inspect the shrubs and flower beds placed just so in the front yard while Bill mounted the steps to the front door. Brent heard the door open and a woman's voice saying good morning, and then Bill introduced himself, no doubt passing a business card to the lady. Then Brent heard the agent say, "I'd like to show the house, Ms. Benning. Is it convenient to do so right now? My client is with me."

Brent nearly choked, and he turned to see the woman at the door, but she was standing inside and he could only see Bill on the front stoop. He didn't want to rush forward to get a clear view of Ms. Benning, and besides, he told himself, she couldn't possibly be Blythe. Things like that didn't happen in everyday life. And there was the chance, of course, that he had misunderstood Bill. He could have said "Bennington," or "Benton," or any number of other similar sounding names.

Blythe looked at the agent's business card, then smiled at him. "It's convenient, Mr. Harkens. Please bring your client inside. I'll be in the kitchen." Leaving the door open in invitation, she walked through the foyer and down the hall to the kitchen.

"Brent, it's okay," Bill called.

Brent slowly approached the front steps. He wasn't sure he wanted to do this. Suddenly he felt somewhat panicky. If the woman's name *was* Benning, then she could be a relative of Blythe's. How old was she? If only he'd been able to get a good look at her without her seeing him. Was he emotionally prepared to meet a Benning, whether she be Blythe's mother or her great-aunt?

This could be a shock of monumental proportions, he realized, and he didn't know how to stop it from happening. His mouth had become uncomfortably dry and there was a suspicious churning in his stomach. He couldn't just tell Bill that he'd changed his mind about seeing the inside of the house without some sort of explanation, and he couldn't think of an explanation other than the truth, which he could not tell a virtual stranger.

Along with those discomfiting thoughts, however, was a perverse desire to meet Ms. Benning, whoever she turned out to be. A battle raged within him as he forced himself to climb the four steps to what wasn't merely a stoop, but was actually a front porch large enough to accommodate several pots of brightly colored flowers and two dark green metal chairs. Brent loved those two chairs on sight, and suspected, with a horrible knot burning a hole in his gut, that he was going to love the entire house.

Telling himself that this Ms. Benning had to be a member of an entirely different clan of Bennings than Blythe's family, he smiled, albeit weakly, at Bill. "Nice place," he commented, sounding casual through sheer willpower.

"Yes, it is. Let's go inside."

Apprehensively Brent followed the Realtor in. Ms. Benning was nowhere to be seen, and Brent was glad, because although he had an almost desperate desire to meet her, he was afraid of the actual event. Being afraid of meeting someone seemed so utterly ridiculous when he thought about it, however, that he immediately became more manly and afraid of nothing. Good Lord, even if the woman was Blythe, which couldn't possibly be the case, they were mature adults, weren't they? But if by some perverse twist of fate she was Blythe, why was she using the name Benning? Hadn't she ever married?

Blythe had caught just a fleeting glimpse of Mr. Harkens's client in the front yard, and her impression was of a tall, well-built man nicely dressed in light blue, summer-weight slacks and a coordinated shirt. Puttering in the kitchen, she also remembered that he had nice hair. Dark hair. Probably in his late thirties, she mused—a professional man. Married with a number of children and looking for a house large enough to accommodate a big family.

Actually, she was quite excited by this drop-in prospect. Something told her that this man might be the buyer she'd been hoping would come along since January. She never intruded when an agent showed the house, because she felt that one salesperson was enough for a potential buyer to deal with.

Of course, if questions arose that the agent couldn't answer, she was always happy to help out.

She could hear the low rumble of masculine voices as Harkens led his client through the lovely, wood-paneled foyer, the elegant living room with its white brick fireplace and formal furniture, the family room containing a large-screen TV, piano and lots of easy-living furnishings, and the cozy little den lined with bookshelves and furnished with comfortable reading chairs and lamps. When she heard them in the formal dining room, which was right next to the kitchen, she drew a deep breath and prepared herself for the moment when they would walk into the charming country kitchen.

But nothing on God's green earth could have prepared her for getting a full frontal view of Bill Harkens's client when the two men finally walked in. Shock turned her into a mindless, immobile, mute object. She felt the blood drain from her face, while her knees grew weak enough to buckle.

Harkens boomed jovially, "Blythe Benning, Brent Morrison. Ms. Benning, if I recall correctly, you are also intending to sell the furniture?" He waited for a response, but when none came—not a word from Blythe, not a peep from Brent— Harkens glanced perplexedly from one to the other.

Brent swallowed hard, barely able to believe his own eyes. *My God, she's exactly as I remembered. Soft blond hair, slender, beautiful!* He finally found his voice.

"Hello, Blythe."

"Hello, Brent." It was hardly more than a whisper. *He's better looking today than he was in college! I never dreamed...never could have imagined. Why is this happening? What is he doing in Coeur d'Alene?*

A frown creased the Realtor's forehead. "Do you two know each other?"

"We did," Brent said quietly. "A long time ago. How are you, Blythe?"

She tried very hard to smile, to act as though she wasn't fighting an almost intolerable urge to run from this room, to run from the house. "I'm fine. And you?"

"The same."

He looked well. He looked strong and healthy and prosperous. How did *she* look to him? Dressed in knockabout walking shorts and a casual T-shirt, Blythe nervously raised her hand to her hair. Realizing what she was doing, she felt the blood rush back to her face, heating her skin to such a degree that she knew she was no longer pale, but rather embarrassingly red faced.

Brent cleared his throat. "I had no idea this was your house."

"It's not. It's my parents' house. I…mean, it *was* their house. They're both…uh, gone now, and I— I've been trying to sell it." She hated that she was stammering and red in the face and unable to get her bearings, but never had she been so discombobulated. It was a wonder she could speak at all.

Bill reminded them of his presence by coughing discreetly behind his hand. Two sets of dazed eyes looked at him. "Brent, would you like to see the rest of the house?" he asked.

Brent gathered his wits. "You'll excuse us, Blythe?"

She nodded. "Of course." She escaped to the den to quiver and shake while Bill expounded on the great kitchen. Huddled on a chair, she wrapped her arms around herself, rocked back and forth and wished with every trembling cell of her body that she had gone to the grocery store when she should have instead of putting off the chore until later in the day. She would not have been here when Harkens and Brent came by. She would have been notified that another prospective buyer had looked at the house, but would not have been told Brent's name, because she never learned the names of viewers when she wasn't home to meet them in person.

And then a horrifying idea burst upon her: what if Brent liked the house? What if he decided to buy it? She moaned under her breath, caught in an agonizing web of fear and guilt. She had done Brent the worst injustice a woman could do to a man. She'd given away his child! What if he found out?

No, he would never find out, not unless she herself told him. No one else knew.

That wasn't altogether true. That home in Utah for unwed mothers certainly must keep records.

But records that old?

And what possible incident or event would make Brent stumble across that home?

You're driving yourself crazy, worrying about something that will never happen. Pull yourself together! You should say goodbye when they're through with the house. To Brent you are merely an old memory. Do not make something of this unexpected meeting that it could never be.

Blythe's thoughts continued in that vein until she heard Harkens and Brent in the hall leading to the foyer, where they had obviously stopped to talk.

"Well, what do you think?" Bill asked.

"It's a great house," Brent replied. "I can't imagine anyone not liking it."

"It's a very large house."

"Yes, but I like space, Bill."

"You'd certainly have it in this home."

"The price is reasonable," Brent mused. "I'd like to think about it for a few days."

"Take whatever time you need, Brent. I wonder where Blythe is. I'd like to tell her we're through, for the time being."

"I'm right here," Blythe said, stepping from the den. She'd heard every word they had said and saw no good reason to apologize for it, either. If they had wanted a private conversation they should have gone outside.

"Blythe," Bill said amiably, "we're leaving now. Thank you for letting us look at the house without the courtesy of a phone call."

"Anytime, Mr. Harkens," she murmured, keeping her eyes on him in an effort to *not* look at Brent.

But he was looking at her, and he was remembering and wondering. Wondering mostly about the past, but the present as well. Had she finished her education? Had she become a teacher? Did she teach right here in Coeur d'Alene? Was she the last of the Bennings? Where was her own home? If she lived and taught school in Coeur d'Alene, why wouldn't she remain in this marvelous old house?

"I, too, would like to thank you for letting us barge in the way we did, Blythe," he said quietly.

Her eyes jerked to him, and she was instantly trembling again. "It's quite all right," she managed to say in a reasonably steady voice.

"Goodbye," Bill said. "I'll keep you informed."

"Goodbye, Blythe," Brent said.

"Bye," she whispered, and quickly closed the front door behind them. That was when she came very close to falling apart. Throwing the dead bolt so that even the key in the lockbox wouldn't open the door, she ran upstairs to her room and fell across her bed. What cruel fate had brought Brent to her very doorstep? Panic nearly choked her. This wasn't happening, it wasn't!

But it *was* happening, it *had* happened and something told her that she had not seen the last of Brent.

A tidal wave of guilt and searing remorse nearly overcame her, and she fervently hoped that Brent would vanish as abruptly as he'd appeared.

What else *could* she hope for?

Chapter Two

Blythe turned onto her back and stared dully at the ceiling. The question she couldn't stop asking herself was what had brought Brent to Coeur d'Alene? In college he had avidly pursued an architectural degree. Was he moving to the area because of his work?

A second question was equally persistent, but personally more painful: what perverse fate had brought him to the Benning home? There were hundreds of houses for sale in Coeur d'Alene, many of them newer and much less costly than this one.

The worst feeling of all was a fear that she would have to see Brent again. If he liked the house and was actually considering buying it, it would only be natural for him to want to inspect it again. Was there a way to ensure her absence, should a second and even a third viewing occur?

The telephone rang, and Blythe glanced at the clock on her bed stand. Two hours had gone by since Harkens and Brent had been here, and she had spent every minute of those hours battling gut-wrenching fears. It had to stop. She was making herself ill over events beyond her control. Sighing heavily, she reached for the phone and said rather listlessly, "Hello?"

"This is Bill Harkens, Ms. Benning. Just thought I'd bring you up to speed on what's going on. I don't have any sort of commitment on your property, but Mr. Morrison seems to be quite taken with it. He said he wanted to think about it for a few days, which is often the case in the real estate business, but it wouldn't surprise me in the least if he decided to present you with an offer. Of course, there are no guarantees, you understand."

"Yes, I understand," Blythe murmured. She felt a sudden urge to pull the house off the market, just until Brent found something else to buy.

But what a foolish thing to do when she wanted so badly to sell it. Surely she could avoid another meeting with Brent. An idea came to her.

"Mr. Harkens, your bringing a client by today without a phone call was fine, but should Mr. Morrison want to see the house again, would you mind phoning first? The house isn't always as—as immaculate as it is today, and—and I'm sure you understand."

"Wouldn't mind at all," Bill said. "I'll make a note to myself to be sure and do that."

After they had said goodbye and hung up, Blythe felt a little better about the situation. With a phone call for a warning, she would not be here when and if Brent decided to inspect the house again.

Pushing herself off the bed, she went into her bathroom to wash her face and brush her hair. Then she gathered her purse, her sunglasses, her grocery list and car keys and left the house to go to the supermarket.

She was fine during the drive, and still all right when she walked into the busy market. But five minutes later it hit her again—Brent Morrison was back in her life!—and if she hadn't been hanging onto the grocery cart, she would have sunk to her knees.

Feeling light-headed, she leaned on the cart, grateful for its support. There were only a few items in it, as she had just started on her grocery list, but there was so much confusion addling her brain that she wondered, rather frantically, if she would be able to finish her shopping.

A young woman with a toddler in the seat of her cart stopped next to Blythe. "Are you all right?" she asked with a concerned expression. "Are you ill?"

Blythe knew she must be pale again, and the way she'd been leaning on her cart had concerned this kindly young woman.

"It's just a little dizzy spell," she said. "I'll be fine in a minute."

"Are you sure? Would you like me to find the store's manager?"

"No, really…thank you…I just need a minute to—to catch my breath. I'll be fine."

The woman didn't seem totally convinced, but she finally nodded and continued down the aisle. Blythe's thoughts began to coalesce. Life was going to go on however she handled, or mishandled, the shock she'd received today. She needed groceries, and if she didn't get them now she would have to come back to the store, either later in the day or tomorrow morning. It was best if she pulled herself together and finished her shopping now.

Breathing deeply to keep herself afloat, and forcing herself to concentrate on her grocery list, she quickly filled the cart and then got in line at the checkout stand. It seemed to take forever, but finally a box boy transferred her bagged groceries to the back seat of her car and she got behind the wheel.

That's when it hit her again—the trembling, the weakness, the sense of unreality.

Only this time it made her angry. *She* had not invaded Brent's life, *he* had invaded hers!

Not that she believed he'd known beforehand whose house he was going to look at—he'd been as shocked to see her as she'd been to see him—but he didn't have the demons to fight that she did, and she couldn't help resenting everything about him. The fact that he appeared to be so in control of his life was a particularly bitter pill to swallow. He looked, in fact, as though he had sailed through the past twenty-three years without one moment of the misery that she'd had to endure.

With an embittered twist to her lips, she started the car and headed for home. Maybe she had no right to resent Brent for anything, but it was a much more definitive emotion than any other she'd felt today, and she clung to it and deliberately kept it at the forefront of her thoughts so that she could drive home without tears blurring her vision.

When she was finally parked in the garage, however, she could sustain her false courage no longer and jumped out of the car, leaving the door hanging open and forgetting to even close the garage door as she ran inside. She got as far as the family room sofa before her legs gave out, and she fell on it, buried her face in a pillow and once again let the past engulf her.

Brent had never been a nervous, edgy sort of man, but he couldn't seem to focus on any one thing that afternoon. He tried to work and then tried talking himself into playing a round of golf, a sport he loved. When even that seemed like a completely uninteresting idea he knew that nothing would settle him down. He wanted to see Blythe again; he wanted to *talk* to Blythe. She still owed him an explanation, he decided grimly, while staring through the window of his motel room. And why would she object to a brief conversation about a relationship that had happened so many years ago? He was certainly over it. *She* was the one who had walked off into the sunset. So surely they could discuss their long-ago romance like two mature adults. They might even be able to laugh about it now.

Well, he had his doubts about that, he thought wryly, but now that he'd seen Blythe again he knew he wouldn't rest until she told him why she'd so suddenly decided to change colleges twenty-three years ago.

Does it really matter? After all these years, why would you even care?

That was the strangest part of this strange day—realizing he *did* care. Although he'd known Coeur d'Alene was her hometown, he also knew that he had not come to this beautiful little city by the lake with any hope of finding Blythe. She had been no more than a faded memory until he'd seen her today.

Now she was all he could think about, but those thoughts were more resentful than anything else, he realized while shoving his hands deep into the pockets of his slacks. The whole thing was so confoundingly bizarre. Why couldn't he just forget it? What possible good would it do for him to confront Blythe at this late date, especially when his body churned with resentment?

But he knew he was going to do it. He *had* to do it. He had to look her in the eye and ask her what had happened twenty-three years ago. He had to hear her answer, whatever it was, even though he might not like it.

The irony of it all was how much he liked the Benning house. If it had been anyone else's home, he probably would have already made an offer to buy it. Now he just didn't know. Did he want to live in the house Blythe had grown up in?

Maybe he'd have a better perspective on that question after he talked to Blythe, he mused with a troubled frown.

Well, there was no point in putting it off, he decided. If he was going to do it—and he was—he might as well get to it. Leaving his motel room, he got into his car and began the drive.

When he finally turned onto Lakeside Avenue, the street on which the Benning home was located, Brent felt a sigh ruffle through him. This neighborhood appealed to him as no other he'd looked at with Bill. No, he did not need a house as large as the Benning's. But he hadn't instantly fallen in love with anything else he'd looked at, as he had with this long-established, beautifully tranquil neighborhood and the Benning home.

The day's almost unbelievable events raced through his mind again. Had some sort of mystical force taken control of his life? What, really, had brought him to Blythe's doorstep? This was like a movie or a novel, he thought, where two people who hadn't seen each other in many years were manipulated by a writer's imagination into meeting again.

It was fate, he decided with a rather grim twist of his lips. Fate had caused the developers to hire him to design the Sunrise project. Obviously he and Blythe had been destined to meet again. He didn't know why destiny had brought it about, and maybe he never would. It was entirely possible that fate had done its job and now he was on his own. Brent shook his head, as denial of his far-fetched theory about fate and destiny overrode his fanciful search for an answer. It was all accidental, he decided, just one of those disturbing twists that probably everyone experienced at some point in their life.

Recognizing that he was getting close to the Benning place, he pulled his thoughts away from conjecture and concentrated on the lovely homes he was slowly driving past. If he bought Blythe's house, the people living in these homes would be his neighbors. Every yard was a showpiece; every house was in perfect condition. It all appealed to his sense of order, and maybe that was what had influenced him most when Bill had brought him here this morning.

Approaching the Benning home, Brent saw that the garage door was up. Inside was a white sedan. What he didn't notice until he had pulled into the driveway was the vehicle's open door. And when he turned off the motor of his own car, he could hear a repeating pinging from the sedan, which he knew was a signal that a door wasn't securely closed. His own car had the same feature, as most late model vehicles did.

It struck a strange note in Brent, because it indicated haste. Someone, most likely Blythe, had gotten out of that car very quickly and gone into the house without shutting the door. Why would she do that?

He got out and rather cautiously entered the garage. After all, his walking in uninvited could be construed as trespassing. But he would chance it, he decided, because if for some unfathomable reason Blythe had simply forgotten to close the door of her car—an unlikely but possible explanation—then she risked running down her battery.

Brent was about to shut the sedan's door when he saw that the back seat contained numerous sacks of groceries. The picture was suddenly clear: Blythe was apparently in the process of carrying in groceries, and would undoubtedly appear at any moment for another load.

He quietly closed the door to stop that annoying pinging sound, then leaned his hips against the back fender of the sedan to wait for Blythe's next trip. She would be surprised to see him in her garage, of course, but she was going to be surprised one way or another by his return visit, and he figured that surprising her out here was no worse than doing it at her front door.

Inside, Blythe was in her bathroom, washing her face in an attempt to look halfway normal because she had done some crying. She had a lot of groceries to bring in, and she never knew when one of the neighbors would drop by, or simply be strolling past the house and stop for a few minutes' chat, should she be outside.

At least her spell on the sofa hadn't gone on for so long that the damages were irreparable, she thought thankfully. Not that she could completely eradicate the redness around her eyes and nose. But a little makeup helped, and just to be on the safe side she put on her dark glasses again before going out to the garage to begin the task of bringing in her groceries.

The second she opened the door between the laundry room and the garage she saw Brent. Oh, no, not again! she thought wildly, and had to forcibly restrain herself from slamming the door shut, almost in his face.

As upset as she was, however, she couldn't be that rude. Instead, she drew upon the bank of inner strength that had supported her through many bad moments during the past twenty-three years, and managed to speak almost normally.

"Hello, again," she said.

Brent pushed himself away from her car. She must have gotten home from the market only a short time ago, he thought, because she was still wearing sunglasses.

"Hi," he said, realizing suddenly that he felt a little nervous. "May I help you carry in your groceries?"

Blythe wanted to say no, because she didn't want him in the house at all when she was there. There was no sign of Harkens, so Brent was on his own, and that indicated to her that he was here more to see her than the house. It was a possibility she should have thought of, but since she hadn't and thus was completely unprepared for this contingency, she was going to have to take Brent's visit a minute at a time and get through it the best way she could.

"Yes, thank you," she murmured. She reached into the back seat for a sack and started into the house. Brent followed her with two sacks, and when they were in the kitchen, she said rather coolly, "Just set them anywhere."

"I'll bring in the rest," Brent told her, and hurried out.

Her emotions mixed, she began taking food from the sacks. One part of her said that she could get through this if she remained calm and aloof, while the other resented Brent's dropping in without warning or invitation. Did he think she would be glad to see him without Bill Harkens's presence preventing a personal conversation? Blythe pursed her lips; there was *not* going to be a personal conversation, however much Brent might attempt to lead her in that direction.

Sorting her groceries so she could put meat into the freezer right away, Blythe looked up when Brent appeared with the final load, two sacks that he set on the table with the others.

"Thank you," she said again, immediately dropping her eyes to the array of food items on the table.

Brent stood there for a few moments, realized that she wasn't going to invite him to sit down and finally asked, "Is it okay if I use one of your chairs?"

"Sure, go ahead," she said nonchalantly, as though she didn't know he'd been waiting for an invitation. His crisp good looks irritated her. He was forty-five and looked ten years younger. She was forty-three and today probably looked ten years older. She hated that she didn't look her best and that there was nothing she could do about it, except hide behind the dark glasses she still wore.

When she picked up a six-pack of soda to put away, her innate good manners nudged her conscience. "Would you like something to drink? These are warm, but I have plenty of ice."

"Yes, thanks." Brent was fully aware of her distant attitude, but he was determined to see this through. Eventually she'd have those groceries put away and would have to talk to him. Either talk to him or ask him to leave, he reminded himself. But would she do that? He doubted it, because he couldn't imagine a reason why she wouldn't talk to him about the past. Truth was, he couldn't come up with a reason for her present coolness, either. Maybe she had one; maybe it was the same one that had caused her to break up with him twenty-three years ago. Whatever it was, he wanted to hear it.

Blythe busied herself with a tall glass, some ice cubes and a can of soda, which, when ready, she placed in front of him on the table.

"Thanks," Brent said quietly.

"You're welcome." *Dammit, you shouldn't have offered him a soda! No telling how long he'll nurse it, sitting there and watching every move you make. And once the food is put away, what are you going to do? Sit at the table with him and reminisce? No way!*

Blythe put one loaf of fresh bread in the freezer and another in the bread box. "Did you want to see the house again?" she asked with her back to him, praying that was the only reason he'd come back so soon.

"No, I wanted to see you," Brent said calmly.

"Really." Returning to the table without looking at him, she picked up several packages of cheese and cold cuts and took them to the refrigerator.

"Aren't you at all curious about me? I sure am about you," Brent said evenly.

"No, frankly, I'm not a bit curious." It was a lie. What had brought him to Coeur d'Alene was a question that had all but eaten her alive for long, miserable hours today. It still lay in the pit of her stomach, feeling very much like a lead weight. But she would bite off her tongue before asking him any question that might start them on a trip down memory lane.

"I find that a little hard to believe," Brent said bluntly. "We weren't just friends twenty-three years ago, if you'd care to remember."

She waved her hand dismissively. "I don't live in the past,

Brent." It was another lie. There were periods where the past was the only place she *did* live.

"Neither do I, but running into you today so unexpectedly…well, I guess you could say that it sort of brought the past to life again. Our meeting again after so long a time didn't do that to you?"

"No, it didn't. Oh, I was surprised to see you, of course."

"Of course," he said dryly. She was putting away the last of the groceries, very neatly stacking canned goods in a cupboard, making sure that each can lined up perfectly with its neighbors. From behind she looked like a young girl, Brent thought. Her figure was as good as it had been in college, slender but shapely, and though her shorts nearly reached her knees, he could see enough of her legs to admire them. He remembered something then. When their romance had been at its peak he had told her that she had the most beautiful legs of all the women on campus. She'd laughed and told him he was silly, and that men in love said the craziest things.

Recalling how much in love they had really been, or he had been, at least, caused an almost painful wrenching in Brent's gut. He watched her puttering with the canned goods and knew she was putting off the moment when she would have idle hands and nothing to deal with but him.

But it was an awkward situation for both of them, not just for her, and he wasn't going to disappear just because she so obviously wished he would. He'd been driven to come back to her house and confront her, and he wasn't going to leave until he got her to talk about the past, however hard she tried to act as though she barely remembered it.

Blythe's final task was to fold the paper sacks and store them in a laundry room cupboard. With that small chore behind her there was nothing left to do, so in an attempt to make the best of a bad situation, she poured herself a soda and joined Brent at the kitchen table.

"Do you always wear dark glasses in the house?" he asked. "Do you have a problem with your eyes?"

Blythe took a sip of her soda. "They bother me at times. It's nothing serious."

"You weren't wearing them this morning."

"No, I wasn't."

"One's eyesight is very important. If your eyes are bothering you in any way at all, you should see a doctor. Unless you already have."

"Let's change the subject. Why did you want to see me?" She had decided to get whatever he'd come here to say to her over with so he would leave. Whatever was on his mind, she would listen to it politely, respond with lies or the truth, depending on what he asked her, and that, hopefully, would be the end of it.

"Do you really have to ask? Blythe, when Bill Harkens brought me here this morning, I had no idea I would be looking at your house. I want you to believe that."

"I do," she said simply.

"And then, when I saw you, it was like..." Brent ran his fingers through his hair. "I don't know what it was like—maybe like a bomb had just gone off. I was beyond mere surprise, I know, and so were you."

"Well, I hardly expected *you* to walk into this kitchen."

"Exactly! It was a major shock for both of us, wasn't it?"

You will never know the extent of my shock. She still felt it and probably would for a very long time. "We were both taken by surprise. Please, let's leave it at that."

"I can't. I haven't thought of anything else all day. Blythe, will you tell me something?"

She grew wary. "If I can," she said slowly, cautiously.

"You never explained why you transferred to another college, and—"

Blythe cut in. "You're wrong, Brent. I phoned you."

"Yes, I remember, but you didn't explain anything."

She knew she hadn't. She'd been evasive and secretive and hurting so much it was a wonder she'd been able to talk to him at all.

But she couldn't explain anything now, either. "I'm sure you're mistaken," she said quietly, belying the almost thunderous beating of her heart. "I phoned *to* explain. I must have done so."

"I don't remember it that way, Blythe." Brent leaned forward with his forearms on the table and an anxious expression on his face. "Tell me what you remember of that conversation."

"I...hardly remember it at all. Brent, it was so long ago."

He looked at her for a long moment. "All right, let's approach it from another angle. Maybe you don't remember the phone call clearly, but you must remember why you transferred."

She deliberately looked confused. "Actually, I don't."

He sat back. "You're kidding."

"Of course I'm not kidding. Really, Brent, what we did twenty-three years ago hardly matters today." Blythe's stomach began aching. What they had done twenty-three years ago rarely left her mind. More precisely, what *she* had done back then rarely left her mind. He had no idea of the enormity of her sins, and if she had anything to say about it, he never would.

She couldn't talk about it any longer. No matter how persistently he asked questions, her answers would remain the same. There was no point in prolonging this uncomfortable meeting.

Making a big show of looking at her watch, she said, "I have a dinner engagement, and I really must start getting ready for it."

Brent was sick-to-his-stomach disappointed. He had learned nothing. He didn't know if he should believe that she remembered so little of the past, but he also didn't know where to go from here to find out.

He got up slowly. "Apparently you never married."

Blythe rose, as well. "What makes you think that?"

"You're still using your maiden name."

"I was married, Brent. That, too, was a long time ago. My husband died. I never stopped using my maiden name because I teach young children, and it seemed easier to let them continue to call me Miss Benning. It just sort of went on from there."

"Did...do you have children?"

A huge lump formed in her throat, and she could barely whisper, "No." *Do you? You must have a family if you want a house this large.*

"You know, our past lives aren't that far apart," Brent said softly.

She wanted at that moment to bombard him with questions, but she held her tongue. He was on the verge of leaving and she had to let him go. Not because she had a dinner engagement—that had been a spur-of-the-moment fabrication to bring their discussion to a halt—but because she was afraid if he stayed and they kept on talking, she would inadvertently say something she shouldn't. Besides, she really didn't want to hear about his wonderful family, and his comment about their past lives not being very far apart couldn't possibly be further from the truth.

The truth as he knew it, of course.

"Well, guess I'd better go and let you get ready for your dinner date," he said.

She saw the forlorn look in his eyes and knew that her evasive answers had not satisfied him. Regardless, she thought a bit defensively, they were the only answers she could give him and he would have to live with them.

"Yes, time's getting short," she agreed. She escorted him to the foyer, said a quick goodbye and really only breathed freely again when he was gone and the front door was closed behind him.

She spent the entire evening hoping and praying that he would not come back again.

Even if it meant that he would not be buying the house.

Chapter Three

When three days had passed without a word from Harkens or Brent, Blythe began to relax. Obviously Brent had decided against making an offer to buy the house, which in a way was too bad. But since it also meant she wouldn't have to see him again, she couldn't feel too disappointed about it.

In fact, she was beginning to feel almost normal once more, and she was enjoying the final days of summer by working outside as often as possible. She'd been sleeping well—without that haunting dream—and she had learned long ago that a restful night usually guaranteed a good day.

Not that she ever completely forgot the past. It was a specter in her mind and an ache in her heart, but she had lived with those factors for so long that they hardly affected her behavior. Actually, it was a miracle that no one had ever caught on to her periodic mood swings. Apparently she was a master at concealing her feelings, she'd come to realize, for not even the counselor at the school she taught at in Connecticut, Muriel Hart, who was also a trained psychologist, had ever come to her and asked if something was wrong.

While mowing and trimming the lawn, and pulling weeds from the flower beds during the pleasant, summery days after Brent's two visits, Blythe recalled that years ago she had come very close to talking to Muriel during one of her bad spells. But she'd had—and still did have—such an aversion to telling her story to anyone that she had decided against it. She had never regretted that decision, because there seemed to be a perverse sort of comfort in knowing that no one else had any knowledge of the unforgivable sin she'd committed twenty-three years ago.

Yes, she regarded giving up her child as a sin and a crime against nature. She knew that if she didn't feel so strongly about that, then she would not suffer such guilt. But she couldn't change her attitude, so she must endure the guilt. Crime and punishment, she had thought very often. She had committed the crime and must live with the punishment.

Only, sometimes she *wasn't* able to live with it, and those were the bad times, the dark moments when she would resent and blame her parents along with herself.

Thankfully, she was coming out of her most recent "bad time." Even Brent's sudden intrusion into her life didn't seem that bad anymore. She had apparently succeeded in destroying his curiosity, for it appeared that he had given up on both her and the house, and her spirits were lifting more each day. It didn't matter that he would find another house and be living in Coeur d'Alene, because she would be back in Connecticut, where she now firmly believed she belonged. There were too many memories here, and unquestionably she'd done better—emotionally, at least—in Connecticut.

So, she thought as she moved the small rug she'd been kneeling on while clearing away weeds, dry leaves and twigs from the flower beds on this bright sunny day, she really must return to her own home as soon as possible. Which, of course, meant leaving her parents' house unsold.

Frowning, she sat back on her heels. She'd wanted so badly to get the house sold this summer, and she couldn't help feeling that she had let her sisters down. The hardest part of what felt like a dilemma to Blythe was that she knew if she phoned

Tamara and Sierra and explained her decision to go home, they would both say she should do it. Her sisters weren't the problem, *she* was—she and her acute sense of responsibility.

Blythe always took a cordless phone with her when she worked outside, and today she had left it on a table on the backyard patio. When it started ringing, she got up, pulled off her garden gloves and hurried to answer it. "Hello?"

"Bill Harkens here, Ms. Benning. I have a favor to ask. Mr. Morrison wants to take another look at the house today, and I have so many appointments scheduled that I wondered if you would mind if he came alone."

Blythe sucked in a sharp breath. She had convinced herself that Brent had lost interest in the house, and to learn otherwise was an unpleasant jolt. And with Harkens too busy to accompany him, there was no way he could "take another look at the house" without her being here to let him in.

She didn't want to see Brent again. The mere thought of doing so made her spine stiffen and the rest of her body get tense.

"Actually, Ms. Benning," Harkens continued, "I suggested having one of my associates take Mr. Morrison to your place, but he said that he preferred doing his looking by himself. If you didn't object, of course. He said that he would really like to take his time this visit, because he feels that he missed a great many details the first time around."

He's using you, Mr. Harkens—he's using you to get to me! She drew another deep breath, this one horribly uneasy.

"I—I'm not sure," she finally said in a rather unsteady voice.

"Ms. Benning, if I may be blunt, your house has been on the market for a long time. I would not let Mr. Morrison get away, if I were you. He's anxious to get settled, and no other house I've shown him has whetted his interest the way your home has. He even made the comment to me that your price seems very reasonable, so if he does make an offer, which I feel is quite likely, I believe it will be very close to your listed price."

Blythe cleared her throat. This conversation was making her

nervous, but if Brent did buy the house, her sense of responsibility would be satisfied and she would be able to return to Connecticut with a clear conscience on that particular issue. Surely she could face him one more time.

"Yes, all right," she said into the phone. "He may come by himself. What time should I expect him?"

"Three o'clock this afternoon, if that time is convenient for you, of course. If it's not..."

"Three is fine. Goodbye, Mr. Harkens." Blythe pushed the disconnect button on the phone and then sank onto a chair. Despair gripped her for a few moments, but she knew that emotion was one she should do her best to avoid, so she jumped up and, yanking on her gloves, hurried back to the bed of flowers she'd been working on.

"Don't think about it," she muttered under her breath. Brent would show up, spend perhaps an hour in looking everything over, and leave again. She would survive seeing him one more time, especially if she refused to let him draw her into a discussion of anything that didn't concern the house. If she managed to do that—and she must—then she would get through one more traumatic experience relatively unscathed.

If she wanted to sell the house she really had no choice, did she? Brent was, after all, the only person who had liked it well enough to even want a second look.

She should be grateful.

At two Blythe put away her yard tools and went into the house for a shower. She'd taken only a brief break for lunch and otherwise had spent the entire day outdoors. In all honesty she felt in better spirits than she had in weeks, and she was determined not to let Brent's three o'clock appointment throw her back into the doldrums.

After a shower and shampoo, she dried and fixed her hair and put on a little makeup. The cosmetics were not for Brent's benefit; she always wore makeup. The simple but attractive skirt and blouse she put on were not for Brent's benefit, either. She often chose a skirt or a dress instead of shorts, slacks or jeans. In fact, she could honestly say that she was doing nothing special just because someone was coming to the house. It was her habit to look nice and she *liked* looking nice.

Of course, when she was dressed she did realize that she looked much nicer today than she had on Brent's previous visits. At least I don't have to hide red eyes behind dark glasses today, she thought wryly.

She was sitting in the small den with a glass of iced tea when the doorbell rang. Remonstrations to act cool and collected raced through her mind again, but they suddenly seemed most ineffective. Brent made her nervous and she might as well stop telling herself that he didn't. Nervous and burdened with guilt. It was difficult to look him in the eye and pretend they were nothing more than old acquaintances.

Secrets were a curse, she thought with a heavy sigh, and hers was especially onerous. She had paid almost all of her adult life for what she had done as a naive, foolish young woman. Why must she also have to deal with Brent at this late date?

And then, for just a moment, the sweetness of the love they had shared so long ago overcame all other thoughts. The memory startled Blythe, for not only had she not expected it, it had been many years since she'd suffered any such emotional invasion.

Inhaling sharply to dispel *all* memory, she placed her glass on a coaster on the table next to her chair and forced herself to her feet. With great reluctance she walked to the foyer and opened the door.

Brent stared. She looked beautiful, and remnants of the deeply rooted feelings he'd once held for her stirred within him. It was a jarring moment, and for a few seconds it was the only thing he could think of.

But reality returned quickly, and he said, "Hello, Blythe."

"Did you deliberately wait for a day when Bill Harkens was too busy to come here with you?" Blythe immediately flushed over her rude question. She hadn't planned to say any such thing to Brent, and her unanticipated rashness was embarrassing. But then she saw unfamiliar streaks of red in

Brent's cheeks and knew that she had inadvertently hit on the truth.

"Uh, sorry," he mumbled. "Guess I didn't think you'd figure it out. Blythe, I really do want to see the house again, but..." He looked away for a moment, then brought pleading eyes back to her. "I also wanted to see you."

She didn't know whether to invite him in or to become even ruder by telling him to get the hell off her front porch.

But deliberate rudeness was not a part of her normal personality, and he was so sadly ignorant of the past that she began feeling sorry for him. Why wouldn't he be curious? Not that she could ever satisfy his curiosity, but she certainly could be a little more understanding of it.

"I'm sorry," she said quietly, and stepped back from the threshold. "Come in."

Heaving a relieved sigh, Brent murmured, "Thanks," and entered the foyer.

Blythe closed the door. "You've seen me, so that part of your visit is over. If you still wish to inspect the house, feel free to wander." She hadn't spoken rudely or bluntly; she'd merely stated their situation as she saw it. "I'll be in the den."

He forced eye contact by silently staring at her until she became uncomfortable. When her gaze finally met his, he said, "I'd much rather have you walk through the house with me."

"Why?"

"Because I have some questions about certain rooms."

She didn't relent gracefully. "Oh, very well," she said sharply. "Where do you want to start?"

"The basement."

"Fine!" She led the way to the kitchen, which contained the door to the basement. Preceding him down the stairs, she then stood by with her arms folded across her chest while he walked around the largest room. It had once contained a pool table, because her father had loved the game, although he'd had very little time to spend on it. The pool table was long gone, but the floor was still carpeted and the room had become a receptacle for out-of-style and no-longer-used furniture.

Blythe decided she should explain the outdated furnishings.

"Any furniture in the house that a buyer doesn't want will be sold by auction or donated to a charity. Most of the things in this room have very little value. They're not old enough to be antiques, and, as you can see for yourself, everything is pretty much worn out."

"It's a good room, though," Brent said. "I couldn't remember its lighting." He glanced at the ceiling. "I see that it has some good fluorescent fixtures. Would you mind turning them on?"

Blythe flipped the switch, and the light fixtures flickered on.

"I've been thinking of making this my workroom," Brent said.

"Your job permits you to work at home?"

"I don't have a job per se, but I need a place with good lighting for my drafting tables and CAD equipment."

He didn't seem to be at all concerned about not having a regular job, so Blythe figured he was probably a freelance architect. Since the term he'd just used was unfamiliar, she asked about it. "CAD equipment? What does that consist of?"

"Computers and printers, specially programmed for architectural designs and techniques."

Blythe nodded. "I see."

Brent was pacing the room off, estimating its size, which was information the listing agent had taken down, along with the size of every other room in the house. But perhaps Brent and Harkens hadn't discussed specific room sizes, Blythe thought.

"It's really a lot bigger than I need," Brent said thoughtfully. He grinned then. "But then the whole house is, isn't it?"

"I wouldn't know. How large is your family?" Blythe had sworn that she would not ask Brent about his family, but the question came popping out of her mouth before she could stop it. Annoyed with herself, she quickly added, "Not that it's any of my business."

"It's not a state secret, Blythe," Brent said with a rather amused expression. "I'm it."

Her mind went blank. "You're what?"

"My family. I'm all there is."

It was so far from the way she'd been thinking of him that she couldn't help showing astonishment. "Well, why on earth would you want a house this size?" she blurted.

"You know, I've been asking myself that very question. The only answer I've been able to come up with is that I like it." Brent walked to the far end of the room and opened a door.

"That room is extremely cluttered," Blythe hastened to say as she followed him. "These file cabinets contain my father's old medical records. They will, of course, be removed before a buyer takes possession."

Brent turned and looked at her. "That's right, your father was a doctor. I'd forgotten. But I don't understand. Wasn't his practice sold to another physician? I mean, it only seems logical that—"

Blythe interrupted. "Dad died rather suddenly. Mother did sell his practice, but the buyer only wanted Dad's records on current patients. When you look at the many file cabinets and the space they take up, it's easy to see why."

"Yes, you're right. So these records are for people who stopped seeing your father for one reason or another, or moved away. What are you going to do with them?"

"I'm not sure *what* to do with them. Hauling them to the dump doesn't seem right. Many of these people could still be living in Coeur d'Alene, and they are entitled to privacy on their medical problems, no matter how long ago they occurred."

"And you're thinking that someone might stumble across the folders at the dump and look through them? Doesn't the city of Coeur d'Alene use the landfill method of handling its trash?"

"I believe it does—actually, I'm not sure—but I still don't feel comfortable with the idea of just filling trash bags with what could be important and very private data on Dad's former patients, and having them hauled to the dump."

"Well, I can't imagine what else you would do with so

much paper," Brent said as he pulled open one of the drawers of a file cabinet. "This drawer is crammed full."

"They all are."

"Could you burn the records in one of the fireplaces?"

"They've all been converted to gas. And there's a very strict city ordinance against outside burning. I've thought of buying a shredder, but it would take weeks to shred so much paper."

"A commercial-size shredder would do the trick in a lot less time," Brent said.

Blythe thought a moment. "Do you know where I could buy or rent a commercial shredder?"

"I would think that any office supply outlet could order one." Brent moved down the line of file cabinets and opened another drawer, and then did so again with yet another cabinet. This time he frowned. "Are you sure these cabinets contain nothing but old patient files? Looks like there are other types of files in this drawer."

"I'm only going on what Mother told me. Dad may have also stored some business files in these cabinets, but they, too, would be very outdated."

Brent pushed the drawer shut. "You know, this room is a much better size for my equipment. Maybe I'll do something else with the big room. It would be perfect for a rec room, don't you think? It's got more than enough space for a pool table."

Blythe smiled poignantly. "Dad had a pool table in that room. But he was so busy with his medical practice I know he didn't get to use it very often."

"Too bad. Well, I think that does it for the basement." They left the small room and reentered the large one.

"You checked the furnace room? Mother had a new gas furnace installed about four years ago."

"I saw it."

"All right." Blythe started up the stairs, with Brent close behind her. "What else would you like to see?" she asked, realizing that they had carried on a very civil conversation in the small room, and in the next instant recalling their wonderful long talks, sometimes far into the night, when they had been lovers.

I'm already looking at it, Brent thought as he watched the swaying movement of her skirts as she ascended the stairs ahead of him. She had matured so beautifully. Blaming any coolness she had shown him on the shock they had both felt at meeting again after so many years, Brent decided that she was the same gentle, tenderhearted woman she'd been in college. He had been madly in love with her then, and he suddenly realized that he could very easily fall in love with her again. It was a happy thought, one with which he could find no fault. She was a widow, he was a widower. They were both childless and alone. True, they were just barely getting to know each other again, but he doubted very much that he would uncover anything about this more mature Blythe that he wouldn't like.

At the top of the stairs Brent closed the basement door. To prolong his visit until a propitious moment arose to bring the conversation around to the two of them, he said, "I'd like to take a closer look at the kitchen."

"Be my guest." They were, after all, *in* the kitchen, and if he wanted a closer look at it, this was a good time to take it. It was nearing four, she saw from a glance at the wall clock; it didn't seem possible that they had been in the basement for almost an hour, but it had to be true.

Remembering the glass of iced tea she'd left in the den— which would no longer be iced, she reminded herself wryly— she said, "I'll be back in a minute or two. Take your time looking things over."

Walking out, she went directly to the den and picked up the glass. Then, holding it, she stood there remembering what he'd said about his family. *I'm it. All there is.* Had he never been married? Why on earth not? Surely not because of the way she'd broken up with him! She couldn't imagine him not having gotten over that long ago.

And yet that phone call had been so cruel. She had hemmed and hawed to elude an honest explanation, and she had lied. Oh, how she'd lied!

Weakly she sank onto a chair. She could tell he thought she was the same person today that she'd been in college, but it wasn't true! It was so far from the truth, in fact, that it would be funny if it wasn't so awful. She had not only given away her baby, she'd given away *his* baby, and if he ever found out about it he would despise her for the rest of his days.

"Dear God," she whispered, as though seeking help from the Almighty. How dare she resent Brent for anything? All he'd done was love her.

She could at least treat him with some respect. She'd been acting as though he were a criminal! Not today so much, but certainly during his previous two visits to the house.

That was over. He did not deserve unpleasantness from her, and he was not going to be on the receiving end of that sort of treatment again. Not that she could or would answer any point-blank questions such as he'd thrown at her before. But they could talk of other things, and besides, their relationship would not go on for long. If he bought the house, she would ask for two weeks to get it ready for closure. If he *didn't* want the house and bought something else, she couldn't imagine a reason why they would be seeing each other again.

She certainly could be civil to the man for two weeks, for heaven's sake.

With that determination solidly fixed in her mind, she got up and returned to the kitchen. Brent, to her surprise, was sitting at the table.

"Did you look at everything already?" she asked, taking her glass to the sink.

"This is the cleanest kitchen I've ever seen. Do you have a cleaning lady?"

Turning to face him, Blythe smiled. "You're looking at her."

That smile did something to Brent. It brought to mind her many soft smiles when they'd been so much in love. Her hair had been soft, her smiles and her voice had been soft, her skin and even her laughter had been soft.

She could sense a change in his mood, and sensed, too, where it could be going. She brought them both back to earth with a simple question. "Would you like something cold to drink?"

Brent laughed. "Cold might be best, but you know what I'd really like? A cup of coffee."

"Then I'll put on a pot." With her back to him, she busied herself with the coffeepot. "Have you seen everything you wanted to in the house?"

"I think so. For now, anyway. Blythe, I've got to ask you something. When the house sells, where will you live?"

She hesitated a moment, then said quietly, "I'll go to my own home in Connecticut."

Brent sat back. "I see." He'd been all set to contact Bill Harkens and tell him to write up a purchase offer, but if he bought the house, then Blythe would leave Idaho. It hit him like a ton of bricks: he didn't want to lose her a second time! That thought confused him for a moment. He didn't *have* her, so how could he lose her?

But that was the whole point, he answered himself. If she left Coeur d'Alene before they got to know each other again, there would never be another chance to do so. He should put off making that purchase offer.

His mental debate wasn't over with that conclusion, however, for it occurred to him that someone else could come along and buy the house while he was maneuvering for time, in which case Blythe would *still* be leaving. His mind raced for a solution to that problem, which at this moment seemed insurmountable.

He became aware of Blythe setting two attractive cloth placemats on the table, one in front of him and the other across from where he was sitting.

"I like the way you do things," he said quietly. "I suppose you've been keeping the yard immaculate, as well as the house? Or do you employ a yard service?"

"I do the yard myself because I like working outside." Blythe checked the coffeepot. "It's almost ready." She brought spoons and a matched sugar bowl and cream pitcher to the table, and next got out two pretty cups and saucers.

"This is a big yard to care for."

"It's a big house to care for, as well, but I haven't had anything better to do this summer."

"Bill Harkens told me the house has been on the market for quite a while."

"It has been. Mother died in January, and I volunteered to stay in Coeur d'Alene and settle her estate. But then I just couldn't do it, so I went back to Connecticut and only returned in June when school was out."

"Volunteered to who?"

"My sisters, of course."

"Sisters, as in more than one? I thought you had only one sister."

"No, I have two sisters. Oh, I see what you're getting at. I *did* have only one sister when…when we knew each other in college." That remark caused an internal wince, but she recovered quickly and forged on. "Tamara, the baby of the family, was born shortly after…after…" Blythe suddenly realized she was treading shallow water with this topic, and it made her terribly nervous. "The coffee's ready."

While filling the cups, she told herself to change the subject. They were getting entirely too close to the one thing they would never be able to talk about. She had decided to be more civil to Brent, but he was becoming a little too friendly for comfort.

She brought the cups of coffee to the table and placed one in front of him. She sat at the second place setting with the other cup. Since she could not talk about herself, they were going to have to talk about him, regardless of her sworn oath not to pry into his life because that would be like giving him permission to pry into hers.

But she doubted that he would be content to discuss world affairs with her, so she asked, trying very hard to make this conversation appear mundane and ordinary, "So, where did you live before coming to Coeur d'Alene?"

Brent took a sip of his coffee before replying. "Seattle's been my home base since college, but I'm rarely there anymore." He told her about past projects in a dozen states, and that he'd been hired by the developers to design the Sunrise project in Coeur d'Alene. "So that's what brought me here," he said.

He lowered his cup and looked directly into her lovely, blue-gray eyes. "After meeting you again I wondered if fate didn't have a hand in bringing me here. What do you think? Do you believe in predestination?"

Chapter Four

Blythe nearly choked on a swallow of coffee. How clever he was about bringing the conversation back to the two of them!

She couldn't let him do this, she thought frantically, and she looked *him* in the eye and said firmly, "I certainly do not believe that fate brought you to Coeur d'Alene so that we would meet again. There's no sense in that sort of theory."

"And you're a completely sensible person."

"Not always, but is anyone?"

"Looking at you now, and remembering the bright, intelligent woman you were in college, I can't believe that you have ever been anything but sensible."

Bitterness crept into her voice. "Well, you're wrong." Internally Blythe wilted. She could not say things like that to Brent without inciting his curiosity. He was obviously extremely interested in the turn of this conversation, and she had only herself to blame.

She altered the tone of her voice, eradicating bitterness from it, along with nearly every other emotion. "More coffee?" Without waiting for a reply, she got up and topped off their cups. He wouldn't stay much longer, she told herself while returning the glass pot to the coffeemaker. He would finish his coffee and leave, and, all things considered, his visit hadn't been so bad. The worst moment had been when she'd said that he was wrong in assuming she was always sensible, but she believed she had smoothed that over well enough.

After resuming her seat at the table, however, she realized that he seemed to be settling in for a long chat.

Smiling at her, Brent spoke almost lazily. "I've been wondering how you ended up in Connecticut."

Blythe shrugged. "The same way you ended up in Seattle, I suppose—a good job offer."

"Right after college?"

"Soon after, yes." He was so persistently pursuing her past, Blythe thought uneasily, and realized again that the only way to avoid talking about herself was to talk about him. "Did you start freelancing directly out of college?"

Brent shook his head. "No, I worked for an architectural firm for about five years before striking out on my own. Blythe, how about having dinner with me this evening?"

He'd taken her by surprise, and she had no prepared answer for something so totally unexpected. "D-dinner?" she stammered, as though it was a word she'd never before heard. She knew she'd just sounded completely brainless, but couldn't help it as her mind raced for a reasonable excuse to refuse. Her heartfelt opinion was that they had already spent too much time together today.

Brent was smiling. "Yes, you know, dinner, food," he said, sounding amused.

"I really can't," she said, ignoring his teasing response and wishing she could have come up with a better answer. "But thank you, anyway."

"Do you have other plans?"

"Yes." She offered no explanation, because she had none.

He sensed that she was lying, and it gave him a start that she would lie to avoid spending the evening with him. Obviously he'd been enjoying her company a lot more than she'd been enjoying his, and that struck him as sad. He would eat alone tonight and so would she, and it didn't have to be that way.

Why was it that way? His eyes narrowed speculatively.

"Blythe, are you dating someone?"

She was totally taken aback and blurted, "No, I am not!"

Brent frowned. "You said that as if the mere idea of dating gives you cold chills."

Realizing her mistake, she hastened to correct it. "All I meant was that I've been much too busy to, uh, do any dating."

"But you have plans for the evening."

She could take no more; she would tell no more lies on this subject. "All right," she said with a distinct light of battle in her eyes. "You've pushed for the truth, so here it is. You make me uncomfortable, Brent. You keep prying and digging into the past, and *that* makes me uncomfortable. What happened between us in college is best forgotten, and it *was* more or less forgotten until you started stirring up old memories. I don't have plans for this evening, but I am not going to have dinner with you tonight or any other night. Our relationship is limited to this house. Either you want to buy it or you don't, and I honestly wish you would make up your mind. I've tried to be civil about this whole thing, but I suspect very strongly that you've been using the house as an excuse to see me."

"Now why do you suppose I would do that?" he asked softly.

Blythe felt a flush heating her face, but she couldn't back down now. "I hope it's not because you'd like to take up where we left off twenty years ago, but your behavior seems to point in that direction."

"Twenty-four years is more accurate."

"All right, twenty-four years! Brent, you're not getting my message!"

"Yes, I am, but I have to ask myself what you're afraid of. As I see it, there's not a damn thing wrong with two old friends having dinner together."

The high color in Blythe's face faded abruptly, until her

skin was no longer rosy but rather a pasty white. "I'm not afraid of anything!"

It seemed odd to Brent that out of the several points he had raised, her being afraid of something had been the one that upset Blythe the most. It puzzled him, because what could she possibly have to fear from a renewal of their long-ago relationship? Besides, all he'd asked for was a dinner date, not a lifelong commitment!

He started wondering again about the explanation for transferring colleges that she had never given him, and could only conclude that something had happened back then that he didn't know about—or didn't remember—and she couldn't talk about.

"I did something that you couldn't accept, didn't I?" he said in a quiet, sad voice.

"What? When? What are you talking about?"

"In college. When you broke up with me. I did something to cause it, didn't I?" He leaned forward, laying his forearms on the table. "Why didn't you tell me about it during that phone call? I would have done anything to earn your forgiveness. Didn't you know that about me?"

She sat there almost hunched in her chair as misery all but overwhelmed her. "You have it all wrong," she said dully.

"I don't think so, Blythe. I believe I have it exactly right, only you're still too kind to tell me about it. Don't be kind, please don't be kind. Be honest, Blythe. Tell me what I did, even if you still can't forgive me."

She realized that she was on the verge of breaking down, and if she fell apart now she just might tell him everything. It was such a horrifying thought that she gained some strength from it.

"There's nothing to tell," she said sharply. "Why won't you accept that?"

"Then tell me why I make you uncomfortable, dammit!"

"I *did* tell you! How many times do you have to hear it?"

He pointed an accusing finger at her. "You've told me nothing! You said I make you uncomfortable, and that my prying and digging into the past makes you uncomfortable. What kind of information is that? Do you realize how you reacted when I suggested that you might be afraid of something?'' She did it again, right before his eyes; she cringed as though struck. "You *are* afraid,'' he said in utter astonishment.

"I am not!''

"Then prove it by having dinner with me!''

They were practically shouting, and each of them realized it at the same moment. There was so much tension in the air it was almost tangible, and both of them suddenly felt very foolish.

"I'm sorry,'' Brent said, speaking much more quietly.

Blythe could hardly believe that she had let him make her so angry. Obviously he was not going to leave her be, and now he believed that she was afraid of the past, afraid of him. She drew in a deep breath. Somehow she had to throw him off the scent, and she could think of only one way.

"I *will* prove that I'm not afraid of you,'' she said with studied calmness. "If having dinner with you is proof of anything, which I doubt.''

"I never said you were afraid of me, Blythe,'' he gently reminded her. "But I still believe you're afraid of something. However, I'm very pleased that you'll have dinner with me, and I promise not to pry while we eat. I've discovered that Coeur d'Alene has some excellent restaurants. Do you still love Chinese food?''

She felt trapped, but she had caused it as much as Brent had. "Chinese is fine, if that's what you prefer.''

"It's what *you* prefer. I'd like this to be a pleasant evening. Do you have a favorite restaurant?''

"No, you choose,'' she said listlessly. "What time?'' It was nearing five, and she felt that she should change clothes.

"You name it.''

She got to her feet. "Seven.''

Brent rose. "Seven it is. Thanks for letting me see the house again, thanks for the coffee and I'm sorry we argued. I don't like arguments and dissension, Blythe, and there's not a reason in the world why you and I should argue about anything. I'll go now and be back at seven.''

She followed him to the front door, feeling totally shattered. He was a strikingly handsome man, and if he were anyone else she would have been looking forward to having dinner with him.

But he wasn't anyone else; he was the one man in this whole wretched world with whom she shouldn't be spending time. He wasn't a bit dense, either, and if she didn't stay constantly alert he just might infiltrate the wall of secrecy she had erected around herself so many years ago. *He* might think this was going to be a pleasant evening, but she knew better.

He crossed the threshold, then stopped on the porch and turned to look at her. "I just realized that you're not wearing dark glasses today. Are your eyes feeling better?"

"Yes." It seemed that all she did was lie to him, and it was starting to get her down.

He smiled at her, and it was a wholesome, generous smile. "I'm glad," he said. "It's really a shame to hide such beautiful eyes behind dark glasses. See you later."

After closing the door, she leaned weakly against it. When they had been lovers he'd often told her how beautiful her eyes were. He'd been complimentary about so many things— her legs, her eyes, her intelligence. He had been her first lover, and he'd been so wonderfully kind and patient with her naiveté in bed.

Abruptly she pushed away from the door, telling herself that she shouldn't be thinking of those things.

After all, they could never be more than the most casual of acquaintances.

And this evening was going to be one of the worst personal trials she'd had to live through in many years. Remembering their romantic past was not the best way to begin it.

Forcing Brent from her mind, she went upstairs to her bedroom to decide what to wear.

While getting ready for the evening ahead, Blythe stopped every few minutes and asked herself how she had let this happen. Her system roiled with dread. Brent's innocence seared her conscience. She remembered him as a hard-working young man, determined to get an education. She recalled the two of them laughing about how difficult it was to arrange their busy schedules so they could see each other. He had worked several jobs while maintaining a four-point grade average. He'd told her that until they'd met he hadn't done any dating, and she had never doubted that every hour he'd spent with her had taken some serious juggling of his jobs, classes and study time.

She also remembered him telling her that he was the kind of man who would fall in love only once in his life. She realized now that he'd been a romantic young man and had probably liked the idea of his first love also being his last, unrealistic as his attitude had been.

They had both been unrealistic, she thought with a heavy sigh while attempting to choose a dress that was suitable for a good restaurant without being suggestive. They'd been very young, naive in different ways and joyously excited whenever they'd managed to steal a few hours together. Falling in love had completely changed her. She had entered her first year of college as a serious young woman with nothing on her mind but her long-time dream of becoming a teacher. After she'd met Brent her education had still been important, but she had become a woman in love, and she had walked around campus and sat in classes in a state of euphoria that was so lovely, so enchanting, that she had dreamily felt the world had become a place of boundless beauty.

She hadn't been able to quite pull herself out of that almost mindless ebullience when she'd learned she was pregnant. Her ability to see the situation as it really was had been heavily influenced by her love for Brent. He'd been financially strapped, exhausting himself with work and classes and struggling to make ends meet, and for a week she had weighed her options without a word to Brent, simply because she hadn't wanted to add to his already overwhelming burdens.

It had struck her one evening that she needed advice, and who else would she go to with a problem of this sort but her parents? They had always been there for her, they were supporting her education, they were wise and sympathetic people and she'd known in her heart that they would come up with a solution that would be perfect for both her and Brent. Never once had she visualized *any* solution that hadn't included Brent. He was the man she loved and the father of her unborn child. In later years, as she had matured, she'd realized that she'd been subconsciously hoping for financial support when she approached her parents, and perhaps if had she talked to her father first, instead of her mother, she might have gotten it. Dr. Harry Benning would probably have been more understanding and kinder than her mother had been.

Oh, why was she thinking about that now? Blythe asked herself impatiently as she yanked a simply styled blue dress from the closet. It was all water under the bridge, and the last thing she needed was another bout of the blues, which happened every time she let herself dwell on the past.

But she couldn't always control her thoughts, and while she brushed her hair in front of a mirror and eyed her reflection, she found herself wondering with a very heavy heart if her son or daughter looked like her or like Brent. Their child could be dark-haired like Brent or blond like herself. He or she could be tall and built like Brent, or small boned and of average height, as she was.

Her face in the mirror suddenly blurred from the tears in her eyes, and she threw down the brush and hurried from the bathroom. She would find something to do until seven; she had to. Staying busy was her only salvation. It was the reason the house was always spotless and the yard a showplace.

It was the reason she loved teaching, because there was always something for an educator of young minds to do to keep busy. She needed, desperately, to get back to her job, her career, her students.

She needed even *more* desperately to leave Coeur d'Alene and never see Brent Morrison again. Ironically, he was the person who could bring this about by buying the house.

Was he going to do it?

"Bill, if I don't buy Blythe Benning's house right away, am I in any danger of losing it?" Brent had made several phone calls from his motel room before locating Bill Harkens, but he'd finally reached him.

"Your guess is as good as mine about that, Brent," the agent replied.

"Well, let me ask you this. Is there any way I can tie up the house without Blythe knowing about it?"

"No. Any offer you might present to me must be passed on to Blythe's listing agent, Abby Decker, almost immediately. She will present it to Blythe. That's the law. I'm not sure I understand the problem, Brent. If you want the house, why delay your offer? Or try to keep it from Blythe?"

"I can't explain, Bill. Let me amend that statement. I'd rather *not* explain."

"I see. Well, it's your business. I can tell you one thing, which I've touched on before. The Benning house has been on the market for some time. Now, a serious buyer could come along tomorrow, but I don't think it's very likely. That's only my opinion and I could be wrong, you understand. Obviously you have a reason for not making an offer now, and I would hate to see you lose the place if you really want it. But that house has never drawn hordes of potential buyers, and there's a good chance that another person like yourself won't come along for months."

"And yet, as you said, someone could come along tomorrow," Brent said rather grimly.

"Exactly."

"Well, thanks, Bill. I'll think it over."

After hanging up, Brent *did* think it over. He sat at the table in his room, doodled on a pad and thought very hard about it. One thing he should keep in mind, he told himself, was that the Benning house was not apt to sell quickly when the Sunrise project was completed and he went on to another. But his quandary wasn't just about buying a house for resale after a year. It was mostly about Blythe, and about keeping her in Coeur d'Alene so they could get reacquainted.

Eventually an idea occurred to him, and he wondered if he should discuss it with Bill. But Bill couldn't speak for Blythe. Not even her listing agent could do that. His best bet was to subtly broach Blythe with the idea during dinner tonight and gauge her reaction to it with his own eyes and ears.

With that decision firmly fixed in his mind, he left the table and went into the bathroom for a shower and a shave.

Blythe tried to be tactful about the large bouquet of roses in her arms, delivered by Brent when he arrived at seven. "Thank you, they're very beautiful," she said, doing her best to squelch an urge to giggle, which in itself was most unusual for her. Truth was, for many years now it had taken something truly hilarious to make her laugh at all.

"You're welcome." He followed Blythe through the foyer, then stopped at the doorway leading to the family room and started laughing. In plain sight, nicely displayed in prominent locations, were three large vases of roses. "I can't believe I forgot about the rose garden in your own backyard."

"It's the thought that counts," Blythe said, and realized that she meant it. Whatever their past connection, and however leery she was of getting involved with him again, he was a nice person. In fact, in her heart of hearts she suspected that Brent Morrison possessed the same traits today that had drawn her to him in college—intelligence, a wonderful if sometimes offbeat sense of humor and a kindly nature. And, of course, his good looks were so obvious she would have to be dense as a door not to notice.

Well, she wasn't dense and it had been a very long time since a man had brought her flowers. Wise or not, she felt cheered up by the bouquet in her arms—felt like a woman, something else that hadn't happened in a very long time.

"I'll put these in a vase," she said. "It will only take a few minutes. Sit in the family room, or feel free to wander, if you prefer."

"I'd like to take another look at the den, if you're sure you don't mind."

"I don't mind at all." Blythe hurried away.

Brent went to the doorway of the small den and leaned against the framework. It was a wonderful little room with its walls of shelves and hundreds of books, but he found himself thinking of Blythe instead of the den. She was even more beautiful now than she'd been in college. Some people aged very well, and he would bet anything that someone meeting Blythe for the first time would never guess her true age. She looked especially young tonight. Blue was definitely her color, he decided, thinking about the pretty blue dress she was wearing.

How his thoughts jumped from her dress to sex he would never know, but that was what happened. He suddenly wanted to make love with Blythe, and everything around him melded into a beautiful fantasy. *She walked up to him, empty-handed because she had placed the vase of flowers somewhere else in the house. She smiled at him warmly, invitingly, and he put his arms around her. She responded with a sigh of breathless anticipation and wound her own arms around him. They kissed. Her mouth against his was a heavenly sensation, but both of them knew they wanted more than kisses, and they started undressing each other.*

"I'm ready when you are."

Brent came out of his trance with a start. He cleared his throat. "I'm ready, too," he said a bit hoarsely, thinking that if she had the slightest inkling of how ready he really was she would probably throw him out on his ear.

What had he seen in the den to affect him so strangely? Blythe wondered uneasily. "Do you like this room?" she asked a bit cautiously, for it was really her favorite room in the house, and she couldn't help hoping that he saw something special in it, as well.

"Yes," he said. "I like this room very much."

She decided that he must have been thinking of something other than the den. It occurred to her then to wonder about his financial status. The house was not inexpensive. Could he have been worrying about its cost, or perhaps how he was going to pay for it? He appeared to be prosperous, but appearances could be terribly deceiving.

On their way out to Brent's car, parked in her driveway, Blythe wondered if she should ask him point-blank how he intended to pay for the house. It could be the reason he was procrastinating on an offer, she realized with mounting concern.

Still, concerned or not, when they were in the car and driving down Lakeside Avenue, she could not force herself to mention the subject that, given Brent's especially thoughtful mood, seemed to her to be the one they were both thinking about.

He spoke first. "I made a reservation at the Lake City Steak House. Do you know the place?"

"I know of its existence, but I haven't eaten there," she answered quietly.

"I have. I think you'll like it. I hope you do, anyway."

"I'm sure I will." It was an automatic response and quite untrue, as she wasn't sure of anything this evening. Certainly she had a horde of misgivings where Brent was concerned. For instance, why would a man with no family even want such a large house?

Her heart sank. She had undoubtedly been right when she'd accused him of using the house as an excuse to see her. What did he want from her? she thought as panic suddenly invaded her system. Would he use unscrupulous methods to learn what had really happened so many years ago? Why would it still matter to him? In spite of his story about being hired for the Sunrise project, had he really come to Coeur d'Alene to find her?

Her own panic frightened her. Breathing deeply, she told herself to calm down. It was all speculation and extremely unlikely. How could she be so egotistical to suppose that he had ever even thought of her to that extent?

He hadn't, she told herself, feeling a little less tense over that conclusion. Their meeting again after so long had been pure accident. He knew nothing of their past and he never would if she was careful. There was, after all, no one but herself to tell him about it.

Dammit, she thought next, she should be able to enjoy having dinner with an attractive man instead of having to watch every word that passed between them.

And maybe she would, she added resentfully. Maybe she

would relax and pretend that her dinner companion was someone else. There were many topics they could discuss over dinner without even coming near her dreadful secret. Surely she was smart enough to control a conversation with anyone for a few hours.

But Brent wasn't just anyone, was he? And he was easily as smart as she was, maybe smarter.

While he drove and chatted amicably about the great weather and what a pretty town Coeur d'Alene was, Blythe sat there numbly and wished she were anywhere but in Brent Morrison's car.

But there again, she had only herself to blame. So what if he had accused her of being afraid of something? No one had forced her to take up his silly challenge to prove she *wasn't* afraid by going out with him tonight. All he'd been doing was fishing for information; she hadn't had to fall into his trap! Oh, yes, he was much smarter than she was, much more clever.

"Here we are," Brent announced while driving into the parking lot of the Lake City Steak House. After switching off the ignition, he turned his head and smiled at her. "I hope you're hungry, because the food here is exceptionally good." He noticed the wan look on her face, and his smile faded. "What's wrong, Blythe?" he asked quietly.

She drew a breath and forced a brighter expression. "Not a thing."

To her surprise he reached out and took her hand. "Let's forget everything but enjoying the evening," he said gently.

The electricity flowing from his hand to hers was so startling that Blythe found herself holding her breath. She looked into his eyes and saw, very clearly, that he felt it, as well. And not only did he feel it, he was absorbed in the moment.

Abruptly she jerked her hand back. "Don't do that again," she said stiffly. "I agreed to have dinner with you, not to sit in your car and hold hands."

Brent tried to laugh off the pain she had just inflicted. "Don't beat around the bush, Blythe. Say what you mean."

"I think I just did that. Are we going in, or aren't we?"

"Yes, we're going in." With an inward sigh, Brent opened his door and got out.

Chapter Five

In spite of her own topsy-turvy emotions, Blythe was impressed with Brent's confidence in the quite elegant restaurant. He discreetly tipped the host and they were seated at a table with a marvelous view of the lake. He pulled out her chair himself instead of relying on the host for that amenity, then took both menus from the man, seated himself and handed one to her.

"If you're in the mood for a steak," he said, "I recommend the filet mignon. However, this place also serves fresh fish. I see that tonight's special is salmon with béarnaise sauce."

"That's what I'll have," Blythe said, setting her menu aside.

"It sounds good to me, too." A waiter appeared, introduced himself and asked if they would care for a cocktail before dinner. Blythe said no, Brent did the same and then he ordered salmon for both of them. "I'd like to see your wine list," he told the young man. Without consulting Blythe on whether she even drank wine, he ordered a bottle of chardonnay with instructions to make sure it was well chilled.

After the waiter had gone, he said with a smile, "I hope you enjoy a dry white wine with salmon."

"Yes, I do, thank you."

While they were eating their salads and sipping wine, Brent realized how wrong he'd been to presume that Blythe was the same soft, sweet woman she'd been in college. She *looked* soft—she looked beautifully soft and feminine, in fact—but while he couldn't doubt her femininity, her softness was apparently limited to her flawless complexion.

Something had changed her. Some event, or series of events, perhaps merely the passing years, had hardened her. It struck Brent as sad, but surely her personal life could not have been any more difficult than his own. If only he could get her to talk to him, *really* talk, about their commingled pasts, about the many years since. So far this evening their conversation had consisted of remarks about the striking decor of the restaurant, the many patrons and the excellent service.

Noticing that her wineglass was almost empty, he refilled it, added a splash to his own glass and returned the bottle to the ice bucket. He also noticed that she seemed to be relaxing. The wine, he thought. He was sipping his wine because he was always cautious with alcohol when he knew he would be driving. Blythe, however, didn't have that deterrent and she appeared to truly be enjoying the wine.

Just how relaxed would she become with three or four glasses of wine? he mused. Should he make an extra effort to find out? Deliberately plying a woman with a delicious wine to get something from her was not normal routine for him, but since all he wanted from Blythe was some honest conversation, he couldn't find too much fault with the idea.

Of course, he thought next, conversation *wasn't* all he wanted from Blythe. He'd honestly never thought it would happen to him again, but he seemed to be falling in love. There was something droll about falling in love twice with the same woman, but feelings for another human being developed without one's conscious approval. Simply put, he couldn't help how he felt.

Over the entrée Brent talked about the Sunrise project.

Blythe found herself enjoying the conversation, and even laughed over anecdotes he dug up about past projects.

She loved his deep, rumbling laugh, and recalled that she had also loved the sound of his laugh twenty-four years ago. Externally he'd changed very little. There were some lines at the corners of his eyes that hadn't been there before, a smattering of silver in his dark hair, and he'd put on a few pounds through the years. He looked almost as he had in college, but then, she had to admit, he could be thinking the same about her, and look how much she'd changed. Just because one's changes weren't visible didn't mean they weren't part and parcel of a person.

Of course, twenty-odd years was a long time, and some change was only natural. Again she wondered why he wasn't married. He was such a fine-looking man, with flair and style and that incredible smile. There had to have been other women since she had walked out of his life.

She sighed quietly, because his love life was something she would never ask him about, and finally, at long last, admitted to herself that the evening was lovely. It felt wonderful to be dining in a good restaurant with a handsome escort again, if only for one evening. The food was delicious, and she knew that the excellent wine had warmed her persistently chilling thoughts. She was, in fact, enjoying herself far more than she'd thought possible.

''About your house,'' Brent said matter-of-factly, taking the wine bottle from the bucket to top off her glass again, ''I think I'm going to buy it. If you agree to certain terms, that is.''

She became vaguely suspicious, but the wine had mellowed her and she spoke calmly. ''What terms?''

''A sixty-day closing, for one thing. And, Blythe, I don't like the idea of the house sitting empty. Correct me if I'm wrong, but I have the impression that once you receive a substantial offer on the place you will immediately return to Connecticut. I'd like you to stay and look after the house until the paperwork is completed and the closing is final.''

She frowned slightly and spoke honestly. ''I was hoping for a two-week closing date.''

"Not practical."

"Why isn't it? Bill Harkens gave me the impression that you were quite anxious to get settled."

"Uh, true, but I need a few months to, uh, to wrap up some things before closing the deal." He should have been prepared for that question and was annoyed with himself for the oversight.

"Brent, if you put a sizable down-payment in escrow, I would be happy to give you early possession. You could be living in the house yourself, and it wouldn't be empty."

Her logic threw him, and he put undue concentration into saturating the last bite of his salmon with the béarnaise sauce. "This is delicious. Did you enjoy the salmon?"

"Very much."

"In Seattle fresh salmon was always, or nearly always, available. My wife was a good cook, and she—"

"Your wife!" Thunderstruck, Blythe stared at him. And then she realized that he'd used the past tense, and she became very still.

"Blythe," he said very quietly, "my wife and four-year-old daughter were killed in a car accident ten years ago."

Blythe's heart nearly stopped beating. He hadn't lost one child, he'd lost two! Tears suddenly burned her eyes and clogged her throat.

"I'm so sorry," she whispered raggedly. "I'm so very, very sorry." Pushing her chair back, she stood and picked up her purse. The linen napkin on her lap fell to the floor. "Please excuse me. I have to…go to the powder room."

Brent rose because she had, and he sat down again with a feeling of bewilderment. Blythe had apologized as though the loss of his family was her fault, which, while considerate, made very little sense. Regardless, he couldn't doubt that what he'd told her had impacted her most cruelly, and he was terribly sorry that he'd chosen tonight to tell her about Debbie and Lori. Actually, he'd done no choosing at all; their conversation had led in that direction and he had merely carried it through.

His gaze flicked across the room, and with enormous shock

bolting through his system he saw Blythe veering from the lady's room and heading for the door of the restaurant.

He didn't have the check yet; they had just barely finished eating their entrées. With great haste he searched the large dining room for his waiter, and when he spotted the young man Brent got to his feet and motioned him over. At the same time he mentally calculated the tab and reached for his wallet. As the waiter approached the table, Brent laid down some bills.

"Do you have my check with you?" Brent asked.

"No, sir, but I can get it."

"This will more than cover it. Keep the change." He dashed across the room to the door and hurried through it. Night was falling and the parking lot lights had come on. People were getting in and out of vehicles, and someone's laughter floated on the evening air. Frantically Brent looked through the maze of cars for Blythe. He spotted his own car, but she wasn't near it. My Lord, he thought, completely at a loss. What had happened in there to cause this?

One side of the parking lot was separated from an attractive apartment complex by a low wall, and in the dimming light Brent finally saw Blythe sitting on the far end of it. Relief nearly staggered him, and he all but ran across the parking lot to reach her.

She heard him coming and listlessly turned her face toward him. Brent's heart sank. He had never seen a more forlorn expression on anyone's face than what he saw on Blythe's. He stopped running and approached her at a much slower pace.

She didn't say anything, so neither did he. Instead, he sat on the wall next to her, and when several minutes had gone by and she still hadn't spoken, he murmured, "It's a beautiful evening, isn't it?"

"Yes," she said in a whispery little voice.

He let a few more minutes pass, then said quietly, "I'm sorry, Blythe."

She released a long, desolate-sounding sigh. "You have nothing to be sorry for."

"And you do?"

"Yes."

"Can you tell me about it?"

"No."

"But it has something to do with me?"

"I can't talk about it. Please don't ask."

Brent sat there perplexed and confused. "How can I help you if you won't talk to me?"

"I don't expect you to help. You couldn't, in any case. No one could."

"All right, maybe I couldn't help, but what could be so terrible that you can't talk about it?" A chilling thought struck him. "Blythe, are you ill?"

She laughed, and it was a bitter sound to Brent's ears. Stunned that she apparently had a reason to feel bitter, and positive now that she was suffering from some horrible disease, he sorrowfully turned to look at her, and he watched her face closely when she said, "No, I'm not ill."

Her answer took him aback; he'd been so sure. Now he was confused again. But there remained in his system a remnant of the sorrow he'd felt before her denial of illness, and without conscious thought he took her hand in his.

"You're a very unhappy woman," he said softly. "And obviously you aren't looking to anyone else to ease your unhappiness. But, Blythe, if no one ever cared about anyone else, or tried to help other people through bad times, this would be a mighty bleak world."

Blythe looked down at their intertwined hands. His was big and warm and comforting around hers, and this time she didn't pull away from his touch. It seemed so ironic that he was the last man from whom she should be seeking comfort and still be the only man from whom she might be able to accept it. Even the man she had married hadn't known of her secret misery; she had not been able to force the words from her mouth. If he hadn't become ill so soon after their marriage she might have reached the stage where confession was not only necessary but sensible, but that chance had been snatched away from her by the brutality of his illness.

Perhaps it was caused by the wine she'd drunk with dinner, but for a few moments she felt as though the last twenty-odd years hadn't happened at all, and that she was sitting with Brent somewhere on campus, holding hands as they had done so often during their brief but passionate love affair in college. One thing she had never doubted was the sincerity of their love for each other, and with Brent's hand around hers this evening she could almost feel it again.

It softened her voice as well as her heart. "I appreciate your kindness, but some things simply cannot be shared."

"Do you think kindness is the only thing I feel for you? Have you really forgotten what we once meant to each other?" Brent raised his free hand and cupped the back of her neck. He could see on Blythe's face that the intimacy had startled her, but still he released her hand and tipped her chin. His kiss was gentle, a mere brushing of their lips, and he heard and felt her swift intake of air.

"I haven't forgotten anything, Blythe, and I don't think you have, either," he whispered before kissing her the way he'd been wanting to, with emotion and affection and all that passes through a man when he is kissing a woman who arouses feelings that have lain dormant for many years.

Blythe was undergoing a similar awakening. Lovely emotions that she had once taken for granted and then had disappeared because of trying circumstances were suddenly alive again in her body. Her lips became softer under his, pliant and giving, and the kiss lasted until they both needed air.

Inhaling, Brent kept his face close to hers and looked deeply into her eyes. "It's the same for us, isn't it? Exactly as it was twenty-four years ago."

She shivered, not because she was cold, for the evening air was only slightly cool. Her shiver was caused by internal upheaval. She should not be kissing Brent. She should not be letting him kiss her.

And she most definitely should not permit him to believe that nothing had changed since their college love affair.

But her emotions, once stirred, would not give way to common sense, and the only objection she was able to make to his advances was a weakly stated, "Everything changes, Brent."

"I disagree. Time changes most things, yes, but not everything. Blythe, I could so easily fall in love with you again."

She lowered her eyes to avoid his. "Please don't say things like that. Our lives have gone in different directions. We are not the same people we were in college. You don't know me, Brent."

He settled his arm around her and brought her head to his chest. "I want to know you. I've been trying to know you since the day I walked into your house and saw you. I couldn't believe my eyes at first, but there you were, and there I was, and things I'd thought long forgotten began coming back. Hasn't it been that way for you? Haven't you started remembering little things, like how often we laughed together? Like how we juggled classes and my work schedules to spend time together?"

This was what she had been fearing most—not a kiss, not an embrace, but a stroll down memory lane. Though her heart was beating much too rapidly and she was almost dizzy from his clean scent and the sensation of his body so close to hers, she sat up and edged away from him.

"I think I'd like to go home now, Brent."

Although she wasn't looking at him, Brent gazed at her for a very long time. She had shut the door again, he realized sadly, and she wasn't going to let him get past it a second time tonight.

"All right," he finally said with a sigh of resignation, and got to his feet. He offered his hand to help her up, and she took it, but only until she was off the wall, whereupon she immediately let go.

Actually, he reasoned as they wound through the parking lot to his car, it was almost a miracle that she'd opened the door at all. He should be pleased that he'd made that much progress, and should look forward to making more during their next time together instead of feeling frustrated. Maybe if he hadn't kissed her, and she hadn't kissed him back, he wouldn't *be* frustrated, he thought while unlocking the passenger door and holding it open for her.

But he *had* kissed her and she had unquestionably kissed him back. Now he didn't know which he wanted more from her—a long, serious conversation about the past, with no holds barred, or more kisses and some serious lovemaking, also with no holds barred. Small wonder he felt frustrated, he thought grimly as he got in the car himself.

Driving her home, he went back to their conversation in the restaurant and said, "I never would have told you about losing my family if I'd had any idea of how hearing about it would affect you. I didn't mean to upset you, Blythe, that wasn't my intention."

"Of course it wasn't," she murmured, wishing ardently that he hadn't chosen that topic to discuss during the drive.

"I keep wondering why it upset you so much."

Since she couldn't explain, she fell back on a generality. "Senseless tragedy always gets to me." After a second she added, "I'm sorry if I embarrassed you."

"You didn't embarrass me. Don't even think it." What she'd done was scare the hell out of him, but he was too kind to lay that on her. His mind changed directions. He didn't want the evening to end this soon, and he asked, "How about taking a drive around the lake before we go home?"

Blythe hesitated; riding around with Brent after that emotionally searing kiss would be like asking for further intimacy. It was dangerous business as far as she was concerned, because she knew she had kissed him back and that nothing had felt so good in a very long time. And dare she forget his talking about falling in love? No, she couldn't chance another such encounter. She simply didn't trust herself.

"Not tonight," she said. "Perhaps another time," she added, just so she wouldn't sound rude.

"Should I take that to mean you'll go out with me again?"

She wanted to appear calm and collected, but Brent wasn't making it easy. Her voice rose just a little. "Brent, dinner together is not going to become a habit."

"We could do other things together besides eat, you know."

Her calculated patience was starting to wear thin. "Your persistence is annoying."

She was speaking her mind, so Brent did the same. "So is your stubbornness."

"Fine," she snapped. "Since we annoy each other so much, we shouldn't attempt any more socializing."

Frustration did strange things to a man, Brent realized. "You just keep adding more questions to what is becoming a very long list in my mind," he told her. "Why are you constantly evasive? What's in the past that you can't, or won't, talk about? Why did you react so strongly to hearing about my wife and daughter? What are you afraid of? Were you afraid before I reentered your life, or did meeting me again cause it? Blythe, I could go on and on."

"Please don't," she said sharply. "I'm not the least bit interested in your list of questions."

"Why not? You see, you just keep making that list longer. Why wouldn't I be curious about you? Why aren't you curious about me? We're not strangers, for hell's sake."

"You're dead wrong about that."

Brent took his eyes off the street long enough to send her a befuddled glance. "You can't mean that."

"Sorry if it unnerves you, but I do mean it. Knowing each other twenty years ago does not mean that we're not strangers now. A lot of water's gone under that bridge, Brent, and water keeps moving."

"What's that supposed to mean?" he barked.

"It means that my life didn't suddenly come to a halt twenty years ago, and neither did yours."

Brent turned onto Lakeside Avenue; they were only a few blocks from her house. The evening was almost over, and had he gotten even one point across to Blythe? Yes, for a few minutes in that parking lot he'd seen progress in their relationship, but that observation, he realized, had been based solely on the fact that she had kissed him back.

Well, isn't that interesting, he thought sardonically. She

wouldn't talk to him in an open, honest way, but she would permit an extremely emotional kiss to happen between them.

He kept silent and so did she. In Blythe's case she was relieved that he'd stopped talking; in Brent's, his thoughts were going a mile a minute. The very second that he pulled the car into her driveway, he unlatched his safety belt and slid across the seat. Before she could get one word out of her mouth, startled though she was, he had his arms around her and was kissing her.

She pushed against his chest and tried to tear her mouth from his, but he was ten times stronger than she was and she finally gave up and let him take his kiss, furiously vowing in the back of her mind that it was the last one he would ever force on her.

But her own body began betraying her. An ache in the pit of her stomach became too much to combat, and she felt as though even her bones were melting. All the passion she hadn't unleashed in years and years was suddenly devouring her, and her hands rose to hold his face while her mouth opened under his and accepted his insistent tongue. She heard herself moan deep in her throat, she heard his hard breathing and the desire racking her body became almost unbearable.

He let go of her as abruptly as he'd grabbed her, and she nearly cried, "No, no, don't stop!"

But he had stopped, and was leaning back against the seat, trying to catch his breath. She sat there, dazed and shocked, knowing she could get out now but was unable to do it.

He finally mumbled, thickly, "Tell me again what strangers we are." Then he slid over, opened his door and got out.

Mobility returned in a rush, and hastily she undid her seat belt and fumbled with the handle of her own door. She had just found it when he opened the door for her. Ignoring his outstretched hand, she climbed out under her own steam and started for the house. Halfway there, she turned and faced him.

"That's far enough. You are *not* invited in!"

He smiled. "Whatever you say. Good night, Blythe. Oh, I almost forgot. Think about the terms I offered you on the house."

"You will never have this house! I wouldn't sell it to you if you were the only buyer on earth!"

His smile became a laugh. "Sure you will, honey. By morning you'll be your normal cold, pragmatic self, and *that* woman wants to sell even though the woman you are now— and believe me, you *are* a woman—despises the ground I walk on and would say anything to put me in my place. Pleasant dreams, sweetheart."

She walked into the house fighting tears.

Chapter Six

Blythe sat at the kitchen table with the newspaper and a cup of coffee, her usual after-breakfast routine, even though the half piece of toast she'd forced down could hardly be construed as a normal breakfast. But she'd put in a terrible night and felt this morning as though she hadn't gone to bed at all. The newsprint blurred before her eyes, and she finally folded the paper, set it aside and let her thoughts go where they would.

She had already gone over last night with Brent so many times that every word they'd spoken, every move each of them had made, seemed etched on her brain, as though she had memorized a play. *Act I, Scene I: Brent Morrison provokes and maneuvers Blythe Benning into having dinner with him.* That thought caused her lips to settle into a thin, tense line.

She could berate herself for being a fool, and she did; she could tell herself again and again that she had not had to *let* Brent maneuver her into anything, and she did; she could curse Brent's brash nerve, and she did; but there was one thing she couldn't do: she could not obliterate the memory of his kisses.

She had suffered feverish, erotic thoughts all night because of them, and she still felt them this morning, on her lips, in the pit of her stomach and in every other erogenous zone of her disgustingly traitorous body.

One peculiarity to ponder was why last night's events hadn't immediately brought on the blues. She felt miserably unhappy, angry and resentful, but the blue funk that had always descended whenever something occurred to remind her of the past was glaringly absent. Not that she wished it weren't, heaven forbid. It was just so bizarre, and she truly didn't understand herself in this instance.

Her most trying question was how she should behave the next time she saw Brent. There was no doubt in her mind that he would finesse another meeting, and it was terribly disconcerting to recognize signs within herself that she wished things were different and she could openly, honestly look forward to another evening with him.

But it just could not be. It could *never* be, so she really must stop wishing for the impossible.

The day dragged by. Blythe usually dashed through the house with a dustcloth every morning, so that the house was always immaculate in case a Realtor wanted to show it. Today she simply could not drum up any enthusiasm about the house, nor could she force herself outdoors to make sure the yard was perfect.

By three, when the phone rang, she was gritting her teeth with nervous energy, but she hadn't even been able to force herself to stack the dishes she'd used for breakfast and lunch in the dishwasher, and they sat in the kitchen sink.

Her pulse leaped when the phone jangled, and she approached the instrument gingerly and cautiously, as though it might bite her. If it's Brent, she thought, I'll hang up. But it could be Sierra or Tamara, or one of the neighbors, and she couldn't just ignore it simply because she would prefer to let the damn thing ring rather than take the chance that it might be Brent calling. Slowly, apprehensively, she brought the receiver to her ear. "Hello?"

"Abby Decker here, Blythe. I have marvelous news. I'm

holding in my hand a very good purchase offer for your house. May I bring it by?''

Blythe's initial relief that it wasn't Brent on the line was short-lived, because she knew the ''very good purchase offer'' that had Abby all giddy and pleased was *from* Brent.

It irritated Blythe that he'd been right about her changing her mind about not selling to him, but facts were facts. The sooner someone bought the house—and he was the only one interested in it—the sooner she could put two thousand miles between them. It seemed even more crucial to accomplish that now than it had been before last night.

''Yes, Abby, come by anytime.''

''Great. See you in fifteen minutes.''

Blythe used those fifteen minutes to stack the dirty dishes in the dishwasher and prepare a pitcher of lemonade. When Abby arrived, Blythe led her to the kitchen, offered lemonade, which Abby accepted, and they sat at the table. Abby was about fifty years of age, Blythe estimated, and so happily immersed in real estate that Blythe envied her ebullience and vitality. Since her first year of college, when her whole life had gone to hell, she hadn't felt one-tenth of Abby Decker's zest about anything. Looking at Abby's big, friendly smile as she dug into her large leather bag, Blythe vowed to try to do better in the ''zest'' department. Abby's enthusiasm was something to admire, not envy, and Blythe felt that she should at least attempt to emulate it.

''Here we are,'' Abby announced, laying a file folder on the table. ''I didn't sell the house, Blythe, an agent from Lowery's North Idaho Realty brought in this offer.''

''Bill Harkens.''

''I see that you've put two and two together. Well, in my opinion this is an exceptionally good offer, but, of course, it's entirely up to you to accept or decline it.'' Abby opened the folder and took out some papers, which she passed to Blythe. ''I'll be quiet while you read. If you have any questions along the way, feel free to ask them.'' She lifted her glass and took a swallow of lemonade. ''This is good.''

"Thank you," Blythe murmured absently. Her mind was completely focused on the purchase offer in her hands as she began reading it. The price was twelve thousand dollars more than she had asked for, which puzzled her until she'd read further. She raised astonished eyes to Abby. "He wants *all* the furniture?"

"Apparently so."

"But some of it is…" She sighed. If Brent wanted that worn-out junk in the basement, what was it to her? However, she reread the clause and said to Abby, "It's so vague. It only says that he wants the furniture in the house. How does he even know what's here? Specifically, I mean. And, Abby, there are some things that could be construed as furnishings that he can't have." Leaving the papers on the table, Blythe got up, walked over to a corner shelf and waved her hand at it. "The miniatures on this shelf, for instance. They belonged to my great-grandmother, and they should be kept in the family."

"Oh, I'm sure Mr. Morrison isn't expecting to get every item in the house, Blythe. He must realize there are things with sentimental value that you wouldn't sell to anyone."

"But those papers don't say that, Abby."

"No, I guess they don't," Abby said slowly. "Tell you what, I'll add a sentence to the furniture clause, and you initial it. When Mr. Morrison initials it as well, the whole thing will be agreed upon."

Blythe returned to her chair. "What will you add?"

"There's not much space, so I'll have to make it brief." Abby thought a moment. "I'll add, 'except for those items Blythe Benning deems personal.' That should do it."

Blythe spoke dryly. "I could deem half the furniture personal, if I were an unscrupulous person, Abby."

Abby looked downcast for a moment, then brightened. "I know what to add," she declared, and busily wrote on the document.

Smiling, she passed it to Blythe, who read aloud, "'The furniture will be inventoried by buyer and seller at a mutually agreed upon time.'" She lowered the papers, feeling as though someone had just let the air out of her balloon. Inventorying the things in this house could take days, and she didn't *want* to spend days with Brent. Not true, she amended. She would love to be able to spend time with Brent, it was just that she should not risk doing it.

But Abby looked so pleased with her own inventiveness, and Blythe couldn't explain her objections, in any case, so she merely sighed and continued reading the document.

She finally came to the closing date and Brent's request that she occupy the house until he could take possession in sixty days. Laying down the papers, she sat back, turned her head and stared out the window. Pricewise the offer was good, *more* than good. Somehow she would get through the inventory with Brent, although the mere idea of spending that much time with him was unnerving. But that aside, some of the furnishings were excellent pieces—the piano, for instance, and all of the furniture in the living room, including a unique mantel clock. A house of this size could not be furnished with new things for twelve thousand dollars, so he was negotiating a good deal for himself. But didn't he have any furniture of his own?

Well, that was neither here nor there. The only part of the offer that truly disturbed her was Brent's request that she occupy the house until closing, which he'd mentioned last night.

"Abby," she said, turning toward the agent, "Brent Morrison told me that he's concerned about the house sitting empty." She was about to add, "It sat empty from January to June and no one bothered it," when Abby interrupted.

"You've talked to the buyer yourself?"

"Yes. We, uh, knew each other years ago. We were…both surprised to run into each other again. You see, Brent came to the house not knowing that I owned it, and…" Her voice trailed off because she was explaining too much to a woman who couldn't possibly be more than politely interested.

Abby smiled. "That must have been a lovely surprise."

"It was more of a shock than a surprise, but that's not my point. I told Brent that I would be willing to give him early possession if he put a sizable sum in escrow. I see by these papers that he has written an earnest money check for five thousand dollars, and nothing at all is said about a substantial down-payment. Five thousand is not nearly enough for early possession, but I really want to return to my own home in Connecticut. What do you think?''

''Hmm, well, you could make Mr. Morrison a counteroffer, stating your own terms. How much money would you *like* him to put in escrow?''

''At least fifty-thousand. Do you think that's unreasonable?''

Abby fell silent and appeared to be thinking it over. ''Blythe,'' she said finally, ''would it be a hardship for you to remain in the house for another sixty days?''

''Not a hardship, no, but it would most definitely be an inconvenience. Abby, you know I'm a teacher. The fall school term is going to start in a very few weeks. I need to be there.''

A small frown played over Abby's features. ''Hmm, yes, I see what you mean. Blythe, I'll tell you what Bill Harkens said when he delivered this offer. He said, 'Abby, Morrison is willing to pay the full asking price, plus twelve thousand for the furniture, because he is also asking for a concession. He stressed how badly he needs sixty days to get his affairs in order before the closing date.' I asked Bill if his buyer had to arrange financing, thinking, of course, that was why he needed the sixty days, and Bill said, 'No, he has the cash to pay for it.' Now, I have no idea why Mr. Morrison needs those sixty days, but perhaps you do.''

''No, I don't.''

''All right, I think the next thing you should consider is how important it is to you to finalize this sale. In all these months, Blythe, this is the first offer to come in, and it's an excellent one. Are you willing to risk losing it?''

An uneasy premonition hit Blythe, and she got up to walk around the kitchen. *He's doing this to keep me here! He doesn't need sixty days, he doesn't need twenty days! He's manipulating me again. This is his way of preventing me from leaving!*

Her thoughts changed directions. *But why would he care if I left or didn't leave? What, really, is going on with that man?*

Does he think I will eventually break down and tell him everything? He knows, or at least suspects, that something unusual happened twenty-four years ago. Is that the reason he kissed me last night and talked about love? Did he think kisses and nonsensical talk would destroy my common sense? I can't believe he actually said that he was falling in love with me again. That is just too preposterous. She frowned. It *was* preposterous, wasn't it?

She turned to face Abby. "I don't know what to do. I'm not thrilled with having to inventory everything, but except for that sixty-day request, you're right about this being an excellent offer, and no, I don't want to lose it."

"Why don't you think it over for the rest of the day? I'll notify Harkens that the offer is in your hands." Abby gathered up her things and rose. "I recall your mentioning two sisters, and that you have power of attorney to make this decision entirely on your own, but it might help if you talked to them about it."

"It might," Blythe said thoughtfully. She should phone her sisters, in any case. They had a right to know that she had finally received an offer on the house.

Abby was all-smiles again. "I'm sure everything will turn out just fine. Call me with your decision."

"I will, Abby, and thank you." Blythe escorted the agent to the front door and said goodbye. Then she went to a phone and dialed first Sierra's number and then Tamara's. Other than a few minutes of personal chitchat with each sister, the two conversations were virtually the same. Blythe explained Brent's offer to purchase, without telling either sister that she'd known the potential buyer in college.

As she had suspected would be the case, both Sierra and Tamara told her that if she didn't want to remain in Coeur d'Alene any longer, then she shouldn't do so. Only she could make that decision. They expressed gratitude for the months she had already given to their mother's estate, and each said that she would never presume to tell Blythe when she should finally say enough was enough. They were sympathetic about her dilemma, but neither had a solution for it.

The calls hadn't helped a bit, Blythe thought with a heavy sigh after they were over. It had been nice hearing her sisters' voices and learning that each was happy and doing well, but the sale of their parents' house was completely on her own shoulders. She couldn't resent the situation, not when she herself had caused it. But last January, when she had offered to see to the estate, it hadn't occurred to her that it might drag on for so long.

Returning to the papers Abby had left with her, Blythe read the offer again. Was she right to assume that with this offer, Brent was trying to manipulate her into staying in Idaho, or was her imagination running just a little bit wild?

He'd told everyone involved, herself included, that he needed sixty days to take care of some loose ends. He'd also told everyone concerned that he was anxious to get settled. The two didn't coincide.

And yet, what if both were accurate? He could be anxious to get settled and still have some loose ends to tie up. After all, what did she really know about his business? His architectural projects?

The weight of her decision was a heavy burden, but if she turned down Brent's offer, how long would it be before she received another one? That accursed inventory was hanging over her head, of course, but once that was done there really would be no further reason for them to see each other.

And then, without warning, a startling disappointment struck her. Her breath caught in her throat and her heart fluttered alarmingly. Oh, dear God, what was happening to her now? she thought frantically. Surely she wasn't going to let a few kisses get to her.

But apparently they had *already* gotten to her, because Brent's kisses were the reason she'd put in an almost sleepless night, and the reason she'd been too edgy to take care of simple chores today. *Why have you been lying to yourself?* she thought with angrily pursed lips. *You loved being kissed, and you would have let him do more than that if it had been up to you. He was the one who backed off, and instead of moping around all day because he dared to kiss you, you should be humiliated by your voracious response!*

So there it was, finally out in the open. Her stomach churned at the truth, and her mouth went dry because she could no longer deny that she felt something very serious for Brent. Groaning in utter anguish, she laid her head on the table. This was too much. Falling in love with a man she could never have was too damned cruel. Hadn't she already paid enough for her sins?

Trembling, she sat up, hurriedly signed her name on the purchase offer and initialed Abby's addition to it. She had no choice but to accept Brent's terms. If she went home with the house unsold she would be constantly worried about it. She would somehow get through the next sixty days, escrow would close and that should be the end of whatever this thing was between herself and Brent. She couldn't call it love; she couldn't even label it a relationship. All she knew was that she couldn't have it.

Going to the phone, she dialed Abby's office number. "I've signed the offer," she said dully. "You may pick it up whenever you wish."

That evening Bill Harkens brought the offer back to Brent. The agent's ruddy face was beaming when he entered Brent's motel room. "Blythe agreed to everything with one minor exception. According to Abby Decker, the listing agent I told you about, Blythe thought the furniture clause was too vague, and she requested an inventory. Here, read it for yourself. You have to initial it, anyway."

Brent read what Abby had handwritten into the document. "So," he said casually, "Blythe and I are supposed to take this inventory together?"

"That's the way it reads," Bill replied. "Apparently there are a few things in the house she doesn't want to sell. Personal mementos, I'm sure."

"No problem there," Brent said. "Yes," he added solemnly, as though he wasn't tickled pink about Blythe's addendum to the offer, "I suppose an inventory is a good idea."

He'd been wondering what excuse he could use to drop in on her again, and it was startling that she herself had given him one. What's more, he wouldn't just be dropping in for a brief visit. The Benning house contained so much furniture that an inventory would take at least a day. It was a heaven-sent opportunity to spend time with Blythe.

"Well, it will accomplish one thing, Brent. There will be no misunderstandings about the furnishings when you take possession," Bill said matter-of-factly.

Brent took out his pen and wrote his initials next to Blythe's. He shoved the papers across the table toward Bill. "So, we have a deal, right?"

"We sure do." Grinning, Bill gathered the papers, got to his feet and offered his hand.

Brent got up and shook it. "Thanks, Bill, you did a good job."

"Wish I could take all the credit," Bill said. "But Abby's fine hand is a big part of it. Listen, Brent, I would advise you to phone Blythe and set up a date for that inventory as soon as possible. Keep the ball rolling, if you know what I mean."

"Oh, I intend to, Bill, believe me, I intend to." He walked the agent to the door and let him out. Immediately he went to the phone and dialed Blythe's number.

She answered on the third ring. "Hello?"

"Blythe, hello. Bill Harkens was just here. Looks like we have a deal."

His cheery voice rubbed Blythe the wrong way. "What we have is *your* deal," she said coldly.

"You didn't have to accept it."

"But you knew I would."

"I had hoped you would, but, no, I didn't know for certain. Anyhow, that inventory idea of yours was very smart."

"Yes," she said with scathing sarcasm. "I'm so brilliant that I astonish myself at times."

"You're mad at me."

Blythe ignored that comment. "Before this conversation goes any further, let's get one thing straight. Inventorying the furniture was Abby Decker's idea, not mine. I thought the reference to furniture in the offer was too vague, and she wrote that line about you and I taking an inventory without first discussing it with me. Obviously she meant well, but then she doesn't know our history, does she? At any rate, I'm not thrilled about the inventory and would like to get it over with right away. Are you free tomorrow?''

"Free as the breeze," Brent said smoothly. "What time would you like me to be there?''

"What I would like and what I have to accept are miles apart," Blythe snapped. "But be here at eight. Goodbye.'' She slammed down the phone.

Shaking his head, Brent hung up. The reason she was mad was because she had kissed him back, and maybe, just maybe, she was also angry because he hadn't gone further than kisses. Not that she would ever admit it, he thought, not even to herself. But she had gotten all worked up in his car and he'd cut everything short.

He'd done it deliberately, and he wasn't sorry about it, either. He had wanted to prove there was chemistry between them, and he'd done exactly that. If Blythe had one honest bone in her body she would face what was happening, and maybe even welcome it. He hated thinking that time and tide had turned her into a secretive recluse, but so many signs pointed in that direction. If he could bring her out of her shell just once her barriers might permanently crumble.

Exactly why she'd erected such staunch barriers he couldn't begin to guess. Maybe she was still mourning the loss of her husband, or her mother. But most people, himself included, eventually got over the death of a loved one. Not that he still didn't have bad moments about Debbie's and Lori's senseless deaths—he probably would for the rest of his days—but he was intelligent enough not to let himself dwell on something he couldn't change. Life went on for everyone but Blythe, it seemed. It was odd and tragic and mystifying, and he would do almost anything to make her happy again, as happy and sweet and loving as she'd been in college. She'd been such a special woman, and he knew in his heart that she could be again.

He also knew that the next time they got into a hot clinch, as they had the other night in his car, things were going to end much differently.

How would she feel about that?

Blythe was positive she was in for another bad night when she went to bed, but she was so worn out from not sleeping the night before that she all but passed out the minute her head hit the pillow.

She didn't come to until seven the next morning, and remembering that Brent was coming to the house at eight, she jumped out of bed and ran for the shower. Moving with all haste, while attempting to ignore her jagged nerves, she rushed through her morning routine.

And then she found herself standing in front of the bathroom mirror and studying her reflection. She leaned forward, bringing her face closer to the mirror, and looked for signs of aging. Her skin was clear but not as taut as it had been only a few years ago. There were small lines around her eyes, and her jaw wasn't nearly as defined as it used to be. Sighing, she stepped back and looked at her naked body.

For years she'd hardly noticed her passing birthdays, and now, all of a sudden, she was worried about how she looked? Because of Brent, she thought resentfully. Damn him!

Furious with herself, she dragged an old denim skirt and a faded red T-shirt from her closet. These clothes would tell him she didn't give a damn *what* he thought of her looks! He'd aged as many years as she had. He wasn't a perfect specimen, either!

But that wasn't true, was it? Brent was the best-looking man she'd ever set eyes on, and it wasn't fair that men aged better than women.

Disheartened, she quickly made up her bed, straightened the room and the bathroom and then went downstairs to the kitchen and put on a pot of coffee.

The day was going to be horrible; there was no other word to describe it. Why in heaven's name hadn't she left that furniture clause alone in Brent's offer to purchase? Was she destined to forever cause her own misery?

It appeared so, she thought with a thinning of her lips. It most definitely appeared so.

Chapter Seven

When Brent got up that morning he realized that he was thinking of the day ahead a lot more sensibly than he had last night. For one thing, Blythe had let him know on the phone that she wasn't one bit pleased about it. He felt certain that she wasn't going to greet him with smiles and cordiality, and him arriving all charged up about the inventory just because it meant they would be spending time together wouldn't be at all wise.

So he put on jeans, a plain blue shirt and comfortable shoes, as though dressing for a day of work. He lingered over breakfast in the motel's coffee shop and then dawdled his way through town on back streets so that he would ring her doorbell right around eight. As pleased and thrilled as he couldn't help being over the prospect of hours with Blythe, he drove with a sober expression, practicing, he told himself with a small chuckle, the exact demeanor he wished Blythe to see when she opened the door for him. He wanted her to believe that he, too, viewed an inventory of the furnishings as an annoying chore, when in fact he felt just the opposite.

But today he would keep his feelings as private as she kept hers and see what happened. She shouldn't be offended if he took his cues from her, he mused while pulling into her driveway, but she gave away so little of her thoughts and feelings that he wasn't sure he would correctly interpret anything she said or did. So far, he hadn't done very well with interpretations, so it really was best, he decided again, for him to project a strictly business persona for today's agenda.

Getting out of his car, he walked to the front door with the expression he'd practiced on his face, even though his big act seemed pretty funny and it was hard not to laugh.

He rang the bell and waited.

Blythe was positive that it was Brent at her door, but instead of immediately going to the foyer and letting him in, she peeked through the drapes in the den to get a look at him before they actually faced each other. If he dared to look thrilled, she thought with barely banked anger, she might not *let* him in.

To her surprise he looked dispirited and a bit impatient, as though he was being forced into something he had no wish to do.

"Well, for crying out loud," she mumbled uneasily as she let the drape fall back into place. She was the one with the right to be upset over this fiasco. What was *his* problem?

Marching almost militantly to the foyer, she unlocked and opened the door. "Come in," she said with neither a smile or a hello.

"Thanks," Brent said curtly, and went in. Her scent immediately invaded his system, and it was all he could do to maintain his stern expression. Blythe shut the door and, out of habit, flipped the lock. "What do you think I'm going to do, try to escape?" Brent said dryly.

"What?" For a moment she didn't grasp his comment, and when she did she stiffened. "If you don't want to do this today, tell me now," she said frostily. "I don't want to get halfway through the inventory and have you suddenly decide you'd rather be doing something else."

"Believe me, I'd much rather be doing something else, but the inventory has to be done so let's get to it," Brent retorted.

Why, he wasn't at all nice today! In fact, his mood appeared to be a mirror image of her own. This was a first, she realized with a peculiar mix of emotions. She hadn't even known that he had a dark side to his personality.

She lifted her chin. If he thought his bad mood would daunt *her* he had another thought coming!

"I have pads and pens in the kitchen," she said coldly. "I'll get them. You decide in which room we should start."

The second she was in the kitchen by herself, away from Brent, she started trembling. All she could think of was how handsome he looked this morning, and of how withdrawn and disinterested he seemed to be. It would be an enormous relief if he'd given up on ever hearing the truth of their past, but had he also given up on her?

She drew a breath, striving for composure. Feeling disappointed because he no longer seemed inclined to chase her around the house was ridiculous. She should be down on her knees, thanking the powers that be.

But she didn't like him in this mood. She would rather have him pressuring her with questions, and trying to charm her with smiles and sly little reminders of the love they had once shared. Was she crazy, or what?

Heaving a sigh, she picked up the pads and pens and headed back to the foyer. She spotted him in the family room before she got there, and walked up to him. "Is this the room you'd like to start with?" she asked while handing him one of the pads and a pen.

"It's as good as any," he said shortly, again indicating impatience with their task.

"I don't like having to do this any more than you do, you know," she said sharply, forgetting her silly ideas in the kitchen.

"Neither of us likes it. At least we agree on that. Correct me if I'm wrong, but I think it's the first thing we've agreed on since our reunion."

"It was hardly a reunion," she scoffed.

"No, but it could have been. Okay, how should we go about this? Have you ever done an inventory before? Of anything?"

"No," she said flatly. "Have you?"

"Yes, quite a few times. I wasn't inventorying furniture, of course, but the procedure is probably the same."

"So what procedure do you suggest?" She didn't speak kindly. How could he kiss her so passionately and then, only a few days later, act as though he'd never laid a hand on her?

"As I understand it there are things in the house you never intended to sell to anyone. Why don't you make a list of those items, as we come to them, and I'll make a list of everything else?" Brent suspected that his plan to infiltrate Blythe's guard just might be working. Obviously she was confused by his distant attitude, but much more interesting than her confusion was that she seemed to be shaken and unnerved by it. Oh, she was trying her damnedest not to show it, but she wasn't a good enough actress to hide *everything* she was feeling.

On the other hand, he thought, she'd been hiding something with unquestionable success. From him and maybe from the rest of the world, as well. What was it? What could possibly be so bad that it had changed a wonderfully sweet and gentle woman into a hard and just barely friendly person?

"All right," she said, agreeing to his suggestion. "Let's get started. I don't plan to keep anything in this room." Her gaze fell on a painting on the wall. It was done by Sierra, who was a professional artist, and even if it wasn't as good as her more recent ones, it should remain in the family. "Except for that painting."

Brent looked around. "Which one?"

"That one of the two girls playing in a flower garden." Blythe had always liked the painting, but for the first time she really saw it. Her eyes widened suddenly. One of the girls was tall, probably around twelve or thirteen years old, the other no more than a toddler. The taller girl had blond hair and the toddler had dark hair. It was a painting of her and Sierra! Had no one seen that before? Blythe couldn't remember the painting ever being discussed in that light.

"It's yours," Brent said flatly. "Write it down." He

frowned at the peculiar expression on Blythe's face as she stared at it. "Is there something special about it?"

"My sister Sierra painted it. She...she's an artist." Blythe was truly stunned by her revelation. She recalled Tamara telling her shortly after her marriage to Sam Sherard that Sierra had sent her a painting for a wedding present, and that Tamara was positive the three girls in the picture were Sierra, Blythe and herself.

Now, here was a second painting of Sierra and a sister—in this case Blythe. Tamara hadn't been born yet, of course. She was ten years younger than Sierra, and in the painting Sierra was only two or three.

But wait, there *was* another child in the painting, a tiny blond girl almost completely concealed by flowers! All but holding her breath, Blythe got as close as she could to the painting to see it better, but it was hanging above a wide table and the light wasn't good.

It was a very large painting in a wood frame, and she knew she wouldn't be able to lift it from the wall by herself. She set down her pad and pen and turned toward Brent. "Would you help me take down this painting? I want to move it over to that window so I can see it in better lighting."

"Sure," Brent agreed, and laid down his own pad and pen. "You needn't help. I'll get the painting, and if you want good lighting you had better open the blinds on that window."

"Thanks," Blythe mumbled almost numbly. Why had she never really examined the painting? Why hadn't anybody? Sierra had always dabbled with oil paints, but she really hadn't started producing until her college days, which meant that Tamara *had* been born when Sierra did this work. But why had Sierra put Tamara in a painting that depicted herself as a toddler?

Brent carried the painting to the window. Blythe had raised the blind, and bright morning light poured into the room. She asked Brent to lower the painting to the floor, and she got on her knees.

Why, she couldn't see the third child at all from this angle! Startled, Blythe moved back a few feet and once again saw the child. Or thought she did. Frowning, she wondered if she was merely imagining a tiny face and form among the many flowers.

A quick glance up at Brent told her that she was perplexing him. She scrambled to her feet, deciding that she would examine the painting again when she was alone.

"Just prop it against that chair," she told him.

They both went to retrieve their pads and pens. "Okay," he said, "you're sure that the painting is the only thing you want to keep from this room."

"Yes. Everything else is yours. Please make a note of each item."

He started writing and realized how time consuming this job was going to be. Not only that, an inventory of this sort should contain serial numbers where pertinent, brand names if known, and probably a description of the item. He was merely writing down "Lamp, rectangular table, circular table, sofa, blue chair, television set," and so on. His list was already a page long and this was only the first room. It was a silly exercise, when all Blythe would have had to do was go through the house and tag those items she wanted to keep.

And yet it was giving him a valid reason for being here, he reminded himself. While he wrote, Blythe sat on the sofa and waited for him to finish with this room so they could move on to the next. He glanced at her and saw that she was still looking at Sierra's painting. He looked at it himself and thought the painting to be quite attractive. It had a pleasing mix of colors, a muted, soft style, and the children had a special glow about them. Sierra had talent, he decided, no doubt about it.

"Is your sister selling her work?" he asked.

His question jarred Blythe out of her reverie. "Yes, for quite some time now. Are you through in here?"

"I think so."

Blythe got up. "Den next?"

"Fine with me."

They entered the den and the first thing Brent said was, "What about the books? Surely you want the books."

"I...don't know. I know there are some first editions...or there used to be." She scanned the shelves. "I don't see them. Maybe Mother sold them." How strange, she thought. Myra had never been short of money that Blythe knew of, but the first editions that had been so highly prized by Dr. Harry Benning were not here. Blythe remembered them quite clearly, and they had always resided on that glassed-in shelf that now contained ceramic knickknacks.

"Your mother could have put them somewhere else," Brent said. "Were they valuable?"

"I believe they were."

"Is there a safe in the house?"

"A safe?" Blythe frowned. "There wasn't a safe while I was living at home, but I suppose Mother could have had one installed after Dad died. It would have to be quite large to hold a dozen books, though, and I can't imagine where it might be. Besides, I'm sure Mother would have mentioned a safe if she..." Blythe's voice trailed off. Myra hadn't even mentioned her years-long illness to her daughters. Why would she have told them about a safe?

An unexpected bitterness erupted within Blythe. Was this another secret? Myra had been far too secretive about too many things. To Blythe's knowledge the secretiveness in the Benning family had started with herself and her "condition," as Myra had delicately labeled her oldest daughter's pregnancy, but Blythe really had no proof of that being the beginning. It had been *her* introduction to keeping a secret, but who could say when her mother's had taken place?

She looked at Brent and suffered an almost intolerable urge to tell him the truth. He had a right to know that he had a son or daughter, living somewhere in this vast world. Her stomach knotted. How she detested secrets!

But she detested what she'd done even more. Today no one got away with telling her what to do, but back then she'd been disgustingly malleable and trusting. She'd grown up believing that Mother knew best, and she had run home trusting in the fact that Myra would make all of her worry and concern vanish.

And she had, that was what was so terrible. Myra *had* made all of her troubles vanish, only she'd also made Blythe's child vanish.

"Blythe, what's wrong?" Before his eyes her face had lost color. He moved closer to her, dropped his pad and pen on a chair and laid his hands on her shoulders. "What are you thinking of?" He sensed that the missing books had triggered a disturbing memory for Blythe, and he realized in that moment that he couldn't go on acting as though he wasn't happy to be here with her.

She looked into his trusting, honestly concerned blue eyes and felt like the dregs at the bottom of a barrel. She had given away her child. She had given away *his* child.

The dam broke and tears began cascading down her face. "Blythe!" Stunned, Brent pulled her to himself and cradled her head against his chest while she sobbed her heart out. "There, there," he said gently while stroking her back. Because her heart was obviously breaking over something, so was his. He couldn't bear her grief, and he would do anything to alleviate it. "Nothing could be that bad, honey," he whispered huskily, feeling choked up himself.

She tried to say something. The urge to just let go and tell him everything was overwhelming. But she couldn't stop crying long enough to speak an intelligible word.

So she accepted his comfort even while thinking that she deserved his derision, his disgust. If he knew the truth he would not be holding her like this.

And it felt so good to be held, to be soothed. She let her pad and pen drop to the floor and wound her arms around his waist. Gradually her tears stopped flowing, and still she stood in the circle of Brent's arms and basked in the comfort he was providing.

The tenor of their embrace began changing. Each of them knew it. Neither of them tried to break the spell. She felt his chest expand against her cheek as he inhaled rather unsteadily. His arms tightened around her, and she took a tiny step forward to get closer to him. Her pulse began racing. Far, far in the back of her mind she knew she shouldn't be doing this, but she wasn't able to stop herself.

"Blythe," he whispered raggedly, and tipped her chin to look into her moist eyes. "Do you have any idea how much I want you?"

She closed her eyes and nodded. It was all the permission Brent needed, and he pressed his lips to hers in a hungry kiss. Her mouth opened under his, and his pulse went wild.

It was an incredible moment for him. He'd hoped it would happen for them, he'd dreamed and fantasized about making love with Blythe, but he had not arrived at her door this morning expecting it to occur today.

Something truly wonderful was happening to Blythe. The inhibitions she'd forced upon herself for so long were disappearing with such swiftness she felt light-headed. The only thought she could hold in her mind was of Brent. She wanted to kiss him forever, to keep him as close to her for the rest of her days as he was this minute.

She leaned into him, raised her hands to his face and kissed him so passionately that he groaned deep in his throat and began tearing at her clothes. Yes, she thought, yes! as her skirt slid down her legs to puddle on the carpet around her feet. He yanked the T-shirt over her head and gave it a toss. Breathing hard, wearing only her bra and panties, she unbuttoned his shirt and drew it down his arms. It, too, fell to the floor.

Their kisses became rawer, rougher as they finished undressing each other. She didn't try to hide her nudity, nor did Brent, and they sank to the floor flushed and feverish with desire. She lay back and held up her arms in invitation, and he wasted no time in complying with what her glazed eyes and sensuously parted lips were pleading for.

He quickly took care of protection. Supporting his weight on his elbows, he watched her face as he slid into her. Her mouth formed a silent "Oh," and there was wonder and amazement in her eyes. He felt the same emotions, and he took her mouth in a long, searing kiss that she gave back with utter abandonment.

He started moving within her, and with each thrust she emitted a soft little moan. Her legs and arms rose to wind around him, and they became as interlocked as a man and woman could possibly get.

"It's so good...so good," she hoarsely whispered. "Don't stop, please don't stop."

"Never!" It was all he could say at the moment. Talk would come later. He kissed her mouth and her face, again and again, and he brushed her hair back from her flushed forehead, but he never once stopped the rhythmic thrusts that were bringing them both to the peak. He couldn't.

When her moans became cries he began moving faster and going deeper. Through sheer willpower he held back his own release until she began clutching and clawing at his back. Then her hips started rising to meet him in a demanding way, and her eyes begged, and he let himself go and they both became a little crazy.

She cried his name, a long, drawn-out "Brent...!" He nearly blacked out from the force of his climax, and then he collapsed on top of her, completely spent.

It took several minutes for Blythe's heartbeat to slow down and for her to catch her breath. It was when Brent finally raised his head, smiled at her and then kissed her that reality returned in a painful rush. What had she done! Oh dear God, what had she done?

Her heart was again pounding, not from passion this time but from self-denunciation. Her lips had gone sandpaper dry. Brent felt their unnatural dryness, stopped kissing her and looked at her with a hundred questions in his eyes.

"Please don't tell me you're sorry this happened," he pleaded.

She sucked in a long, quaking breath. She couldn't meet his eyes. She was heartsick and sorry and knew if she told him how awful she really felt that she would hurt him terribly. He hadn't forced her, after all. If anyone was at fault here, it was her.

"Blythe," he said gently. "Don't you know that I'm falling in love with you?"

"No!" Panic appeared in her eyes. "You don't know what you're saying!"

"Of course I know what I'm saying. There's a damn good chance that I never really fell *out* of love with you."

"That's not true. You loved your wife!"

"I did, yes, but maybe I also loved you."

"That's an insult to her memory!" She had to stop him from talking about loving her, she had to!

"No, it is not. We had a good marriage, and I held nothing back. But isn't it possible that you were always there, somewhere in my mind? Blythe, you were my first love, and now you're going to be my last. I can't be unhappy about that, honey, I just can't be."

He *couldn't* love her; she didn't deserve his love. Tears began coursing down her temples. "I have something to tell you." Confession was the only thing she could think of that would make him see her as she was—a sinful, despicable woman who had given away their child.

He studied her truly forlorn features, and a fearful premonition struck him. He'd wanted to know her secret, he'd badgered her to tell him why she'd changed so much and now it appeared he was going to hear it all. Instinctively he knew he wasn't going to like it.

"Don't tell me anything you don't want to, honey," he said quietly. "You're entitled to your privacy."

"I'm entitled to nothing," she said with such bitterness it stunned Brent. "Let me get up," she said in that same acrid tone.

"All right," he said slowly, and left her to pull on his clothes. He noticed that while he was putting on *all* of his clothing, she merely yanked on her skirt and blouse. She tucked her underthings in a pocket of the skirt, sat on a chair and didn't even try to smooth down her hair. Her mood frightened him, and he wasn't easily frightened. But this was different than anything he'd ever encountered, and he wished to high heaven that he'd kept his damn mouth shut about the past. What difference did it make now, anyway?

He took a chair facing hers and sat back, attempting to look unbothered and nonchalant. In fact, he even managed to smile.

"Are you ready to hear it now?" she asked with a malignant twist of her lips. "And don't smile at me. You'll never smile at me again after you know the truth."

"That's not true, Blythe. I care deeply for you."

"Don't say that! Dammit, what's wrong with you? Don't you have any idea what happened twenty-four years ago?"

"No," he said quietly. "Should I?"

She looked away and realized that she still didn't have to tell him anything. But she couldn't *not* tell him when he so foolishly believed that he had never stopped loving her. That she'd been worthy of his love. He had her up on a pedestal, and she was worse than the dirt under his feet. He had to know. She couldn't live with his talk about love. Look what had just happened between them. If that wasn't encouragement for a man to bare his soul, nothing was, and she couldn't tell herself it wouldn't happen again as long as he was pursuing her and behaving like a love-struck teenager. All she deserved from him was derision and worse, and there was only one way to destroy his romantic fantasies.

She turned dead eyes on him. "I've never told another person about this, not even my husband. My parents knew because they were a part of it, but no one else does. I've lived with it for almost twenty-four years. I never thought you and I would ever meet again."

A cold chill went up Brent's spine. "Blythe, don't tell me, please. Whatever it is, it's way in the past."

"You have to hear it all," she said. "You said I was evasive, and I was. It was a shock seeing you again, but I managed to get over it. Your interest in the house was another shock, but I reminded myself how much I wanted to sell it, and I got over that, as well. What I would never be able to get over, what I cannot let go on, is your thinking that you're falling in love with me again. You see, I detest myself for what I did, and your persistent attentions only increase my guilt. I don't deserve your love and respect, and I cannot accept either.''

She looked him straight in the eye. ''The reason I left college so suddenly was that I was pregnant. I had our child, and I gave it up for adoption.''

Chapter Eight

Brent went statue still. The color drained from his face. His body was suddenly ice-cold. He stared at her for a long time and finally mumbled, "No, you couldn't have."

"Your first reaction is disbelief? Why? Because I'm such a wonderfully pure woman I couldn't possibly be capable of doing something so sickening?" Blythe's mouth twisted. "Believe it, Brent. It happened."

"But...but why?"

"Today I don't know why. Today there's no sensible reason for what I did."

"Was there a sensible reason before?" He heard the thickness of his own voice, and marveled that his benumbed lips would even take direction from his benumbed brain.

"Looking back, no."

"Then why did you do it? Why didn't you come to me?"

"I *said* 'looking back.' Do you think the past looks the same now as it did when it was the present?"

"Of course not, but my God, Blythe, did you think I

wouldn't marry you? What *did* you think I'd do, wash my hands of the whole thing? We were in love!''

''And you were holding down two jobs to get an education!''

Brent held up his hands. ''Let's not get angry.''

''Don't try to convince me you're not angry.''

''All right, I'm angry! But let's not yell at each other. Tell me what happened.''

She looked everywhere but at him and spoke in a robotlike monotone. ''I wasn't unhappy when I discovered I was pregnant, but it did worry me. You were overworked and tired most of the time. You were already stretched to the limit, and I didn't want to give you another burden.''

''A burden! You visualized yourself and our child as a burden? What in hell was wrong with you? You knew I loved you, and what had I ever done to make you think I wouldn't love our baby?''

''I didn't say you wouldn't have loved our baby, dammit! I was worried about money! And how hard you were working, and how little time you had to spare!'' She took a breath and tried to calm herself. ''Look, I'm not making excuses for what I did. All I'm trying to get across to you are the things that kept going through my mind at the time.''

''And for how long did these *things* go through your mind?'' Brent asked with cutting sarcasm.

She couldn't object to his sarcasm, nor to his anger. He had every right to detest her, and she knew that he would before this was over.

''For about a week. If you care to recall, I was financially dependent on my parents. You might also recall that I, unlike you and many of our friends, stayed in close contact with my parents. I felt, at the time, that I could tell them anything.''

''So instead of coming to me, you went home to them.'' Brent got up and began walking back and forth in front of her.

''Only for advice. I—I didn't expect what happened.''

The break in her voice caused Brent to stop pacing and look at her. ''Are you saying your parents forced you to give up the baby? That's pretty hard to swallow, Blythe. You were almost twenty years old, for God's sake!''

He was so very, very right. She'd been far too old to let anyone convince her that black was white.

And yet that was what happened. There was no way to make him understand it. How could she explain the influence of her parents, of her mother in particular? Brent had grown up so differently. His father had been disabled very young and had lived in a wheelchair. His mother had worked at a menial job to add to the modest pension his father had received since his accident. Neither of his parents had had the energy to influence their son about anything. Brent had grown up knowing that if he wanted an education beyond high school he would have to pay for it himself. He'd virtually been on his own since childhood.

No, he could never comprehend *her* family life, the pervasive pressures to always behave properly. *You are only as good as how others perceive you, Blythe. Reputation is your most valuable asset. Your father is an important man. We must never do anything to shame him in the eyes of the community.*

"Well, whether you want to believe it or not, I was a very naive almost-twenty-year-old," she said sharply.

He couldn't dispute that remark, for he remembered that she had been naive about many things. Feeling totally drained, he flopped down onto a chair. He'd brought this on himself, he thought darkly. No, he never could have imagined the reality of Blythe's secret, but why in hell hadn't he left it alone?

"Where did you have the baby?" he asked after a long stretch of discomfiting silence.

"In a home for unwed mothers in Utah. My father arranged it."

"Was it a boy or a girl?"

"I don't know. I signed the adoption papers before it was born, and I never saw it."

Brent raised his head from the back of the chair. "You never saw it, not even in the delivery room?"

"I was sedated. I…I heard the baby crying, and I remember begging to see my baby, but no one would bring it to me."

For several moments he felt an almost choking sympathy for her, for what she'd gone through, for giving birth to a child and never once holding it in her arms, and then he remembered that she could have come to him, and the sympathy vanished.

He got up. "I'm not going to finish the inventory today. It doesn't need to be done, anyway. Just tag anything you want to keep. Don't get up. I know my way to the front door."

Without a dram of life in her body, Blythe sat there and listened to him leaving. He hadn't said that he couldn't stand the sight of her one second longer, but she knew he'd been thinking it.

It was, she thought with profound sadness, as her emotions began functioning again, precisely what she deserved.

So why did it hurt so much?

Brent lay on his bed in his motel room and stared at the ceiling. He couldn't remember the drive from Blythe's house. Obviously he'd made it on automatic pilot, because the only thing he could still think of was what she had done. Somewhere lived another child of his, an adult now. He'd nearly died himself when Debbie and Lori had been killed. He remembered wishing for blessed oblivion, but he'd had to go on, day after day, week after week, living in a house that echoed with ominous silence.

His first conscious step toward healing had been to sell that house and buy another. It was the one he still owned in Seattle, and it was where he had gradually returned to normal. His work had been a lifesaver, he'd realized later, but during those first terrible months immediately following the fatal accident he'd known nothing but grief.

It had been a senseless, unnecessary tragedy, and what Blythe had done was almost as bad. She should have come to him. Her reasons for going to her parents instead of him churned in his brain and seemed too inane to be believed. They hadn't been children. Young, yes. Financially insecure, yes. But they would have managed.

And they would not have lived twenty-odd years without

their child. Who had adopted it? Had Dr. Benning arranged the adoption, as well as the place in which the baby would be born?

Fury rose in Brent's chest, all but choking him. Cursing Blythe's parents, he got off the bed and wandered the room. He hadn't felt this kind of pain in years, and it was disheartening to realize that no matter how hard a man tried to elude the harsher realities of life, they were always out there, waiting to pounce on him when he least expected it.

He could never have imagined this, though. He'd known that Blythe wasn't the same woman he remembered. He'd even accused her of being afraid of something.

What she'd been afraid of, he thought angrily, was of him finding out the truth! She hadn't expected to see him again, any more than he'd expected to see her. It had been a shock for him, but *shock* was too mild a word for what she must have felt when he walked into her house.

This was not something he would be able to think about for a few days and forget, he thought grimly. He couldn't even put Blythe and forgiveness in the same sentence. Why had she made love with him, when she must have known she wasn't going to let it go any further than that?

Or maybe she hadn't known. Dare he be kind enough to think she might not have known her own mind until he'd started talking about falling in love? It was as though she didn't *want* to be loved. Why else would she have breached her own wall of silence and told him everything?

He realized that he was thinking more rationally now. Anger still burned within him, but that might be a permanent condition; he could live with it.

He stretched out on the bed again, locked his hands behind his head and went over the day's events until he had memorized every word Blythe had said, every nuance, every tone of voice. It renewed the pain in his soul, but it accomplished something else, as well.

It created a question: had Blythe ever attempted to find their son or daughter?

* * *

After Brent left, Blythe sat in the den for a long time, feeling too lifeless and empty to move so much as a finger. What was there to do, anyhow? Tag the items in the house she wanted to keep? she thought cynically. Why bother? Brent probably wouldn't buy the house now, and did she care if he didn't? No, she did not. In truth, she cared about nothing.

The emptiness she felt wasn't pleasant, but at least she wasn't almost mortally depressed, she realized after about an hour. *Why* wasn't she depressed? It was strange that she hadn't immediately sunk into a dark pit, as she'd done so many times over the years. In fact, while she couldn't deny the emptiness in her system, she also felt relief! Now *that* was more than strange, and how should she interpret it?

Interpret nothing! Accept it and get off this damn chair!

Obeying her own instinctual voice, she got up, went to her bathroom, undressed and stepped into the shower stall.

Days passed. Brent forced himself to work on his plans for the Sunrise project. The developers came to town and they met with him to check on his progress and to kick around ideas. As busy as Brent was able to keep himself, Blythe and her heartrending story remained firmly fixed behind every other thought. His emotions were in turmoil. Sleeping well was impossible. There were moments when he wanted to go to Blythe and make her tell him about their baby again, as though a second narrative would reveal some small fact that would ease his pain.

He tried very hard to understand what she'd done. Almost desperately he looked for logic in something that he felt in his soul was completely illogical. He knew that he was searching for a way to forgive her, a way for him to get over the shock she'd handed him, and it was almost as much of a shock to finally face the truth of his feelings: he still cared for her.

How could he? he asked himself repeatedly, without ever coming up with a reasonable answer. But he was again looking for logic, he realized, and was there any logic in personal feelings? Bottom line, he was almost mortally wounded by what Blythe had done, but he couldn't hate her for it. It was a startling revelation, but it seemed to free his thoughts from the rut they'd been in. And the question that had occurred to him before, the one about whether or not Blythe had ever attempted to find their child, began eating at him with a persistence he wasn't able to ignore.

Blythe functioned in two speeds, slow and slower, during those same days. She couldn't get out of her mind the stunned, disbelieving expression on Brent's face when she'd told him what had really happened twenty-four years ago, and a hundred times she wished that she hadn't told him, only to reverse herself a hundred times and decide that it had been her only recourse.

Accepting his affection, his love, with that destructive secret in her heart would have been the worst kind of deceit anyone could inflict on another human being. She'd done the right thing, she kept telling herself, the only thing she *could* have done.

Regardless of the "rightness" of her actions, she felt utterly miserable about having hurt Brent so badly. She listlessly wandered the house and wished she could think more clearly. Obviously Brent was out of her life. He might still want the house, he might not, but in either case it was time that she figured out what *she* should do next.

It was while she was under the pulsing spray of hot water in her shower one morning that her mind cleared. Relieved over the first set of definitive thoughts she'd had in days, she dried off quickly, donned a robe, went to the kitchen phone and dialed Abby Decker's office number. Luck was with her. The receptionist told her that Abby was there, and transferred the call to the agent's desk phone.

"Blythe, hello! How are you?" Abby said in her cheerful way.

"Fine, Abby. I've made some decisions and I need your help."

"I'd be glad to help, Blythe. What would you like me to do?"

"I'm going home, Abby, back to Connecticut. Mr. Morrison

may take early possession of the house, if he still wants it. Please pass that information on to Bill Harkens. If Mr. Morrison doesn't want early possession, the house will have to sit empty until he does want it. I'm not going to go into my reasons for believing he may back out of the deal, but you should know it could happen. I'm going to take the things that I want to keep in the family with me, so anything that is left in the house will be his.

"Now, if he does change his mind about buying the house, please return his earnest money. I don't want it. And if that should happen, I would like you to keep the house on the market. You have my Connecticut address, and if the house doesn't sell before the listing agreement expires, just send me another and I will sign and return it to you. I'd like you to continue as my agent.

"Let me see, what else? Oh, yes, the basement storage room. I've been negligent about getting rid of my father's old medical records. They should be shredded, Abby, and would you happen to know of anyone that might have a commercial-size shredder who would be willing to do the job?"

"My," Abby exclaimed, "you *have* been making decisions! Off the top of my head, Blythe, I can't think of anyone who even owns a large paper shredder. But I'll look into it."

"I think the job will be costly, Abby. You've seen the room and its many file cabinets. Even with a commercial shredder, there has to be several days of work involved. Please don't worry about saving me money. I'll pay the bill, whatever the cost.

"I'm going to leave all the keys I have to the house, so they will be available for either Mr. Morrison or another buyer. They will be in the cutlery drawer in the kitchen. Have I missed anything? Do you have any questions?"

"I think you've covered everything very well. Of course, I can't help wondering what brought this on. You sound terribly down in the mouth. I don't mean to get personal, Blythe, but—"

Blythe cut in. "I just want to go home, Abby, that's really

all there is to it. When we're through talking, I'm going to make a flight reservation.''

"You're going to fly to Connecticut? What are you going to do with your car? You can't just leave it behind, can you?''

Blythe's heart sank. She'd been using her mother's car, and Abby was right. She couldn't leave it at the house, nor could she leave it at the airport. It seemed so silly that she'd been planning to drive to Spokane and the airport without considering what she'd do with the car. "I—I guess I didn't think about the car," she stammered.

"Would you like to sell it? I've been looking for a good used car, and I know yours is in excellent condition.''

"Abby, that would be perfect!'' She could take a taxi to the Spokane airport if she had to. It was, after all, only about thirty-five miles away.

"Do you have any idea of price?''

"None, absolutely none. Abby, I've got a zillion things to do before I leave, and I'm going to try to get a flight reservation for tomorrow. I know you're busy, too, but would you mind calling some car dealers and asking about price? You know the brand and year of the car. If you'd be willing to go by the values listed in the vehicle blue book, I certainly would be.''

"I'll do it right away. I'll call you later, okay?''

"Thanks, Abby. Bye for now.'' Hanging up, Blythe reached for the telephone book to look for the number of a travel agent. Now that she had a viable plan of action in mind, her urgency to be on her way was increasing by leaps and bounds. She didn't anticipate Brent ever trying to see her again, but an accidental meeting would be as ghastly as one that was planned. Making love with him had been an act of insanity. So was his talking about falling in love. She'd had to make him understand it could never be, and now he knew the truth and she never needed to worry again that he might find out.

That was why she'd felt that curious relief, she decided with tears running down her cheeks. Drying them with her fingertips, she studied the ads for travel agents, finally chose one and started to dial the company's number.

And then what she was doing brought her up short. Her sisters! Blythe could pick and choose those things in the house that she thought should remain in the family, but Tamara and Sierra might have other ideas on that score.

Well, she would call them next, Blythe thought as she finished dialing. In ten minutes she had a flight reservation for tomorrow, and she broke the connection with the travel agent and immediately dialed Sierra's number.

"Blythe!" Sierra exclaimed excitedly. "I was going to call you. Clint and I have been talking about a trip to Coeur d'Alene this coming weekend. I want the two of you to finally meet, and—"

"Sierra, I won't be here this weekend. I'm sorry, but I'm going home tomorrow. I already have a confirmed flight reservation."

"Oh. Well, maybe we can come to Connecticut sometime."

"You sound disappointed. I'm sorry, Sierra, but I have to go home."

"Please don't apologize. You've been so generous with your time that Tamara and I will never be able to sufficiently thank you."

"You don't need to thank me, either of you. I'll call you when I get home, okay?"

"I would like that. Blythe, did you accept the offer you received on the house?"

Blythe's heart sank. If her own problems didn't drive her over the edge, this damn house just might do it. But she couldn't fault Sierra's curiosity, and she answered the best she could. "Yes, I did, but now I have—uh, reason to believe the buyer may back out of the deal."

"Really? Oh well, someone will buy it sooner or later."

"Well, bear in mind that nothing is final at this point. What I'm trying to say, and doing a bad job of it, is that I don't know for certain that the buyer *will* change his mind. It's…just a feeling I have. If he does go through with it, though, he will also want the furniture. His offer was explicit on that point. Sierra, there are some things in the house that I feel should stay in the family. Is there anything you'd like to have for yourself? Not the actual furniture, you understand, which the three of us agreed to sell. But things like Grandmother's miniatures, and…well, I'm sure you know what I mean.''

''Yes, I do know. I can't think of anything, Blythe. You're taking the miniatures home with you?''

''Only so they won't remain in the house. You may have them, if you wish, or Tamara may want them. Sierra, I'm also taking the painting you did of the two girls that hung in the family room. Let me ask you something about it. Is there a third child in the flowers, or am I imagining things?''

''That old painting? Goodness, I did that so long ago I just barely remember it. Let me think a minute.'' After a brief silence, Sierra said, ''I believe I did put a third child among the flowers.''

''And the painting is really of you, Tamara and me, isn't it?''

Sierra laughed. ''Probably. I did quite a few paintings of the three of us.''

''Do you recall why you depicted Tamara as a shadowy figure?''

''Heavens, no. I was probably trying out a new technique.''

''Then there's nothing symbolic in the rendering,'' Blythe said quietly. What had she been hoping to hear? Why did that painting bother her so? Was it because her own child was no more than a shadowy figure in her mind, and seeing her own thoughts on canvas had taken her by surprise?

''Maybe at the time I was attempting something symbolic,'' Sierra said. ''But I honestly don't remember, Blythe. I'm sorry. You said you were taking the painting with you? If I recall correctly, it's not that good.''

''I think it's wonderful,'' Blythe replied. ''Besides, you painted it, which makes it special for me. Well, if there isn't anything specific you want from the house, Sierra, I'll go ahead on my own judgment.''

''Yes, please do. Blythe, you sound…I can't find the right word, but it worries me. Are you all right?''

''I will be, Sierra. I just need to go home.''

After they said goodbye, Blythe called Tamara. It was almost painful to repeat virtually the same conversation that she'd had with Sierra, with the exception of the painting, but Blythe felt duty bound to keep her youngest sister informed of her plans.

Tamara's laughter had become bubbling, Blythe realized as they talked. Her happiness was almost tangible, even over the phone. How wonderful for her.

Like Sierra, Tamara couldn't think of anything she wanted from the house, and the biggest difference in the two phone calls was Tamara's emotional invitation for Blythe to come to Texas for a visit. "I want you to see my babies, Blythe. I want you to meet Sam. Please come. You could fly here first and then go home."

Blythe could feel herself choking up. She would like very much to see Tamara's triplets in person, but now was not the best time for her to be holding babies. She was hanging on by the tips of her fingers as it was. She needed desperately to be alone in her own home.

"I hate to say no, Tamara, but I really must go home."

"You'll come sometime, though, won't you?"

"Yes, of course I will."

"Christmas would be a good time. Oh, Blythe, wouldn't it be incredible if the three of us could be together for Christmas? I wonder if Sierra would consider it."

"She might. We...we have time to talk about it, Tamara. Christmas is still a long way off."

"Only a few months, Blythe, and time goes by so quickly. I can't remember if we ever spent Christmas together, can you?"

"I don't think we ever did. One of us was always doing something else, if memory serves."

"That's how I remember it, too. Promise me you'll think about it."

"You have my word."

After saying goodbye and hanging up, Blythe sat there feeling limp as a dishrag. Her emotions were in shambles, and she knew nothing was going to change until she got on that plane. Maybe not even then, but she hoped it would.

Dragging herself to her feet, she went to get dressed. She was just starting to pack the miniatures in a small box when the phone rang. It was Abby Decker.

"I spoke to Bill Harkens and told him what you said. He will pass it on to Mr. Morrison. I also have the high and low blue book value of your car. I'm thinking that we can come to an agreement somewhere in between. I can't get away for a while, but I'd like to come by sometime this afternoon. I have the cash to buy your car, so once we settle on a price, we should be able to wrap it up in a few minutes."

"Come by anytime, Abby. I'll be here. Oh, I will be gone for about a half hour. I have to pick up my ticket at the travel agency. So if I'm not home when you get here, I won't be long."

"If you're not home when I get there, I'll wait."

"Thank you, Abby. Goodbye."

Blythe resumed packing the miniatures and thought of what else she should take with her. There couldn't possibly be a safe concealed somewhere in the house, because her mother's important papers—the deed to the house, the title to the car and her life insurance policy—had been easily found in a fireproof strongbox in her bedroom. Which meant, thinking logically, that Myra must have sold the first editions collected by her husband.

After the miniatures were ready for shipment, Blythe checked the painting and wondered how she was going to pack it. Inspiration struck and she began removing the canvas from the frame. Once freed, the canvas was easily rolled into a tube, and she secured it with strong rubber bands. She would wrap it in heavy paper and take it on the plane with her.

She was definitely making headway, she thought. Now all she had to do was to pick up her ticket and pack her clothes. She should have everything ready to go by tonight.

Brent opened the door of his motel room and saw that it was Bill Harkens who had knocked on it.

"Hello, Bill. Come on in."

Harkens stepped inside. "Brent, Abby Decker asked me to pass on a message from Blythe," he said.

Brent's nerves started jangling, and his lips thinned. "What's the message?"

"Blythe is leaving for Connecticut tomorrow. If you want early possession of the house, you have it. In my opinion she's being very generous...Brent?" Brent was already out the door. Bill followed with astonishment on his face, and made sure the door was securely shut behind them. "Brent, what's going on?" he called.

"Nothing you'd be interested in, Bill," Brent called back as he hurried to his car. "Talk to you later."

Blythe had just shoved a load of soiled clothing into the washer when the doorbell rang. "There's Abby," she mumbled under her breath. Quickly rinsing her hands at the laundry room sink, she hurried to the foyer to let Abby in.

Only it wasn't Abby she saw standing there, it was Brent!

She thought her heart would stop beating on the spot. "I—I don't want to see you," she said raggedly, and pushed on the door to close it again. Or tried to. Brent caught it and pushed it open.

"What do you want?" she asked, fearing another emotional scene between them, which she was in no condition to face.

"We need to talk." Without further ado he pushed *her* aside and walked in.

She totally lost her cool. "How dare you?" she shrieked. "I swear I'll call the police and tell them you forced your way into this house!"

"Go ahead, and I'll tell the whole damn town that you gave away our baby!"

Chapter Nine

They stood there glaring at each other. But too much had happened recently, and Blythe could take no more. A wave of weakness overcame her. Her legs crumpled, blackness threatened and she felt herself sinking to the floor.

Startled but quick on his feet, Brent rushed forward and caught her. Scooping her up in his arms, he carried her to the family room sofa, where he laid her down, then ran to the kitchen to dampen a towel. When he returned, she was struggling to sit up.

He pressed her down again and placed the damp towel on her forehead. "Take it easy," he told her gruffly. "Rest for a few minutes."

It was Blythe's first experience with fainting—or nearly fainting—and while her mind was no longer blacking out, her body was trembling. She "rested," not because Brent had told her to, but because she didn't have the strength to do anything else. Certainly she had no energy to waste on anger. Apparently she had reached the end of her rope.

Brent moved a chair over to the sofa and sat down to keep

a close eye on her. She was pale and looked as helpless and hopeless as anyone he'd ever seen.

"I'm sorry," he said quietly. "I didn't come here to cause something like this."

At the moment she didn't care why he'd come. She closed her eyes.

"Blythe! Are you fainting again?" Alarmed, Brent leaned forward and put his hand on her arm to give it a small shake. She shrank back to elude his hand, and he slowly withdrew it. His nerves settled down some. "Let me get you something to drink," he said. "How about a glass of water?"

Her mouth seemed unusually dry, so she nodded. She heard him get up and leave the room, and she permitted her eyes to open. She raised her hand to the towel on her forehead and thought about that scary moment when she'd felt consciousness deserting her. Her body had given her a warning, and she had best heed it.

She would start by letting Brent have his say without rebuttal; she could not deal with any more disagreements. Her emotions were stretched beyond normal limits and it had to stop.

Brent returned with a glass of cool water, and she raised herself up on an elbow to take the glass and drink from it. "Thank you," she murmured, and lay back again. Lowering the glass to her chest, she held it with both hands.

Brent resumed his seat. "I came here with a question, but maybe you're not well enough to answer it."

"I'm not ill." *What does it matter what I tell him now? I didn't faint without a reason, and he might as well know that I'm at my wit's end.* "I've been nervous and jumpy all summer. I guess it finally caught up with me."

"I think you've probably been nervous and jumpy for twenty-four years."

She looked at the glass in her hands. "Off and on, yes, but it's been worse this summer."

"Because you've been here?"

"Probably. Memories are too close in this house. At first I enjoyed being here, but then the dream..." She stopped.

Thinking about the dream was bad enough; talking about it made it seem too real. "Please don't ask," she said without looking at him. "I really don't want to talk about it."

"I don't have to ask. You said enough that I know you've been bothered by disturbing dreams. Blythe, when you've got a lot on your mind bad dreams are to be expected."

"True," she said, agreeing because his opinion made sense, but mostly because she hoped for a closure of that subject. "I can sit up now," she said.

"If you're sure." Brent reached for the glass in her hands. "Let me hang on to this."

Blythe pushed herself up and was relieved that she didn't feel dizzy.

"You're feeling better," Brent observed.

"Much better." She finally raised her eyes to meet his. "You said you had a question."

Brent studied her. She was still pale, and he didn't want to bring about another fainting spell. For the first time since she'd told him about their child, he was beginning to grasp what she had been living with—guilt, remorse, self-denunciation. Probably a day never passed that she didn't berate and despise herself. It was a hell of a way to live, and he'd have to be completely coldhearted not to feel sorry for her.

And yet she had brought it on herself. He would *never* understand why she hadn't come to him instead of running home to her folks.

But that destructive decision was far in the past and no longer a salient point. The question that had brought him here this afternoon was what mattered now.

He sat up straighter. "This has bothered me for days now. Did you ever attempt to find our child?"

Tears instantly filled Blythe's eyes. Her voice cracked. "Yes. I wrote several letters to the home and pleaded for information. Their replies weren't unkind, merely uncooperative. The law was the law, they said. The adoption was legal and I had given up all rights to my baby. And to any knowledge of its whereabouts."

"When did you write those letters?"

"During the first few years after...after I..." She choked up.

"I'm almost certain that the laws have changed since then," Brent said. Even though he felt some sympathy for what she'd gone through, he was not going to be influenced by tears. He spoke without inflection. "In fact, they may have changed before then and the people running the home weren't abiding by the law at all. I've had no reason to look into it before this, but I know that I've heard and read about adopted children locating their birth parents, and vice versa. They could only accomplish that if their adoption files were no longer sealed."

Blythe's eyes widened. "You're suggesting...?"

"I'm not *suggesting* anything. I'm telling you what I'm going to do. I'm going to go to that home in Utah, read your file and find out who adopted our baby. But I need further information from you to do it. What's the name of that town in Utah?"

"Breighton." She spelled it for him. "It's about a hundred miles north or northeast of Salt Lake City, a little town on a back country road. I remember that the terrain was mountainous." Her heart was pounding. "You're really going to do this?" This conversation was so vastly different than what she'd expected when seeing him on her front porch. She sensed nothing personal from him, other than normal concern because she had nearly fallen flat on her face. He would do the same for a stranger, she told herself, but there was something almost miraculous in the simple fact of him speaking to her civilly.

"Yes," Brent said flatly.

She hesitated, but couldn't stop herself from asking, "May...may I come with you?"

It was Brent's turn to hesitate. He shouldn't still care about her and obviously couldn't control his feelings, but did he want to spend time with her? Certainly he hadn't forgiven her, but she had as much right to look for their child as he did. He spoke quietly. "It might not turn out successfully, you know."

His somber mood did not diminish Blythe's developing excitement. "But it might! Oh, Brent, it might! When are you

going? Are you flying or driving?'' Hope such as Blythe
hadn't felt in years and years coursed through her veins.

''Flying makes more sense than driving,'' he said slowly,
realizing that she was already seeing herself in Breighton. He
sighed. ''It has to be close to eight hundred miles from here
to Salt Lake City. I'll rent a car when I get there.''

''Do...do you object to my going with you?'' Her voice
was barely more than a nervous whisper. If he said yes, that
he objected strenuously, there would be nothing she could do
about it. One thing did occur to her, however. ''This is something I should have thought of doing a long time ago,'' she
said tremulously. ''And if you prefer I don't come with you,
then I will go by myself.''

Brent looked away for a few moments, and Blythe's heart
sank. He *didn't* want her going with him. She heaved a sigh
and said, ''It's okay. I don't blame you.''

He brought his gaze back to her. ''No, it's all right. If you're
going anyway, we might as well go together.''

''You're sure?''

''Blythe, right now the only thing I'm sure of is that I'm
going to Breighton. You can come with me. Let's leave it at
that.''

''Thank you,'' she said softly, and noticed how he had
started avoiding looking directly into her eyes. She couldn't
fault him for that, either. He wouldn't be human if he didn't
resent what she'd done. Again she felt the same helplessness
she'd experienced when attempting to explain, the other day,
her parents' influence during her younger years. Brent had
been so independent his whole life that he couldn't possibly
comprehend anyone being so easily manipulated, as had happened to her.

But why dwell on the irrevocable? She forced her thoughts
in another direction and started thinking of her flight plans to
Connecticut. She would have to contact the travel agent and
cancel her reservation.

Brent had been watching her furtively. A weighty melancholy gripped him. It was so strange how they'd met again,
strange that he'd found himself falling in love with her again

and stranger still that he could still care about her after learning what she'd done. He felt himself softening toward her, which he was in no mood to convey, and he spoke gruffly.

"I'd like a cup of coffee. Got any made?"

Blythe started to get up. "No, but I'll put on a pot."

"Stay put and rest some more. I know where the coffee-maker is, just tell me where you keep the coffee."

"In the cabinet directly above the coffeepot." She was surprised that he'd asked for coffee, surprised that he was here at all, for that matter. Why hadn't he phoned for the name of the town instead of coming over? Had he wanted to see her? She'd been so adamantly against seeing him again, and so positive that he must feel the same. And yet here he was.

And they were planning a trip to Breighton. How incredible, almost unbelievable. Her pulse raced with anticipation of what they might uncover. She would, at the very least, learn whether she'd borne a son or a daughter, and it should also state in her file who had adopted her baby.

She began remembering things. *"Our babies are placed only with couples of the highest moral fiber. You need never worry that your child will grow up without love or financial security."*

She recalled asking if her child would know he or she was adopted, and had been told, *"That is strictly up to the adoptive parents."*

She was biting her lip when Brent came back. "What's wrong?" he asked.

"I...I've been thinking. Brent, have you considered the possibility that our child was never told he or she was adopted? We—you and I—could cause a lot of trouble."

A frown appeared between Brent's eyes, and he sat down slowly. "No, I didn't think about that." After a moment he leaned forward. "I *have* to know what happened to our baby. Maybe that's all I need to know, but I do have to know that much. Let's not look for problems we may never run into."

He was determined, she saw, and more than that, he was right. Neither of them could just do nothing now. They *had* to find out as much about their child as they could.

She nodded. "When do we go?"

"Let's call a travel agent and find out what flights are scheduled for tomorrow."

Blythe pushed herself up from the sofa. "I'll do it. I have to call the travel agent I used for my Connecticut flight, anyhow."

Blythe's excitement was subdued while they drank coffee at the kitchen table twenty minutes later, but it was there, all the same. They had reservations for a flight at nine o'clock in the morning. Blythe had also made arrangements for a rental car in Salt Lake City. All that remained to be done was a little packing.

"What do you think?" she inquired. "Should I pack for two days?"

"If all goes well, that should do it. But maybe it wouldn't hurt to pack for three or four days. We really don't know what we're going to run into in Breighton. Do you recall how to find the home, once we're there?"

"I think so. Unless the town has grown so much nothing's the same, of course." That idea concerned her. "Oh, I hope that's not the case."

"Don't worry about it. We'll find it." Brent drained his cup and got up for a refill. Holding his cup, he looked out the kitchen window. "I doubt if I'll get much sleep tonight," he murmured.

Blythe heaved a melancholy sigh. She deserved the emotional pain she'd lived with for so many years, but Brent did not. He couldn't possibly love her now—could any man forgive what she'd done?—so she had accomplished what she'd hoped for with her confession. And yet it seemed so sad. If she had told him she loved him, too, and had said nothing about the past, he would be happy right now instead of standing at her window looking as though a gust of wind could blow him over.

But that would have been an even worse sin than the one she'd committed twenty-four years ago. She could not be that deceitful, no matter what the cost to herself. It still seemed utterly amazing that they had made love, and she kept wondering how it had happened. Why she had *let* it happen.

Regardless, it was a memory to cherish, one to take out and think about at low points in her life.

This, though, was not a low point, however badly she felt about Brent's emotional upheaval. She was alive again, a feeling she hadn't had since the day she'd signed those adoption papers. Alive and hopeful. Worried, as well, but it wasn't a depressed or despondent worry she felt, but rather a natural and normal concern for an adventure into the unknown. There were, after all, no guarantees connected to tomorrow's trip, even though Brent was positive the home would have to give them access to her file.

The front doorbell chimed, breaking Blythe's chain of thought. Brent turned from the window. "Expecting company?"

"Abby Decker." *Oh, dear, what should I do about the car now?* Blythe got to her feet and then stood there looking at Brent instead of hurrying to the door to let Abby in. "I told Abby she could buy my car," she said, sounding every bit as confused as she felt.

"You really weren't coming back, were you?" Brent said with a hard glint in his eyes.

She could scarcely look at him. "I...no, I wasn't."

"Because of me."

"It—it was time I went home," she stammered.

"You were running away, Blythe. Don't you think it's time you stopped running and faced whatever demons you imagine to be breathing down your neck?"

Her mouth fell open. "That's not fair!"

"Maybe not, but it's the truth. You ran twenty-four years ago and you're still running. This time it was because I talked about falling in love with you. Do you think it's disloyal to your guilt to be happy about anything?" Why was he saying things like that to her? he asked himself. Why should he care if she was happy or not? He heaved a sigh.

Blythe bristled. He had every right to pass judgment on what she'd done twenty-four years ago, but he was not qualified to judge how she had lived her life ever since. "That's an absurd statement! It doesn't even make sense. Whoever heard of being disloyal to guilt?"

The doorbell chimed again. Brent set his cup on the counter and folded his arms across his chest. "Well? Aren't you going to answer the door?"

"Yes!" Racing from the kitchen to the foyer, she opened the door. "Abby, hi. Come on in."

Abby was looking at Brent's car in the driveway. "You have company. Would you like me to come back later on? This evening, perhaps?"

"No, now is fine. Please come in." Blythe led her to the den. "Have a seat, Abby." They settled themselves in chairs, and before the Realtor could say anything, Blythe rushed into an explanation. "My plans have changed, Abby. I can't sell the car right now, but if you still want it when I can sell it, it's yours."

Abby was clearly disappointed. "I have the cash in my purse."

"I know, and I'm very sorry I did this to you. But I was so positive about leaving tomorrow, and then something came up that I never expected to happen, and well, that's about it," she finished lamely.

"Are you now planning to stay until the house closes?" Abby asked.

"I…honestly don't know." Brent hadn't mentioned the house, but she really shouldn't count on him buying it now. "Abby, things are really up in the air right now. All I can do at this point is to promise that you can buy the car when I no longer need it. I wish I could be more definitive about it, but…" She stopped talking because what else was there to say?

"Well, whatever your unexpected surprise was, it put a sparkle in your eyes." Abby rose with a smile, proving again that she was an exceptionally nice woman. "Stay in touch, okay? I really do want the car."

Blythe got to her feet. "You may count on it." She managed a weak smile. "I really do want you to have the car.

Ready-made car buyers don't come along every day, do they?''

Abby smiled again. "No, I guess they don't."

After escorting her to the door, Blythe headed back to the kitchen and entered the room with a downcast expression. She felt bad about reneging on her deal with Abby, but what else could she have done? Unquestionably, she needed the car for as long as she was in Idaho.

Looking at Brent, she tried to recall what they'd been talking about before Abby's arrival. When it came to her, she stiffened slightly.

"I think we should set something straight," she said coolly. "My unhappiness—"

Brent cut in. "What I said was that you won't *let* yourself be happy."

"Because I would feel disloyal to my guilt. For your information, I haven't had anything to be happy about!"

"You were married. You must have been happy then."

She sank onto a chair. Brent was right. She hadn't been happy even then. Oh, there'd been moments of happiness, but they'd been so fleeting, so brief. Always, in the back of her mind, was her guilt. Her remorse. Her bitterness toward herself and her parents, each in varying degrees and usually attacking her at different times.

Brent felt a twinge of guilt himself. He'd obviously hit her where it hurt, and hurting her gave *him* no relief at all. In fact, it made him feel worse.

"Forget it," he said gruffly. "This is getting us nowhere. I'll pick you up at seven in the morning. That will give us plenty of time to drive to Spokane and get checked in before our flight."

She nodded mutely.

Brent looked at the forlorn picture she made for a few seconds, deeply regretted his big mouth, wished wholeheartedly he could recall his unkind remarks, then gave up on the whole thing and walked away, calling over his shoulder, "See you in the morning."

Blythe stayed where she was for a long time. It was obvious

from Brent's cruel remarks that he despised her now, and she
suspected she was going to hear a lot more of the same during
the next few days.

But she was only getting what she deserved from him, and
she could endure anything if it meant locating her child. Or at
least finding out its gender, and if it had been adopted by a
kind couple. Perhaps her greatest fear over the years was that
her baby had been adopted by people who didn't know how
to love a child. If she ever learned that her child had been
emotionally or physically deprived or abused, it would be the
final straw, one with which she feared she would not be able
to cope.

Sighing, she got up from the table. It was time to get her
packing done for tomorrow's trip.

Blythe hardly slept that night. She was too keyed up, too
anxious, and when she did fall asleep she would almost immediately wake up again to worry and fret about tomorrow.
What would they run into in Breighton? Would the people
operating the home hand over her file when she and Brent
asked to see it? Could it possibly be that simple? If it turned
out that way, why in heaven's name hadn't it occurred to her
to go there on her own? It had apparently been Brent's first
thought. Why hadn't it been hers?

Instead she had all but wallowed in self-pity and resentment
for more than twenty years, blaming herself, blaming her parents, never completely accepting what she had done but never
really doing anything about it. She had believed that there was
nothing *to* do about it, especially after that exchange of letters
with the home so many years ago. In essence, she had given
up without a fight. What kind of woman could do that and
still bear the burden of so much guilt? How did she have the
nerve to suffer regret and remorse when she'd done nothing
to help herself *or* her child?

And why had she never brought up the subject with her
mother? Neither of them had ever spoken of it after the fact.
It was strange now, remembering that her mother had been
pregnant at the same time that Blythe had carried her own

child. And then Myra had been happy with her new baby, Tamara, and had never expressed one word of sorrow that her oldest daughter didn't have *her* child.

Of course, there had not been much opportunity for them to talk about anything in those days. Blythe had gone directly from the unwed mother's home in Breighton to a new college. She'd found jobs or taken extra classes during the summers to stay busy and avoid even seeing her family. After graduation she had taken a teaching job in Connecticut. Not for the private school she taught at now, but at a public school. Throughout her adult life, she had continued to elude a homecoming. It wasn't always possible. She'd come home for her father's funeral, of course.

But all of them—Myra, Sierra, Tamara and herself—had always talked in generalities whenever any of them were together. There had never been any closeness between Blythe and her two younger sisters, and there'd been very little closeness between Blythe and her mother. In truth, the three Benning girls had become much closer than they had ever been since their mother's death in January, which seemed terribly sad to Blythe now. She should have made peace with her mother, she thought unhappily, while rolling and tossing during that seemingly endless night. She should have insisted that Myra talk to her about the past instead of holding everything in and bearing her guilt and bitterness in stony silence. It was a secret that had fractured the Benning family. At the very least it had kept Blythe separate from her mother and sisters.

Blythe's worries jumped to her sisters. Tamara and Sierra thought she was going home to Connecticut tomorrow, and if they should try to reach her there they could become alarmed, especially if they also attempted to phone her in Coeur d'Alene.

She would have to call them in the morning, she decided, and tell them that she had delayed her journey home for a few days. That would defuse the situation, and she doubted that either of her sisters would question her about why she was putting off going home. They were wonderful women, each of them, and Blythe had come to love her sisters as she should have all along.

So many wasted years, she thought with a long, weighted sigh. So many *unnecessarily* wasted years. All because she had fallen in love in college with a studious, hard-working young man whom her mother had been positive had not been good enough for her. That was what it had really boiled down to, Blythe had come to believe. Without even meeting Brent, Myra had decided he wasn't good enough for her oldest daughter.

If only Mother could meet him now, Blythe thought with another heavy sigh. He was intelligent, handsome, apparently financially well off and decisive about his work and what he wanted from life. Right now he wanted information about their child, and Blythe strongly suspected that by hook or by crook he was going to get some answers. She had to admire his determination.

She admired more than Brent's determination, though. She knew herself well enough to also know that she would not have made love with Brent without having had feelings of love. She still had them. She felt Brent's presence in her soul, where it seemed to have taken up residence. Maybe it had always been there, she mused uneasily. Maybe the love she'd felt for him in college had never really left her.

No, she could not let herself think in that vein. She couldn't deal with any more heartache, and heartache was the only thing she would ever get from Brent.

But he talked about falling in love with you!

That was before you told him what you did, if you'd care to remember. Dammit, don't get any silly notions in your head!

"Silly notions are for kids," she mumbled disgustedly. "You're forty-three years old, for crying out loud."

Brent was awake, too, but he was enduring his insomnia on his feet, pacing the motel room and grumbling under his breath, because seeing Blythe this afternoon had diminished his anger over what she'd done. He had to hang on to anger;

it was the only thing that might stop him from making a fool of himself with her again.

How had life gotten so complicated so quickly? He'd arrived in Coeur d'Alene feeling good about the Sunrise project. Now here he was, up-to-his-eyeballs involved with a woman he never could have imagined seeing again, and sick-to-his-stomach concerned for a son or a daughter he'd known nothing about. It wasn't fair, dammit, it just wasn't fair.

Then again, he thought with a dejected sigh, had anyone ever said life was fair?

He had to find out what he could about his child, that was a given. But he didn't have to even *like* his child's mother!

Why then did he?

Chapter Ten

When Blythe saw the sign Welcome to Breighton the tension she'd felt during the flight and then the drive from Salt Lake City increased tenfold. With her heart pounding and her sweaty hands clutching a tissue, she said in an unsteady voice, "I don't remember that sign."

"It might not have been there twenty years ago." Brent was driving into town very slowly. The first buildings they passed were gas stations, then there were several small used-car lots. "You said the home is on Ash Street."

"That's right. There's a string of tree streets—Maple, Elder, Oak and more—and the home is at the very end of Ash Street, on a large wooded lot with an iron fence around it. The house is old and constructed of gray rock."

"Sounds gloomy."

Blythe thought about it. *She'd* been gloomy, and broken-hearted, but not because of the home itself. "Actually, it wasn't," she murmured. "There were about a dozen young women when I was there, and each of us had a small room of our own. The food was good, and there were a lot of planned activities. We…were treated kindly.''

''Well, it's not a big town. We should be able to locate the tree streets without too much trouble.'' Brent glanced at Blythe. They were driving through what appeared to be the center of Breighton. There were stores and businesses, mostly situated in old buildings. ''Does anything look familiar?''

''Not really,'' she said quietly. ''I rarely left the home. Oh, I just remembered something. There was a store on Ash Street that I used to walk to for magazines and sundries. I think it was about four blocks from the home. But if I recall correctly, I never came to the downtown area. There was no reason.''

''You had money to buy magazines and things, then?''

''Mother gave me money for incidentals.''

''That was big of her,'' Brent said with some sarcasm. He couldn't make himself say anything nice about Blythe's parents. He'd never met them, but resentment for what they had forced upon Blythe, and upon himself, burned a hole in his gut.

Blythe didn't try to defend her parents against Brent's rancor. If anyone was entitled to feelings of hostility, it was Brent. They had talked very little on the plane—what was there to say? Small talk wasn't feasible, and the topics that were on Blythe's mind were so jarring and had such far-reaching, nerve-racking ramifications that she couldn't bring herself to speak of them. She was sure that Brent felt the same—how could he not?

The drive from Salt Lake City had been almost as silent, but now they were in Breighton and had to join forces if they were going to accomplish their goal.

''So, what do we do, drive around and find Ash Street on our own, or stop and ask for directions?'' Brent said.

''Oh, there's the Mormon church off to the left! See the tall steeple? The tree streets are on the other side of the church.''

''Okay, great.'' Brent made a left turn. ''Was the home affiliated with the church?''

''Not at all. We were encouraged to attend the church of our choice, but that was the only reference to religion that I can recall. No, I believe the home was a privately owned institution. The women in charge were caring, pleasant people. As I said before, the girls were treated kindly. The rules were lenient and aimed toward making us feel good about ourselves.''

''Those kindly, lenient rules didn't work in your case, did they?''

''No, they didn't,'' Blythe said quietly, again ignoring the sarcasm she heard in his voice. They were passing the beautiful old Mormon church, and she began watching for street signs. ''There's Maple Street,'' she announced. ''Ash is two streets down. When we get there, take a right.''

Her stomach was churning, her heart pounding. In all those many years she had never once visualized herself returning to Breighton and to the home. She had avoided even thinking of the months she'd spent waiting for the birth of her child. Now a memory engulfed her. She had heard other girls crying at night, and had known that they, too, were suffering over giving up their baby before it was even born.

But not all the girls *had* given away their babies. Some had left the home carrying their baby in their arms. Those had been the girls Blythe had envied, and on those nights Blythe, too, had cried herself to sleep.

They were finally on Ash Street. ''It's at the very end of the street,'' Blythe said, trying desperately to speak normally, which wasn't possible when her entire body was trembling.

Brent drove with a grim expression. They were almost there. Pray God the home is still functioning, he thought. He stopped in front of a large, gray stone building. ''Is this it?''

A large sign above the massive front doors read Breighton Senior Center.

Confusion hit Blythe. ''It—it was,'' she stammered. There was a parking area that hadn't been on the property before, and she saw elderly people going in and out of the building. Hysteria threatened. The home was no longer here! ''Maybe—maybe they moved it to another location.''

''And maybe it just doesn't exist anymore,'' Brent said tersely. He pulled into the parking lot and turned off the motor.

"I'm going to go in and ask someone about it. Do you want to come with me, or would you rather wait in the car?" His heart softened some when he looked at Blythe's stricken face. "Maybe you'd better wait out here. You don't look very steady."

"I—I'll wait," she whispered, afraid that her legs wouldn't hold her up if she tried to get out of the car. What had happened to the home? she thought frantically. And to its records?

Brent nodded and got out, and with her heart in her throat she watched him go into the building. Every second that he was out of sight felt like an eternity. She kept looking at her watch and then at the door. A group of older women came outside, laughing and talking. It was a bright, sunny day but Blythe felt as if she was in a smothering fog. The fifteen minutes that Brent was in that building felt like fifteen hours.

When he finally came out she could tell from the taut lines of his face that he'd learned very little, if anything.

He climbed in the rental car. "That was a dead end. One woman remembered when this was a home for unwed mothers, but she said the home closed about fifteen years ago. She knew nothing about who the owners had been, or what happened to them, except she's positive they don't live in Breighton now because she claims to know everyone in town." He sounded discouraged. "So, what do we do now?"

"If...if the owners left town, what do you suppose they did with their records?"

"Your guess is as good as mine. Maybe they shredded them, as you're planning to do with your father's old medical records."

They sat there, trying to digest this enormous failure. After a while Brent said, "I wonder if the city hall, or town hall, or whatever they call it around here, would have any information."

"Like the names of the home's owners?" Hope gripped Blythe again. "Oh, Brent, it's worth a try."

Brent started the car, backed from his parking space and entered the street. After asking directions to the city hall at a convenience store, he easily found it.

"Why, it looks like a brand-new building," Blythe commented in surprise as Brent pulled into a parking slot.

"Yes, it does," he agreed. "Do you want to come in with me this time?"

"Yes, I think I do."

They were in the "brand-new" building for approximately five minutes. They'd been told by an apologetic clerk, "All of Breighton's town records were destroyed in a fire a year ago. The old city hall burned to the ground, and so did everything in it. It's been an awful mess, because everyone who currently holds a license to do business in Breighton had to physically bring it in so we could start new records. I'm sorry, but there's nothing I or anyone else could tell you about a business that operated so many years ago."

Back in the car, Brent and Blythe exchanged defeated looks. "We might as well go home," he said with a discouraged sigh.

Blythe agreed, and they drove back to Salt Lake City and boarded the first available flight to Spokane.

Neither of them had even once opened the suitcases they'd brought with them.

It was dark and approaching ten o'clock when they drove into Coeur d'Alene that night. They'd had a four-hour wait in the Salt Lake airport for a flight to Spokane, it had been a long and painfully disappointing day and Blythe was exhausted. Regardless of physical weariness, however, she felt an overwhelming rebelliousness. She could not simply sit back and accept today's abysmal failure, as though it were of small import. Someone somewhere knew why the home had closed, what had happened to the owners and whether or not the records had been destroyed.

She turned to look at Brent, whose profile appeared stony and grim in the dim light from the dash. "I'm not giving up," she said quietly but emphatically.

"Do you have a plan?"

He sounded as tired as she felt, and her heart sank. Today's failure couldn't begin to compare with the failure she'd made of her life, and now she had dragged Brent into it. She never should have told him anything. He'd been a happy man, and what was he tonight? Certainly not happy. She could have let him talk about falling in love with her without getting crazed about it. Why had it seemed so crucial that he *not* love her? Why had confession seemed to be the right—and only—way to destroy his feelings?

Now he was as miserable as she was, and she felt awful about it. "Brent, I—I'm so sorry."

He sent her a startled glance. "Pardon?"

"I hurt you terribly by telling you about the baby," she said brokenly. "I should have left it alone. There's nothing more you can do to find our child, and I can say that I'm not giving up till I'm blue in the face, but I don't have the foggiest idea of what to do next. That's why I'm apologizing. I've caused you so much unhappiness, and it was completely unnecessary." After a moment she whispered, "Both times."

Brent swallowed the sudden lump in his throat and spoke hoarsely. "You can't live in the past, Blythe. Neither of us can."

"You probably never even thought of *our* past until I told you about the baby."

"I thought of our past the second I saw you again."

"But your memories were so unrealistic. I knew that was happening, and that you were trying very hard to reconcile the woman I am now with the one you remembered. You couldn't do it, of course, because I'm not even close to being the same person I was before…before the baby." She choked up. "You'll never be really happy again, I know you won't, and it's my fault."

Brent spoke sharply. "Do you enjoy punishing yourself?"

Blythe's head jerked around. "What?"

"I think you heard me. Everything is always your fault, isn't it?"

"Well, who else should I blame?"

"How about circumstances? How about your parents? How about a home for unwed mothers that pushed adoption instead of providing its young women with some much-needed counseling? How about blaming me for accepting that ludicrous phone call instead of coming after you and making you tell me what was really going on?''

"I should be blaming you? Brent, that's ridiculous!''

"The whole damned thing is ridiculous, Blythe," Brent mumbled darkly. "It was from the start. That's your parents' fault. My accepting your lame explanation on the phone is my fault. That archaic home for unwed mothers is far from fault-less, too, believe me.''

"You're making it sound as though I bear no responsibility at all for what I did! It was all someone else's fault. Well, you're wrong, Brent. I'm the one who signed the adoption papers, and no one was standing over me with a hammer.''

"No, but I'd bet anything that you had been so brainwashed by then that signing those papers actually seemed to be your only sensible option.''

He sounded so bitter that Blythe winced, but then she re-alized that his bitterness was because of what had been done to her! He actually believed that she wasn't at fault, and how could he? My God, she thought sadly, he's the same tender-hearted boy he was in college.

"Why are we having this serious discussion now when we barely talked all day?'' she asked. They were almost to her house, and she was grateful that the grueling trip was nearly over. She wanted to crawl into bed and stay there for days. She wanted to sleep and sleep, and then wake up with a clear head and the ability to formulate a plan for finding their child. She'd been unforgivably remiss about not searching for her son or daughter before this, but now that the search had begun she could not end it without answers.

"We were both tense all day," Brent replied.

"That's no explanation. I'm *still* tense. You must be, too.''

He drove onto her street and, after a minute or two, pulled into her driveway. Leaving the motor idling, he turned in the seat to face her. Looking at her, he wished to high heaven that he hadn't gotten her hopes up. He could have asked her the name of the town in Utah without telling her he intended to go there. She might have suspected something, and then again she might not have. Her dejection and misery now was his doing.

Regret gripped him for a moment, then he thought of what could have been between them and suffered a resurgence of anger. He tried to keep it out of his voice, but couldn't quite do it. Blythe heard it quite clearly when he said, "Come on. I'll walk you to the door."

Blythe suffered the delivery room dream again that night, only she didn't wake up sobbing as she'd always done. Something within her had changed, she realized. She was emotionally stronger than she'd been—a blessing, to be sure, but what had caused it? Knowing Brent again? Having finally shared her secret with another person?

Actually, she reasoned, she no longer had a secret. Even though she still felt badly about causing Brent the same kind of pain she'd been living with, she now had someone with whom she could talk about the past. She probably didn't deserve to derive comfort from that fact, but it was comforting, nonetheless.

She marveled that he was big enough to even speak to her. She had believed with all her heart that he would despise her, and it seemed like a small miracle that he didn't. He'd been shocked and stunned by her confession, but then he'd rebounded and had apparently started thinking not of her deceit, nor of himself, but of their child. He was a man in a million.

Regardless, he was wrong about everyone else being at fault for what she had done. She'd been old enough to make her own decisions, and she had let her mother's will overwhelm her own. How differently her life would have turned out if she had immediately returned to school when her mother started taking over. It wasn't what she had expected from her parents, but she had not had to lose all sense of self and permit it to happen. If only she'd walked out of this house and gone to Brent. In truth, she should have gone to Brent right away instead of coming home at all.

Of course, that wasn't a new thought. Over the years it had haunted her time and again. She could have contacted Brent while she was staying in the home, for that matter, and why hadn't she? Shame? Fear? Loss of self-esteem? Truth was, her mother had taken over so completely that Blythe hadn't had the courage to rebell, and she'd gone along with Myra's plans as complacently as a sheep being led to slaughter.

In a way, none of it had seemed real, Blythe recalled with a tear sliding down her temple. Reality hadn't really hit home until her baby had been born and no one would let her see it. The baby had apparently been whisked from the delivery room into the arms of its adoptive parents. Blythe didn't know that as fact, but she did know that her baby had not remained in the home, for she had wandered the halls looking for it and had hung out at the nursery until told to stay away. Then it had been time for her to leave, and she had walked out of the building too numb to even weep.

Lying in her bed in the dark, Blythe wiped her teary eyes. She could not say that her mother had brought her to the home, then turned her back on her. Myra had kept in touch and had even been there for the baby's birth. She had been pregnant herself with Tamara. In fact, she had given birth to her youngest daughter within days of her trip to Breighton to be with Blythe during *her* delivery.

Blythe knew in her soul that Myra Benning had truly believed that she'd done the right thing for her oldest daughter. Perhaps that was the reason Blythe had never been able to hate her mother. No, any hatred she felt was for herself, along with disgust, a degradation of spirit and more guilt than any person should have to bear.

Blythe wasn't the only one enduring troubling thoughts that night; so was Brent. He had awakened for no good reason, and once he started thinking about Blythe and their child, he couldn't shut off his mind enough to go back to sleep.

His most tormenting feeling was regret over involving Blythe in yesterday's fiasco. Not that he'd gone to her house with any plans to ask her to go with him. Regardless, he'd run her hopes off the scale, and the emotional drop after their complete failure had to be horrible for her. It was bad enough for him, but he'd only been living with this thing for a few days. Blythe had carried it around for over twenty years.

"Dear God," he whispered raggedly. How had she survived it as well as she had? Why wouldn't she be a different woman today than she'd been in college? She'd been so soft-hearted, so sweet and gentle, so far from the kind of woman who could give away her child and then forget it that the mere idea was unthinkable.

But, dammit, he *should* have thought of it. He should have realized that more was going on with Blythe back then than a sudden desire to transfer colleges. Yes, he'd been hurt by that phone call, but why had he become focused on his own shattered feelings and pride, without once considering that Blythe had been keeping something from him?

He sighed with the weight of the world. Like Blythe herself had said, it was all water under the bridge. Instead of lamenting the past, he should focus on correcting the present. Just how he should go about doing that was a complete mystery, but there had to be a way.

It was what he would concentrate on. There *had* to be a way.

Blythe was up only a short time in the morning when she thought of Sierra and Clint, and the fact that they had wanted to come to Coeur d'Alene for the weekend. Going to the phone, she dialed her sister's number.

"Who calls more than I do?" she said dryly when Sierra came on the line.

Sierra laughed. "Every one of your calls is more than welcome. Did you have another change of plans?"

"It probably seems to you as though I can't make a decision and stick to it. But yes, I do have another change of plans. I'm going to be here through the weekend, after all, and I would be thrilled beyond measure if you and Clint came for a visit."

"Oh, Blythe, that's wonderful! I know Clint will agree, so I'm going to say yes without consulting him. He wants very much to meet both you and Tamara. I've told him about my two beautiful sisters, and I think I've got him curious.'' Sierra laughed before continuing. ''Count on seeing us on Saturday, okay? Clint said it was about a five-hour drive, so if we get an early start we should be there around noon. Blythe, I am so excited. We have so much to talk about, and I can hardly wait to see you.''

''I'm anxious to see you, too, Sierra.'' Blythe realized how true that statement was. Among all the dreary feelings in her system was some much-appreciated anticipation.

They talked for a few more minutes, then said goodbye. After hanging up, Blythe sat there staring into space. There was no question that a large part of herself was looking forward to the weekend, but neither could she deny the pain she felt. Her life had taken such a bizarre turn this summer. It occurred to her that she had lost Brent not just once but twice, and both times had been her doing. He'd angrily asked if she enjoyed punishing herself, and although she had argued with him about fault and blame last night, she had to wonder today if he wasn't more right than wrong.

All these years she had lived with the belief that she deserved punishment, and that her secret unhappiness was a justified penalty. But had she accepted her misery too meekly, just as she had accepted her mother's demands twenty-four years ago?

It was a traumatic subject, and Blythe tried to sidestep thinking about it by making plans for the weekend. Good food was a must, and she got off her chair and went to the cupboards and refrigerator to check her stock of groceries.

It was a welcome break from the drudgery of her former thoughts.

Brent sat in a booth in the motel's coffee shop and scanned some of the plans he'd been drawing for the Sunrise project. After a few minutes, though, he set the papers aside; he really couldn't think of anything but yesterday. In truth he was beginning to doubt the wisdom of everything he'd done since coming to Coeur d'Alene. Did he want the Benning house now, for instance? Could he live in that house and not constantly be reminded of what Blythe's parents had done to her?

He ordered another cup of coffee and gave it some serious thought. Try as he might, he couldn't see himself being comfortable living in Myra and Dr. Benning's house. Never before in his life had he disliked people he hadn't met, and he definitely did not like the Bennings. In fact, he resented them so much that even his coffee tasted bitter.

He told himself to look at the situation more rationally. The Bennings were both dead. The house now belonged to their daughters. He wasn't buying it from Myra and Dr. Benning, he was dealing strictly with Blythe.

But the whole thing kept eating at him. He'd fallen in love with that damn house, and he was committed on paper to buying it. What he'd like to do was drop in on Blythe and tell her how he felt about it now. She would understand, he was pretty sure, and she'd probably let him out of the deal without any problems.

But dropping in on Blythe wasn't as simple as it had once been. There was too much between them now to just knock on her door without some sort of okay from her to do so.

The whole thing was a damn mess, he thought disgustedly. He had no idea what to do next to locate their child. Blythe was miserably unhappy, and why wouldn't she be? He, too, was unhappy, and now he didn't want to buy her house, which would probably make her even *more* unhappy.

Getting up from the booth, Brent shoved his papers into his briefcase and took his check to the cashier. He left the coffee shop and headed for his car.

Maybe a round of golf would clear his head.

Chapter Eleven

Blythe had two empty days to fill until the weekend. The house was clean, she had more than enough food on hand to prepare good meals for Sierra and Clint, and she was too on edge to just sit around and wait for Saturday.

There *was* one thing that needed doing, she reminded herself—moving out of the family room that heavy wood frame that had contained Sierra's painting. The only place in the house for it was the large room in the basement, she decided, and she began inching it across the carpet and then the hard surface of the kitchen floor. At the head of the basement stairs, she placed a small rug under the frame and cautiously slid it down the stairs, one step at a time.

Finally she leaned it against a wall behind an overstuffed chair in the basement room. If Brent didn't want it, he could discard it or give it to a charity, she thought, along with everything else. Every stick of furniture down here was old, worn and mismatched. It was a catchall room, and the only reason it was full of junk was because her parents had never thrown anything out.

Glancing at the door to the smaller room, Blythe felt a rising impatience. The rows of file cabinets in that room were a perfect example of her parents' penchant for keeping everything that had ever passed through their hands. Those records should have been destroyed many years ago. Now it was something *she* had to do, and she couldn't help resenting that fact.

Berating herself for having put off what still seemed like a monumental job, she went to the door and opened it. Walking in, she moved among the metal cabinets. In January she had taken only one look into the room. Shuddering at the time, she had quickly shut the door. Her second look was when she'd shown it to Brent.

It occurred to her now that she could procrastinate no longer. Brent should not have to deal with this room, and if he took early possession of the house and she went home...?

Leaning against one of the cabinets, she realized that she was still counting on Brent buying the house. But if he'd changed his mind, wouldn't he have said so by now? Actually, it was out of her hands until he did say something.

She pondered leaving Idaho and found that it wasn't nearly as appealing as it had been. Brent had accused her of running away, and he could be right. Maybe she'd been running all her life. If that was true, what would she be running from this time? Brent?

But so much had changed. Brent was no longer pressing her for a personal relationship. They had spent all day yesterday together and nothing remotely personal had occurred.

She bit down on her bottom lip. Obviously her confession had destroyed his developing feelings for her, which was precisely what she had hoped to do, but her reason for keeping him at arm's length no longer existed. Didn't he realize that? Or maybe he did and it just didn't matter. She had known beforehand, after all, that he would not be able to forgive her.

Still, she would like to see him, she thought poignantly, and wished that he would just drop in, as he used to do. That was a silly wish, of course. Brent might have argued with her about fault and blame, but deep down he had to know that there really was no one to blame but her. How could he possibly overlook the fact that she was the person who had signed the papers that had given their child to strangers? No, he wasn't apt to just drop in.

There was, however, one very good reason *not* to avoid each other—their child. Working together, they just might come up with some ideas on how to find a missing person.

A missing person, Blythe thought sadly. The term fit the situation so well, but it tore at her heartstrings.

Pulling herself together, she turned her attention back to the chore of cleaning out this room. Whatever the timing of her return to Connecticut, she could not leave this mess for Brent—or some other buyer—to deal with. Actually, she'd like to kick herself from here to Spokane and back for putting off this chore. What on earth had she been doing all summer?

Her lips pursed. She'd read in the den for countless hours and not noticed that her father's first editions were missing. She had sat in the family room too many times to keep track of and not noticed the intricacies of Sierra's painting. Had she completely lost touch with reality during her stay in this house this summer?

Well, she thought with a heavy sigh, standing here and beating herself up was getting her nowhere. She forced her attention back to the job she could no longer put off.

All the cabinets were the same tan color, she noted, and not unattractive as far as file cabinets went. Perhaps someone would buy them. After they were emptied and washed down, of course.

And then she noticed that one cabinet was *not* the same as all the others. Frowning, she approached it and saw that it was a fireproof model. She took the handle of the top drawer and was surprised when it didn't slide open. Brent had easily opened several drawers in different cabinets the day he'd inspected the house, but this drawer was locked. In fact, all of the drawers in this cabinet were locked! How strange. Where was the key?

She began looking around for a key, and the longer she looked and didn't find one, the more anxious she became about it. What was in that fireproof cabinet? Even the deed to the house had been in a strongbox in her mother's bedroom. What had been more important to Myra Benning than that?

Remembering Brent checking the contents of some drawers, Blythe also recalled him saying, "Blythe, there are files in this cabinet that don't look like medical records." She'd been so nervous with him in the house that day, and she'd told him that those files were probably old business records of her father's.

Now she hastened to look for that particular cabinet, and when she located it and peered into the drawers, she saw that her guess had been correct. Old tax returns, bank statements and accounting records from her father's medical practice were all there, carefully labeled by year.

But that eliminated the possibility of the fireproof cabinet containing business records, she realized uneasily. So what *was* in it? And why was it locked?

Blythe frowned, because she'd gone through everything in the house this summer, other than this one room, and she hadn't run across a key that she had not been able to match with a lock.

Obviously, though, she hadn't been as thorough as she should have been, because this cabinet had a key and she hadn't found it. It unnerved her, and she spent the rest of the day peering into cupboards and drawers throughout the house. Her mother's bedroom contained furniture, a few knickknacks and nothing else, as Blythe had packed up Myra's clothing and given it to her church. Blythe had been positive that she had checked every pocket of every garment, but since she hadn't even noticed the missing first editions until very recently, she was no longer confident about anything she had done in the house this summer.

Eating dinner that evening, she felt discouraged about the key, angry because she had procrastinated on that basement room and self-pitying about her life in general, all at the same time. It was a lethal mix of emotions, and she stabbed at her food as though her salad, rice and veal chop needed killing.

Thank God Sierra is going to be here this weekend, Blythe thought. She needed someone so badly, someone who loved her and didn't know what a terrible person she was. She needed someone to smile at her and maybe even to laugh with. Surely she and Sierra could find something to laugh about.

Laying down her fork, Blythe put her elbows on the table and her face in her hands. She was so alone, so terribly, frighteningly alone. She had lived that way far too long, pretending that everything was all right when it wasn't. It would be so easy to just give up and let the demons eat her alive.

Tears began seeping through her fingers, and she didn't care that they were falling onto her plate. She wasn't hungry, anyway. She honestly couldn't remember the last time she had come to the table really hungry. She lived a lie. Everything she did was a lie. The people she worked with in Connecticut thought she was a wonderful, decent woman, and she wasn't. Her own sisters looked up to her, and they shouldn't. No one should.

Do you enjoy punishing yourself?

"Shut up! Go away," she mumbled at the voice in her head quoting Brent's question from yesterday. She would have to be insane to enjoy what she was going through right now, and she wasn't totally insane yet.

Then again, maybe she was. Her tears flowed harder, and her shoulders shook from the severity of her sobs. In the back of her mind she knew she had to pull herself together. But she didn't have the strength to stop herself from crying, and maybe she really didn't have the desire to stop, she thought with another spate of sobs.

The doorbell startled her. Grabbing a napkin, she wiped her eyes. She didn't want to see anyone, she didn't want anyone to see her right now, but whoever was on the front porch kept ringing the bell, and it occurred to her that Sierra and Clint might not have waited for the weekend to come. It could be them out there, and if it was, Sierra would probably understand that her older sister might have reasons to cry, having lived in their parent's house all summer.

Taking a minute to dampen the napkin with cold water and press it to her eyes, Blythe finally went to the foyer and opened the door.

It was Brent, and he saw immediately that all was not well. "I tried to call," he said, wondering if she'd been crying over yesterday's failure. She had to be as frustrated about it as he'd been all day. "But your line's been busy for hours."

"I haven't used the phone all day." She was so glad to see Brent that she wanted to hug him, but of course she couldn't do that. "Please come in." Her voice was thick and her nose stuffy. She knew her eyes had to be red and swollen, but what did it matter? So he'd caught her crying. Surely he had to know that she suffered moments of sheer misery.

"Blythe, you look like you're ready to keel over. What's wrong?" He stepped into the foyer and she shut the door.

"It would be much simpler and take a lot less time to tell you what's right. Would you like a cup of coffee?"

"Yes, thanks. Blythe, if you haven't been on the phone, then there must be a problem with it. I'm going to check your line, okay?"

"Go ahead. I'll be in the kitchen."

Brent went through the house, checked every extension phone and finally found one that was off the hook. He walked into the kitchen a minute later.

"The phone in one of the bedrooms was off the hook."

"The bedroom with the green bedspread?"

"Yes."

"I was in there today and must have accidentally bumped the phone."

Under the bright ceiling light in the kitchen, Blythe's red eyes were much more apparent. "You've been crying."

"So I have," she retorted, and set his cup of coffee on the table.

"And you haven't finished your dinner," he said, eyeing her plate of food.

She picked up the plate and dumped the food into the garbage disposal. "Sit down and have your coffee." Pouring herself a cup, she sat across the table from him.

Brent took a sip from his cup. "You've had a bad day, and it's my fault."

"*Your* fault!" she scoffed. "My God, how could you possibly think you bear any fault in this?"

"I should have gone to Utah by myself," he said quietly. "I didn't have to tell you I was going." He'd decided during the day that he could never live in this house. That was the reason he'd tried to call Blythe, finally giving up after hours of getting a busy signal, and driving over instead. But looking at her now, he knew this was not the time to be delivering that sort of message.

"If you'd gone without telling me, I—I..." She couldn't bring herself to say that she never would have forgiven him, even though she knew it would have caused her great anguish. If she'd found out about it, of course.

"It would have made you terribly unhappy," Brent finished for her with a heavy sigh. "Blythe, you're unhappy anyway. Do you know that I haven't seen one genuinely carefree smile on your face?"

"It's not likely to happen." Blythe knew that if they kept on talking about it, she was going to break down and cry again, which would only make them both feel worse. She was glad to see Brent, glad not to be alone, and she didn't want him to leave. She introduced a new subject, one that would depress neither of them. "My sister and her husband are going to be here this weekend."

"Which sister is that?"

"Sierra."

"The painter."

"Yes. Her husband, Clint, is a rancher in Montana."

"I'd like to meet them," Brent said, surprising himself.

"You would?" He'd surprised Blythe, as well, and she found herself stammering. "Well—well, sure...why not? Uh, why don't you come, uh, for dinner...on—on Saturday? Unless you have other plans."

"I have no other plans and I'd like to have dinner with you and your family. Thank you for the invitation." Brent had to wonder why he was doing this to himself. He might still care about Blythe, but he knew he hadn't gotten over her long-ago deception and there was a damn good chance that he never would. Why was he asking for more heartache by getting involved with her family?

But Blythe couldn't read his mind, and a lovely warmth seemed to suddenly float within her. Why, she wasn't alone at all, not really. Not with her sister and brother-in-law coming for the weekend, and Brent in the picture. His even wanting to be in the picture had to be some kind of miracle, but it appeared that he had not given up on her, and if anyone had ever needed a miracle, it was her.

"You're a very special man," she said softly. "You don't hate me, do you?"

His eyes met hers across the table. It took a minute for his thoughts to gel. He realized that she wasn't asking for forgiveness, but for friendship. He could at least give her that. "No, Blythe," he said gently. "I don't hate you."

Something bloomed within her. She felt as though he'd just given her a precious gift. "You were angry at first."

"Yes," was all he could say, because the anger hadn't entirely dissipated.

"You had a right to be. What I did—"

He cut in, startling himself as much as her. "It wasn't your fault." Was he beginning to forgive her? If not, why did he insist on defending what she'd done? Confused by his own ambiguity, he frowned.

She sighed. "Brent, it *was* my fault."

He startled himself again. "You were naive."

"Naiveté is no excuse."

He cleared his throat. "You were manipulated."

"I didn't have to let anyone manipulate me."

"You were young." His frown deepened. Why was he doing this—trying to make her feel better about the past?

"Not that young."

"Do you *want* me to blame you?" The anger in his gut was surfacing again, and he'd spoken harshly.

She visibly shrank and whispered, "I want you to face the—the truth."

He knew now what was happening—the conversation they should have had immediately after her confession. It felt good to finally be bringing it all out in the open, and he said gruffly, "The truth as you see it or as I see it?"

"They—they should be the same." Her eyes fluttered to his and away again. Her heart was pounding; she hadn't been at all prepared for this debate.

He leaned forward and pinned her with a hard look. "But they're not, are they? You haven't discussed this with very many people, have you?"

"You're it," she said timorously.

"Are you saying your sisters don't know?"

"Them or anyone else. You're the only one I've told."

His lips twisted angrily. "No wonder you're ready to explode. Why in hell didn't you ever talk about it with anyone?"

"I…couldn't."

He shook his head. "I just don't understand you, Blythe."

"Don't you think I know that?" This time she met his gaze straight on, and her eyes contained an expression that Brent read as self-protective defiance.

Oddly, it pleased him. So, you're finally of a mind to defend yourself, he thought as he leaned back in his chair with a peculiar sense of satisfaction. "You and your mother must have talked about it," he said, determined to pull every tiny detail out of her while she was in this mood. Her barrier was disintegrating, almost before his eyes, and he wanted to crush it, to destroy it so completely she could never hide behind it again.

Blythe suddenly looked unnaturally distraught, and he wondered if he hadn't gone too far. He relaxed a little when she began talking, although her voice was noticeably strained and bitter.

"Never," she said. "And I'm sure she didn't tell Tamara or Sierra anything about it, because Mother was a master at keeping secrets. She was seriously ill for six years before she passed away and never once hinted to any one of us that she wasn't well. Her death was an unexpected shock, especially for Tamara. She flew home to see Mother right after Christmas and found her unconscious on the floor."

Brent tried to keep his own voice from revealing the bitterness that *he* felt for Myra Benning. "That had to have been hard on Tamara."

"It was."

"I guess I don't understand family members hiding things from each other. Your sisters could have been a great comfort to you through the years."

"We hardly knew each other. We've become closer since Mother died than we ever were while she was alive."

"Then maybe you should tell them now."

Blythe looked appalled. "And risk losing their respect? I don't think so."

"Blythe, other women have given up their babies for adoption and gotten over it."

She spoke sharply, almost disdainfully. "Oh? You know that as fact?"

"No, I don't. But there are so many adopted children, and I find it hard to believe that every birth mother lives with the guilt that you do. Time is a great healer, and—"

Blythe broke in. "In some cases time is an enemy. Every passing day means that my child is one day older. It's one more day of not knowing if my son or daughter is a happy, well-adjusted person. Was he or she told of the adoption? If so, is he or she despising the parents that gave him or her away? Think what that would do to you, Brent. Think what it could be doing to our child."

Though her eyes were teary again, Blythe lifted her chin. "I'm going to find my child, if I have to hire a detective or an attorney or anyone else who might know how to go about it. I should have done it a long time ago. I'm so empty, Brent, and I know in my soul that I'm going to stay empty until I know where my child is living, and whether he or she is reasonably happy. Does he or she have a career, a spouse? Maybe I have grandchildren by now."

She got up, went to the counter and pulled some tissues from a box. She wiped her eyes and blew her nose. "I can't help being passionate about this."

"You have a right," Brent said quietly. He'd pressured her unmercifully, and maybe it was time he let up. After all, this wasn't just her problem anymore, it was his, too. "You keep talking about *your* child, only using the pronoun *our* once in a while. But he's mine, too, Blythe, and I'd like you to know that I'm with you, whatever you do to find him."

"Or her. God, if only I knew *that* much!" Her voice turned caustic. "Mother must have known, because she was there when I gave birth."

Brent looked shell-shocked. This was something he could not have imagined. "Your mother was there and didn't tell you the sex of the baby? I have never heard of anything so cruel. How could *any* woman do something like that to her own daughter?"

"If you only knew how often I've gone over it in my mind," Blythe said wearily. "The only answer I have is that she believed she was doing the best she could for me. I don't want you thinking she was a monster, because she wasn't. She loved my father and she loved us, her daughters. She was just…different. She was so concerned with propriety and what other people might think of the Bennings, as though we were…I don't know…royalty or something. Other kids could play in the mud and get dirty, but not us. Not me or Sierra, anyway. I left home when Sierra was ten, and I know Mother was the same with Sierra as she'd been during my childhood. I don't know how she was with Tamara, because I wasn't around then."

"Talk about a dysfunctional family," Brent muttered. "My family was far from perfect, but it was due to circumstances beyond anyone's control. My dad…" He stopped, because Blythe probably remembered him talking about his precollege background. Besides, they weren't discussing his family now, they were discussing hers, and he wanted to stay on track.

"I guess we were a dysfunctional family, but that wasn't a common term in my day." Noticing Brent's empty coffee cup, Blythe went for the pot and refilled it. The hour was getting late, but she still didn't want to be alone. In fact, if Brent wanted to talk all night she would be grateful. Not wanting to be alone was a new twist in her personality. She'd spent most of her adult life alone and it had never bothered her to this degree. After topping off her own cup, she sat down again.

"Blythe, have you ever talked to a professional?" Brent asked.

A wariness entered her eyes. "A professional what? A therapist?"

"Some kind of counselor."

"No, I never did. I thought of it once or twice, but I couldn't talk about this with anyone, not even a professional."

"You're talking about it with me," he said softly.

"Yes, but you're my baby's father."

"That's not the reason you told me, though, is it? You thought if I knew what a horrible person you were I would stay away from you."

Her face took on a pink color. "I really don't want to talk about that," she said unsteadily. "Except to say that I have nothing to give anyone. I told you I'm empty, and it's the God's truth."

"You made love with me." He knew he was pressuring her again, but why in hell shouldn't he? She *had* made love with him, and for a few minutes that day in the den his head had been filled with beautiful thoughts and dreams. She sure as hell could have picked a better time to unload on him. Oh, he knew why she'd chosen that particular moment to tell him the truth of their past, but it had been a brutal awakening for him, and it still hurt so much he suspected he would never be the same man he'd been before that day.

Though still flushed and obviously embarrassed, she put up a brave front. "Which only proves I'm still a human being."

"It proves a hell of a lot more than that," he said grimly. "How many men have you slept with since your husband died?"

Her facade of courage collapsed as she gasped. "None!"

"Except for me. Maybe you don't want to face it, or even think about it, but you weren't empty that day." The stunned look on her face told him he really had gone too far this time. He got up from the table. "I'm sorry. Guess there are some things we *can't* talk about. I'd better be going. Don't get up. I can let myself out. Good night.''

He was nearly at the front door before Blythe's mind cleared enough for her to realize he was leaving. ''No, wait!'' she cried, jumping up to run after him.

Brent stopped and turned. ''What is it?''

''I...I don't want you to go.'' Try as she might, she could not shed her dread of being alone tonight. Tomorrow she'd be fine again, she told herself, but tonight she needed a friend. ''Stay, please,'' she whispered.

''Why, Blythe?'' He sounded cold and knew it, but if she ever decided that she wanted more than an impersonal friendship with him, she was going to have to say it. He couldn't predict how he would react to hearing such a thing from her, but it definitely was going to have to come from her. In his mind he'd been burned enough. He watched the play of emotions on her face and realized that she was having a hard time saying anything. Well, so be it, he thought, resigned with the status quo.

''Because...because...''

She couldn't say any more than she already had. She'd asked him to stay and his only response had been a rather curt ''Why, Blythe?''

''Forget it,'' she said with a forced smile, weak though it was. ''I know you have to leave.''

''I don't *have* to do anything. Do you want to talk some more?''

''No, I guess not.'' She moved around him and opened the door. ''I'm glad you came by.'' She frowned then. ''You said you'd been trying to call all afternoon. Was there something...?''

Yes, I don't want to buy the house! He couldn't say it. Not tonight.

''It wasn't important. Good night,'' he said brusquely. This time he stepped around her, and for a second her nearness and scent shot through his system as swiftly as a lightning bolt. Gritting his teeth, because he had honestly thought that sort of thing was over for them, he walked through the open door and left.

"Good night," she called after him, and when his car was far down the street, she slowly shut and locked the door.

She had a lot of somber thoughts to take to bed with her, but the one that made her weep into her pillow was that she had indeed lost Brent for a second time. The only reason he was speaking to her at all was to gather as much information as he could that might help him find his child.

If that's true, why did he accept your invitation to have dinner at the house on Saturday night with Sierra and Clint? Actually, he all but asked for an invitation!

How odd, she thought, turning over in bed and wiping her eyes. How very odd. Why would he want to meet Sierra and Clint if he cared nothing about her?

Brent's visit flashed through her troubled mind. Why had he again taken the position that the past wasn't her fault? Did he truly believe that?

She heaved a long, befuddled sigh. The distance between them now was too obvious to pretend it didn't exist, and still he had come by to check on her because he'd tried to call and gotten a busy signal since two this afternoon. Why had he tried to phone her in the first place? And considering their present detached relationship, wasn't his worrying about her at all another oddity to ponder?

Recalling him saying that he didn't understand her, she whispered brokenly, "I don't understand you either, Brent. I really don't."

Chapter Twelve

Blythe awoke the next morning thinking about her and Brent's conversation last night much differently than she had before falling asleep. It really had been a healthy give and take, she decided, even though her emotions had gone up and down while it was going on. But it had cleared the air some; there was nothing about that awful time that Brent didn't know now, no omitted details, no remaining secrets. It made *her* feel better, she realized, and hoped it had done Brent some good, as well.

Should she let herself think of Brent as a friend now? They did, after all, have a common goal, and it only made sense for them to be on friendly terms while they searched for their child. She wouldn't let herself visualize anything between them beyond friendship, although she still wondered why he wanted to meet Sierra and Clint. She wished she could read his mind, because she suspected that there were things going on with Brent that he might never be able to express verbally.

With a resigned sigh—she might never again know what Brent was thinking—she got up and started her day.

After breakfast she tidied the kitchen and realized that loneliness was again sneaking up on her. Pouring herself another cup of coffee, she sat at the table and pondered what was happening to her. She had lived alone for most of her life; why was this insidious loneliness attacking her now? She'd felt lonely before, of course, but not to this extent. It hit her then: she didn't *want* to live alone anymore. Brent being here and talking to her, even about troubling topics, had been a comfort last night. She needed someone important in her life, she thought sadly, a man to talk to, a man who would listen when she talked, a man that she loved and who loved her.

But she would be a fool to ever think that man might be Brent. Sighing heavily, she turned her thoughts to private detectives, and how a person went about finding one. Word of mouth was best, but she didn't know a single person who had ever hired a private detective. Should she just look in the phone book?

She was suddenly struck by the enormity of what she was determined to do. Trying to find her child was going to be like looking for a needle in a haystack, even worse than that because she didn't know where the haystack might be. It *had* been in Breighton, Utah, but that particular haystack didn't exist anymore.

Covering her face with her hands, she moaned. It was never going to happen, was it? Why was she kidding herself? Why was she letting Brent kid *himself?* Deep down she believed that he was as determined to locate their child as she was, and he had to be as miserably frazzled about it as she felt.

Why, *why*, had she told him? Her moods changed daily, she knew, even hourly. What appeared sensible yesterday seemed inane and hopeless today. What in heaven's name should she expect from tomorrow, or next week?

Brent phoned around four. "How are you?"

Just hearing his voice caused an ache in the vicinity of Blythe's heart. She could tell herself that friendship was all she dared to expect from Brent from now to kingdom come, but she would never forget their lovemaking, and what might have been if she had kept her mouth shut. "I'm all right. How are you?"

"I'm fine. What are you doing?" All day Brent had been bolstering his courage to tell her that he no longer wanted to buy her house, and he had dialed her number telling himself that it should not be this hard to do. But it *was* hard, probably because he didn't want to cause her any further unhappiness. He had a whole new point of view on the past because of some disturbing memories last night after he'd gone to bed. Most of the time when they had made love years ago he had been conscientious about protection, but there'd been several occasions—and he had recalled them quite clearly last night—when he'd been so excited, so anxious to hold her that he had skipped it. He'd known she hadn't been using the Pill, and her pregnancy was entirely his fault. No, she had not handled it responsibly, but he hadn't done so well in the responsibility department, either.

"Looking for a key." Blythe's spirits rose, simply because he seemed to be interested in what she was doing. The fact that he'd phoned yesterday, too, and then come over when he couldn't reach her, was also uplifting.

"A key to what?"

"One of the file cabinets in the basement room is a fireproof model. It's locked, and I haven't been able to find the key for it."

"A fireproof model? Guess I didn't notice it. Blythe, how about forgetting that key for tonight and having dinner with me?" They could talk again, and maybe he'd finally be able to tell her how he felt about the house.

"Uh—" She was thrilled that he wanted to see her, but he'd taken her by surprise. It wasn't that she didn't want to spend time with him, or eat with him—quite the opposite— but she really was in no mood to get dressed up.

"Brent," she finally said. "Unless you're set on having something special for dinner, why don't you just come over here and eat soup and sandwiches with me?"

"Meaning you don't want to go out."

"I really don't. It's nice of you to ask, but..."

"Blythe, you should get out of that house more than you do. How are you feeling?"

"What you're really asking is am I in the same down-in-the-mouth mood that you've seen me in so often. I'm not, Brent."

"I'm glad to hear that," he said quietly. "Blythe, I didn't call just to ask you out to dinner. I drove to Spokane today and talked to a private detective. I thought we might talk about it over dinner." *Among other things, such as your house. And maybe you should hear what I've remembered about the past. You wouldn't have gotten pregnant if I hadn't been so rash!*

Blythe's heart skipped a beat. "You saw a private detective? What did he say? Does he think he can help us?"

"He thinks he can, yes. What he brought up right away was the baby's birth certificate. He said that if the people running the home had adhered to the law, the birth certificate would have been filed with the state. We should have thought of that when we were in Utah."

"Oh, my goodness, maybe he *can* help us! Why didn't we think of the birth certificate?" Blythe's hopes were running high again.

"Anyway, he wants to talk to you. He has questions, date and time of birth, for example, and whether the baby was born at the home or in a hospital."

"It was born in the home. It had its own maternity ward."

"And doctors and nurses?"

"One doctor and several nurses."

"Well, those are the kind of questions he needs answers to. If you can remember the names of anyone, the doctor, especially, who was at the home when you were, write them down. I told the detective that I would bring you to his office on Monday. Is that all right with you?"

"Yes, Brent, yes! Oh, this is incredible. Now I can hardly wait for Monday. I wondered today about finding a reliable private detective, but you didn't just wonder about it, you went out and did it! I am so grateful, Brent, thank you."

"Well, *I* wondered about asking you to go with me, but it didn't seem right to raise your hopes before I talked to the man. I did that by taking you to Utah with me, and it turned out badly. I didn't want that to happen again.''

''Brent, I'm much stronger than I appear to be.''

''No, Blythe, you're not. To be honest, I think you're running out of strength.''

Although thrilled with his concern, Blythe realized that he was right. She was winding down, just like an old clock. In her mind's eye she could see that clock exploding into a hundred pieces, and she feared it could happen to her. She'd carried the burden of guilt for too many years; it was beginning to catch up with her.

Beginning to? No, the beginning started a long time ago. I am much closer to the end than the beginning.

But that wasn't a hundred percent right, either. Blythe knew that her physical strength could be giving out because of stress and internal pressures, but her emotional resolve seemed to have gotten much stronger. As far as beginnings and endings went, there was one part of her that was pure steel and indestructible—her love for the child she had never held in her arms. And there would be no end of that for as long as she drew breath.

She didn't debate Brent's observation. Her thoughts were too complicated to explain over the phone.

''So,'' she said, putting a lilt in her voice, ''are you coming for supper?''

''No, I don't think so. I have a lot of work to do, and maybe I'd better get to it. I'll be having dinner at your house tomorrow night, and I don't want to wear out my welcome.''

''You couldn't,'' she said softly, and realized how true that simple statement was. She was suddenly filled with love for Brent Morrison, without doubts, without questions, without reservations, and it was a startling sensation that brought tears to her eyes. She wanted to savor it, to think about it, and she murmured huskily, ''But we'll do it your way. See you tomorrow. Come around five.''

After hanging up, she sat there and thought about love and how badly she had botched her chances of ever attaining it. She remembered how much she had loved Brent in college, and that she had convinced herself that she had loved her husband when it really hadn't been true, not if she compared what she'd felt for Richard to her feelings for Brent.

She put her head down on her arms, but she didn't cry. Her heart wept, her soul wept, but her eyes remained dry. Apparently she had finally accepted her fate.

Blythe was up early the following morning, almost breathless with excitement over Sierra and Clint's impending visit. She toured the house, making sure that everything was spotlessly clean, even checking Sierra's bedroom again, although she had done that the day before yesterday when she put fresh linen on the bed, and, apparently, knocked the phone off the hook in the process.

Satisfied with the condition of the house, she went outside and mowed the lawn. At eleven she went in again, took a shower and fixed her hair and makeup. After choosing a dress to wear for dinner that evening, she put on a pair of slacks and a pretty blouse. Finally there was nothing more to do except wait, and she watched the clock and looked out the front windows at least a dozen times in the next hour.

When at last she saw a dark blue car with a Montana plate pull into the driveway, she flew out the door. Sierra jumped out and ran to her. It was an emotional few moments for the two sisters while they hugged each other and laughed and cried at the same time.

Clint stood by and smiled, until Sierra wiped her eyes and said, "Blythe, this is my husband, Clint Barrow. Clint, this is Blythe."

Blythe offered her hand, but Clint ignored it and hugged her instead. "We're family. I think a hug is in order here."

Laughing for the pure joy of it, the three of them went inside. "Oh, Blythe, the house looks wonderful," Sierra exclaimed in the family room. She took her husband's hand. "Come on, darling, I have to show you the rest of it."

Blythe went to the kitchen and put on a pot of coffee to brew. It was noon, time for lunch, and she set the table for three and began laying out cold roast beef, ham, cheese, lettuce, tomatoes and anything else that would make a good sandwich.

Sierra and Clint walked in. "Oh, Blythe," Sierra said, looking at the laden table. "You shouldn't have gone to so much trouble."

"It was no trouble at all. Clint, I made fresh coffee, but maybe you'd prefer something else to drink. There's soda and iced tea in the refrigerator."

"I'll have coffee, Blythe, thanks."

Sierra went to the refrigerator and took out the iced tea pitcher. "Blythe, iced tea for you, too, or a soda?"

"I'm going to have coffee, Sierra. I think everything's ready. Let's sit down."

They made huge sandwiches, and Sierra and Blythe talked nonstop, about the drive from Montana, about the changes in Coeur d'Alene, about Tamara's triplets and a dozen other topics. Blythe liked Sierra's husband very much. Clint Barrow was a laid-back peach of a guy, unusually good-looking and obviously very much in love with his wife. There was a glow about Sierra that Blythe had never seen before. She, too, was in love, and it showed in her beautiful dark eyes every time she looked at her husband.

Blythe was so happy for her sister that her own problems seemed far away. They would return, she knew, but for the present she was thoroughly enjoying the simple pleasures of eating and talking with Sierra and Clint.

"I understand you have a son," Blythe said to Clint.

"Tommy," Clint replied. "He's at home right now getting ready to leave for his first year of college."

"Which is why we have to get back to the ranch tomorrow," Sierra added. "We have to be there to say goodbye."

"Of course you do," Blythe murmured. It was wonderful that Sierra had a stepson, and incredible that Tamara had triplets. Blythe didn't envy her sisters, but their good fortune was so opposite to her own life that she again began thinking of the horrible mistake she'd made twenty-odd years ago.

But she couldn't dwell on that now. Quickly she forced a

smile. "After lunch, how about the three of us hiking down to the lake?"

"Great!" Sierra exclaimed. "I can't even remember the last time I walked the lakeshore." To Clint she said, "It's very beautiful along the water, darling. I'm sure you'll like it."

Clint smiled and lovingly touched his wife's arm. "We'll do whatever you want."

Blythe and Sierra sat on the sandy beach while Clint explored farther. "He's giving us some time alone," Sierra said with a warm and loving expression. "He's so wonderful, Blythe. I've never met another man to compare."

"I'm very happy for you."

Sierra looked at her older sister and smiled. "I know you are." Her smile softened. "It's your turn, you know. You give so much of yourself, and it's time you got something in return. Blythe, do you ever think of how distant Tamara, you and I were with each other when Mother died?"

"We didn't know each other, Sierra."

"I know, but it seems almost criminal that we didn't. And we had those awful secrets. Or rather, Tamara and I did. She was pregnant and I was going through a divorce, and neither of us could talk about it. You were the only one of us who didn't harbor a secret." Sierra shook her head and sighed. "So much wasted time."

In the next instant, before Blythe could even make a comment on "secrets," although her heart had nearly stopped beating over the word, Sierra said, "You mentioned that the buyer of the house might back out of the deal. Has anything changed in that regard?"

"I—I'm not sure. Sierra, he's going to have dinner with us this evening."

Sierra blinked in surprise. "The buyer is? Have you become friends with him and his family?"

"He doesn't have a family," Blythe said quietly.

Sierra's face lit up. "Blythe, are you and he *more* than friends?"

"We—we knew each other in college," Blythe stammered.

"You're kidding! Is he from Coeur d'Alene?"

"No. His name is Brent Morrison, and when he first looked at the house he didn't know who owned it. It was all—quite a surprise. For both of us."

"Well, I would imagine so! You're saying that you hadn't seen each other in twenty years and you met again because he came to see the house? Oh, Blythe, that is so romantic. And did you like each other in college, and when you met again did all of your old feelings come rushing back?"

Blythe couldn't help smiling over Sierra's exuberant imagination. "You'd like that scenario, wouldn't you, Mrs. Romantic?" she said teasingly.

"I would indeed!"

Blythe got up and brushed the sand from her slacks. "Come on. If we're going to have any dinner at all tonight, I've got to do some cooking."

Sierra rose and called, "Clint! Honey, we're going back to the house now. Do you want to come with us or would you like to stay here at the beach for a while longer?"

"I'll come with you," Clint called back.

While they were waiting for Clint to join them, Sierra looked at her sister. "You're not getting off the hook this easily, Blythe Benning. I want to hear all about Brent Morrison, and I'm warning you now that I will not rest until I do."

"Sierra, you've already heard it all. There's nothing more to tell."

"Yeah, right," Sierra drawled. "I'll believe that when hell freezes over. I knew there was something different about you. You're in love, aren't you? It's in your eyes, Blythe. Oh, I couldn't be more thrilled. It's about time you married again."

Blythe sighed. "Don't put the cart before the horse, Sierra. Inviting a man to dinner does not a romance make."

Sierra smiled a bit smugly. "I have the feeling that the romance was there long before the dinner invitation. Keep in mind that this discussion is far from over, Blythe. I intend to hear it all." She smiled as Clint walked up, and she took his arm. "We have to go back to the house and make dinner, darling. And guess what? We're having a guest, the man who is going to buy the house. Isn't that marvelous?''

Clint looked a bit perplexed, but he smiled at his wife. "If you say it's marvelous, then it is.''

Blythe smiled, albeit weakly. She'd had to let Sierra know who Brent was, but she had also opened a can of worms by doing so.

The evening might not go as smoothly as she'd been hoping, she realized uneasily as they began the walk back to the house. She had whetted her sister's curiosity, and why wouldn't Sierra be curious about such an unusual event as Blythe and Brent running into each other again after so many years?

Darn it, she thought, she should *not* have invited Brent to have dinner with her family! Now she was going to have to watch every word, be on her guard every minute.

And she was so very, very tired of guarding her past. Weary of pretending that *she* hadn't had the biggest secret of all when she and her sisters had come together last January for their mother's funeral. How much longer could she bear to live with lies?

"Blythe, are you all right?" Sierra was looking at her with questioning eyes. "We're practically running. Are we that short of time?''

Blythe slowed her steps. "I'm sorry. We're not short of time at all. I don't know why I was walking so fast." Moving in between Sierra and Clint, she took their arms. "I'm so glad you're both here.''

"And we're glad to be here," Clint said. "We sure would like you to come to the ranch and visit us sometime, Blythe.''

"Oh, we would," Sierra said eagerly. "Will you do it?''

"Yes, of course I will. Right this minute I can't promise when that will be, but I would love to see the ranch.''

"And us, too," Sierra said with a laugh.

"Well, I'm not so sure about the two of you," Blythe said teasingly, and they all laughed. It was a moment of total alliance, and Blythe began feeling better about the evening ahead.

There really was no reason why it shouldn't turn out well. All four of them were, after all, intelligent, reasonable adults.

Chapter Thirteen

"**D**inner was superb, Blythe," Sierra said with a contented sigh. "The whole evening was." Brent had left, Clint had gone to bed and the two sisters, wearing nightclothes and bathrobes, were curled up on chairs in the family room.

"It went well," Blythe agreed.

"Brent and Clint got along great, didn't they?"

"They seemed to. But I have a feeling that Clint gets along with most people."

"Oh, he does," Sierra exclaimed proudly. "Everyone likes Clint."

"Especially you." Blythe was smiling.

Sierra laughed. "I like him, I respect him, I love him." Her laughter faded. "I'm so very, very lucky, Blythe," she said softly. In the next instant a devilish light twinkled in her dark eyes. "Why didn't you tell me how good-looking Brent is?"

Blythe had known a discussion of Brent was inevitable when Sierra suggested they stay up and talk for a while. There'd been no chance of a private conversation while the two men were present, and throughout the evening Blythe had been aware of Sierra's scrutiny of Brent. Thus, Blythe had prepared herself for exactly that sort of remark from her sister.

"A lot of men are good-looking, Sierra," she said calmly.

"But they're not invited to dinner, are they?"

"Well, no."

"You're having trouble admitting your feelings for Brent, aren't you? How come? It's obvious that he thinks a lot of you."

Blythe was taken aback. "Did you get that impression this evening?"

"Don't *you* have that impression?" Sierra looked a bit puzzled.

"Frankly…no. But there are circumstances…" Her voice trailed away.

"Blythe, I would swear Brent is in love with you. You really don't sense it?"

"There's so much more to it than you could possibly know, Sierra," Blythe murmured. One of the highlights of the evening had been Brent's arrival, when she'd opened the front door for him and he had smiled and squeezed her hand. For one wonderful moment everything had seemed perfect, which wasn't even remotely feasible. Because she had finally admitted and faced *her* feelings for Brent, she had obviously read far too much in *his* smile and warm handclasp. At least she was clearheaded enough to know that.

"You're referring to the relationship the two of you had in college, aren't you?" Sierra grinned impishly. "Come on, tell me about it. Were you and Brent in love before?"

Blythe was becoming uncomfortable with the conversation. She'd thought she could control its direction, but Sierra was too bright and intelligent not to have figured a few things out.

"You are much too perceptive, little sister," Blythe said teasingly, in an attempt to keep things light.

"Blythe, we *are* sisters. You can tell me anything, and since I'm dying to know what went on between you and Brent in college, it would be terribly unkind of you to send me to bed to lie awake and wonder about it all night."

"You're not only perceptive, you have a flair for the dramatic," Blythe said dryly.

Sierra laughed. "You're absolutely right. Isn't it wonderful that we're finally beginning to understand each other? I wish Tamara were here, too. The three of us have got to get together, Blythe. Clint and I have been talking about a trip to Texas, and it would be so great if you could go at the same time."

"Yes, it would. Maybe we can work it out."

"Let's try. Now, getting back to Brent, I see it like this. The two of you were madly in love in college, and then something happened to pull you apart. A spat? A misunderstanding? It was probably something silly, and both of you have regretted it ever since. It really is incredibly romantic that you met again after so many years."

Blythe heard herself saying quietly, "It wasn't something silly, Sierra." That was when an overwhelming urge to tell her sister everything struck Blythe. Sierra was mostly teasing with her questions and romantic ideas, but Blythe couldn't laugh about something that she had suffered over for twenty-four years. And why shouldn't Sierra know the truth? At this point, why shouldn't *everybody* know the truth?

Her mother's voice was suddenly in her head: *"You must never speak of this to anyone, Blythe. People would laugh behind your back. You would not be able to cope with the shame and humiliation of bearing an illegitimate child."*

Blythe realized that she felt no shame at all. At one time, yes, but shame had gradually been overcome by much more powerful emotions—grief, remorse, guilt. She looked at her beautiful sister and knew in her soul that Sierra would understand.

Blythe dampened her dry lips with the tip of her tongue. "There's something I'd like to tell you, but first I'm going to get myself a glass of wine. Would you join me?"

The gravity in Blythe's voice instantly sobered Sierra's expression. "Yes, I'll have some wine," she responded, speaking as gravely as Blythe had.

When Blythe came back from the kitchen with two glasses

of wine, she saw that Sierra no longer looked lighthearted and teasing. Blythe gave one glass to Sierra and returned to her chair with the other.

"I've worried you," Blythe said. "If you'd rather not hear this, my feelings will not be hurt, Sierra."

"If it concerns you, it concerns me," Sierra said, speaking in an almost hushed tone of voice. "It's something serious, isn't it? Blythe, are you ill?"

"No, it's nothing like that." She recalled Brent asking that very question when he'd realized that *something* was wrong with her. Apparently illness was everyone's first thought when they knew a problem existed but didn't know what it was.

Sierra breathed a relieved sigh. "Thank God." She took a swallow of her wine.

So did Blythe before she spoke again. "You asked if Brent and I were in love in college. We were, Sierra. He was a wonderful young man, handsome, intelligent and fun to be with. He made me laugh, he brought me to life and…I loved him." Blythe stopped to think a moment. She had loved him so very much, and it felt now, talking about it like this, which she had never done with anyone, that she had stepped back in time.

But that was silly. She wasn't nineteen and dreamily, starry-eyed in love, she was forty-three and realistic. Abruptly bringing herself out of her sentimental reverie, she continued. "He worked very hard, holding down two jobs to pay for his education. Sometimes it was difficult for us to juggle our schedules so we could be together, but even that was fun. It lasted for…almost three months."

"Why only three months?"

Blythe hesitated. Once said, it could never be taken back. But it was bursting within her; she could not keep it contained.

She looked down at the glass in her hand. "I…got pregnant." Her eyes rose to see what damage she had inflicted upon her sister, but she saw only empathy on Sierra's lovely face. Courage rebounded within her. She wanted Sierra to know it all, wanted Tamara to know it all. If they had been closer, her sisters would have heard her secret long before this.

"What happened?" Sierra asked softly.

Blythe spoke as evenly as she could manage, trying very hard to keep emotion out of this. "At first I was thrilled, but in a few days I began thinking more sensibly. Or so I thought. I knew I could go to Brent and that he would marry me, but he was barely making ends meet. How would he support a wife and child? You see, I *believed* I was thinking sensibly, but I wasn't. After it was all over I came up with so many good ideas. I could have gotten a job and still attended classes. I could have quit college altogether and worked full time. There were married couples with babies on campus. I certainly could have managed as well as they did. There were choices, you see, and I chose the wrong one."

"Oh, Blythe, you had an abortion," Sierra said sadly, with tears running down her cheeks.

"No! Sierra, I could never have done that, although what I did do was probably as bad. Instead of going to Brent, I came home. I was so naively certain that Mother and Dad would come up with a simple solution. I think that deep down I was counting on them offering financial support, but that's not what happened. Mother was…appalled. That's the only word for it. I had shamed the Benning name, and she asked me if I even knew who the baby's father was, as though I'd been sleeping with every man on campus."

"Oh, Blythe, how could she have said something like that?"

"I don't know, Sierra. I'll never know. But neither will I ever know why I permitted her to take over. It was as though I'd lost all sense of myself. I was nineteen years old, and Mother made me feel like I was twelve again." Blythe continued the story to the end. "And so I signed the adoption papers and gave up all rights to Brent's and my child. So you see, Sierra, last January when you, Tamara and I were here in this house, hardly talking because we barely knew each other, and you and Tamara were guarding secrets, I had the biggest secret of all."

"Yes, you did," Sierra said with a sob. "Blythe, you always seemed so serene, so in control of your life. My own life had so many ups and downs, and I didn't always handle them well. I admired your tranquillity, but it was a lie, wasn't it—a facade? You weren't calm and collected, you were numb. How could I have been so dense?''

"We hardly saw each other, certainly not often enough for you to see beneath my facade, as you put it. And you're right, of course, I have lived with a facade, a mask of pretense and camouflage.''

"How you must have suffered,'' Sierra said sadly.

"Not one single day has gone by since it happened that I haven't thought of my child.''

"And Brent still doesn't know? Is that why you won't let yourself love him again?''

I do love him, but he will never love me. Blythe stared down into the wine in her glass. "Brent knows. I told him one day because…because he started talking about falling in love, and I couldn't let that happen. I—I didn't deserve his love.''

"Oh, Blythe,'' Sierra said sorrowfully.

"Please don't feel bad. I didn't tell you about this to make you feel bad. Besides, Sierra, there's a slim chance my story might have a happy ending. Brent is determined to find our child, and we've been working on it. As for a personal relationship…well, I really doubt that it's possible. He took the whole thing pretty hard and it changed things between us.''

"I suppose it did,'' Sierra said with a sigh. "Still, it seemed tonight that he…'' She stopped to frown. "I would have sworn that I sensed something very real between you.''

"I think what you sensed is our common resolve to find our child. It really is the only thing on which we're single-minded.'' Blythe couldn't erase the wistful note from her voice. Twice she'd had Brent's undivided attention, and twice she had destroyed it. She doubted that there would ever be a third time.

"Possibly,'' Sierra concurred softly. They fell into their own thoughts until Sierra asked, "And your child is how old now?''

Putting aside all thoughts of Brent, Blythe sat up straighter. "Twenty-three.''

"The same age as Tamara."

"Yes, Mother was pregnant with Tamara the same time that I was…pregnant."

"That was the time she left Dad and went to Colorado. I was ten, or almost ten, when she went, and I couldn't figure out what was going on."

"I don't think any of us will ever figure that one out, Sierra. Mother was an expert at keeping secrets, and she never talked about it with anyone, that I know of."

"She didn't with me, I know," Sierra murmured while wiping her eyes. "Blythe, is there anything I can do to help? It kills me to think of how selfishly Tamara and I left you here in January to take care of Mother's estate. Why didn't you tell both of us to go to hell?"

"You are not to blame yourself for that. Tamara, either. I volunteered for the job—you must remember my doing that."

"Yes, I do remember," Sierra said with a reflective expression. "The question now is *why* did you volunteer? Surely you don't have good memories of this house."

Blythe smiled. "The house never caused me any unhappiness, Sierra."

"Of course it didn't. But don't you see Mother and Dad in every room?"

"No, not at all. I see Mother and Dad in my head, and that's where the bad memories live, not here in this house. Besides," she added, "not all my memories of Mother and Dad are bad, Sierra. I loved them both, very much."

"So did I, Blythe, but I wonder if I would still feel that way if they had done to me what they did to you." Tears filled Sierra's eyes again. "All those years of not knowing where your child was, *how* he was. And the guilt nearly killed you, didn't it? You feel guilty right now—I can see it in your eyes."

"Only the guilty have something to feel guilty about, Sierra," Blythe said gently. "I wasn't too young to tell Mother to mind her own business, and walk out of this house. I *let* her manipulate me. My God, do you think I would let anyone do something like that to me today? Of course I wouldn't. So, yes, I do feel guilt, and remorse and bone-deep sorrow, but it's only what I deserve.''

"You have got to stop thinking like that! You deserve to be happy as much as anyone else does.'' Sierra paused a moment. "Have you told Tamara?''

"I've told Brent and now you, and the next time I see Tamara I'm going to tell her, as well. And if you wish to tell Clint, feel free to do so. I don't want any more secrets in my life, Sierra. I don't know exactly how I reached this point, but I really don't care who knows about my past now. I wish I had felt that way all along,'' she added thoughtfully, realizing that she had caused a great deal of her own misery by not speaking of it.

"I've changed,'' she said slowly, "and maybe Brent has something to do with that. It was such a shock to see him again.''

"I can well imagine,'' Sierra murmured.

They talked until midnight, sometimes emotionally, sometimes in quiet, subdued tones. Sierra detailed her frightening experience with amnesia, but ended her narration on a cheerful note. "If it hadn't happened I wouldn't have met Clint, so some stories do have happy endings, Blythe. I have a feeling things are going to turn out well for you and Brent.''

"I suppose nothing is impossible,'' Blythe softly replied. "But I really have no hopes in that direction. If we actually succeed in finding our child…'' A huge yawn interrupted her. "I'm exhausted. So are you. We should go to bed.''

Sierra yawned, too. "Yes, we should. Clint wants to get a fairly early start in the morning so that we're home in time to say goodbye to Tommy.''

They got up from their chairs and Blythe began switching off lights. At the foot of the stairs they paused to hug each other.

"Remember, Blythe, if there's ever anything I can do to help you and Brent, all you have to do is call.''

"Thank you. Sierra, I'm so glad you came.''

"I am, too. Now, don't forget our plan to get together with Tamara.''

"I won't forget. You know, during one of our telephone conversations she said something about everyone going there for Christmas. That would be special, don't you agree?"

"It would be very special, Blythe. I'll talk to Clint about it."

They were about to ascend the stairs when Blythe remembered something. "Oh, I almost forgot! Sierra, can you stay awake for another few minutes?"

"Of course I can. What is it?"

"Come to the den." Blythe switched on the den's ceiling light and also the lamps in the room, as she wanted lots of light. After unrolling Sierra's painting, she propped it up on the small sofa.

"Oh, for goodness' sakes," Sierra exclaimed, and bent over to examine her own work.

"Do you see the third child in the flowers?" Blythe asked.

"Yes."

"Is it Tamara?"

Sierra straightened up. "It must be. The other two girls are obviously you and me. Blythe, I slathered so many canvases with paint through the years that one blurs into another in my mind. I know this is my work, but I honestly do not recall doing it."

"Then there's nothing symbolic about the hidden child. I— I actually wondered if perhaps you had known of my child, and…that maybe…" She saw the frown that had suddenly creased her sister's forehead, and her heart skipped a beat. "What are you thinking?"

"I'm remembering something. When Mother came home from Colorado with a baby, I became very excited. Tamara was so tiny and beautiful, and I kept wanting to touch her. I was still interested in dolls, and here, in my own home, was a real live baby doll. I was completely entranced. Sometimes Mother would let me hold Tamara, but more often than not she would shoo me away, and tell me to go outside and play.

"The day I'm thinking of, she was feeding Tamara a bottle in the kitchen and I was watching. Dad came in and Mother told me to go outdoors and get some sunshine. 'Stop hovering,

Sierra,' she said. 'You're forever hovering.' I remember that my feelings were hurt and I went out the back door and sat on the patio. The kitchen window was open because it was such a warm day, and I could hear Mother and Dad talking. I wasn't deliberately listening, but it was a quiet day and their voices carried through the open window. I didn't hear complete sentences, but I kept hearing your name and the word *baby*.

"Well, for some reason I started thinking they were saying that Tamara was your baby, so I went back inside and blurted, 'Isn't Tamara our baby? Is Blythe going to come and take her away?' or words to that effect. The shocked looks on their faces told me that I had made a grave error. Mother handed Tamara and the bottle to Dad, took me by the arm and led me upstairs to my room. She sat me on my bed and gave me a stern lecture about listening to other people's conversations, and that I was never, ever to repeat the awful questions I had asked in the kitchen."

Blythe's own frown got deeper as Sierra talked. "I've always wondered if they had ever discussed my baby. They never did with me, but what you overheard sounds like they talked about it between themselves. At least they didn't just forget that I'd had a child." She thought a moment. "That conversation confused you, though, didn't it?"

"I believe it did. Bear in mind that I was only ten years old at the time, and it wasn't long before the incident was forgotten. Apparently I never *completely* forgot it, however, because I recall it now quite vividly." Sierra studied her painting again. "Makes me wonder about that shadowy child in the flowers," she murmured.

"In what way?"

"Well, it's hard to explain. When I start a painting I have certain ideas about how I'd like it to turn out. But many, many times the finished product is vastly different than what I had intended. This will probably sound silly to you, but it's almost as if sometimes the brush in my hand has a mind of its own. This painting, for instance. It isn't at all logical. I depicted you as about twelve and myself as a toddler. Why did I put Tamara in the picture at all? She wasn't even born yet.''

''Maybe it was an afterthought. She is, after all, barely discernible in the flowers.''

''That's possible,'' Sierra murmured. ''I wish I could remember when I did this painting.''

''You did another painting of the three of us. You sent it to Tamara for a wedding present.''

''It was one of my better efforts. I went through a period where I did quite a few paintings of the family. Most of them weren't good and I threw them out.''

''That must have been when you did this one.''

''I...don't think it was. Oh, hell's bells, how would I know? In a brutally honest critique of this painting, Blythe, I'd have to say the best part of it is that shadowy child. I'm speaking of technique now.''

''You must have thought it was good when you did it, Sierra, because you gave it to Mother. What did she say about it? Was Dad still alive then?''

''I...believe he was. Yes, I'm positive of it. I remember them saying that they liked the painting, but you know something? Neither of them ever mentioned the third child. I don't think they ever saw her.''

''Well, I didn't either, until just recently.'' Blythe saw Sierra attempt to stifle a yawn. ''Come on, I'm keeping you up. Let's go to bed.''

''I'm sorry I don't remember more about the painting,'' Sierra said as they left the den. ''That third child bothers you, and you have enough on your mind without that.''

''It isn't your fault that I'm bothered by almost everything, Sierra. I like the painting and I'd like to keep it. Unless you want it, of course. It is your work, after all.''

''Keep it with my blessing.''

Halfway up the stairs, Sierra stopped Blythe with a hand on her arm. She whispered, ''Thank you for telling me what you did. I know it was hard for you to do. I feel very close to you now, and I...I love you, Blythe.''

"I love you, Sierra." They hugged each other for an emotional moment, then continued tiptoeing up the stairs.

In her room, Blythe silently shut the door, slipped out of her robe and slippers and crawled into bed. Once settled in, however, she realized how wide awake she was. Dozens of small details that had made up the evening raced through her mind—Brent's cordiality with Sierra and Clint, how well dinner had turned out and the enjoyable hours all four of them had spent on the patio afterward. Then, when Brent had taken his leave, she had escorted him to the front door. He'd thanked her for a wonderful evening and had told her how much he liked her sister and brother-in-law.

"I think they like you, too," she'd said.

Brent had leaned over and kissed her on the cheek, surprising her. "I hope they did. Family is important. Good night, Blythe. I'll see you on Monday."

That, of course, had been another highlight of the evening, even though Brent's behavior was rather confusing. She knew now that she was in love with him, but she couldn't believe that he'd forgiven her enough to let himself ever be more than a friend. And yet she had picked up some unnerving signals from him tonight. Or was her imagination running wild and he'd meant nothing at all with that little kiss on the cheek and that squeeze of her hand?

Disturbed by questions without answers, she forced her thoughts to go elsewhere. The Monday afternoon appointment with Ray Grant, private detective, was exciting; Blythe was anxiously looking forward to it. But more satisfying to ponder right at this moment was tonight's talk with Sierra. *I feel a hundred pounds lighter!*

It was true. Lying in her bed, Blythe realized that her mind was clearer than it had ever been. She felt unburdened, as though freed from heavy shackles that had weighted her down for years and years. Unloading her secret on Brent hadn't made her feel this way, but then why would it have? She had *hurled* the information at him, and her intentions had not been altruistic.

Talking to Sierra, to her sister, was different than anything

Blythe had previously experienced. How truly wonderful it was to have a sister that she could *talk* to. And she was even more fortunate than most, because she had two sisters. One day soon she would also talk to Tamara about the past.

As far as that painting went, it was lovely and she would keep it forever, but there was really nothing mysterious about it. Talking to Sierra about it had eased her mind on that.

With a rare sense of inner peace, Blythe turned on her side and finally closed her eyes.

Chapter Fourteen

Blythe felt an aching emptiness as Clint and Sierra drove away. It was early morning, barely seven, and she understood their need to get home, but the day loomed long and lonely without them. Blythe stood on the sidewalk until their car was out of sight, then, sighing, she picked up the newspaper lying on the driveway and returned to the house.

In the kitchen she poured herself a cup of coffee and sat at the table with the newspaper. But it held little interest for her today, and she didn't unfold it. Something was nagging at her, she realized after a few minutes, something she couldn't put a finger on. What could it be? She hadn't felt this way yesterday, and last night's dinner party had certainly been successful and enjoyable. Then she and Sierra had talked.

Blythe frowned. Whatever was needling her had something to do with her and Sierra's long discussion. But they had talked of so many things. What had been said that had somehow surfaced in the night to badger her today? Why couldn't she pinpoint what it was?

Well, she couldn't sit around by herself all day and worry

about it. She would get ready and go to church, then she would take a drive somewhere. Anywhere. The destination didn't matter; getting out and away from this big empty house did.

Brent worked on his drawings and waited until two in the afternoon to phone Blythe. He knew Sierra and Clint were leaving today, and he figured that after they had gone Blythe would be feeling down. She might even be glad to hear from him, though, in truth, he had some doubts about that. They weren't the same with each other. She had literally lashed him with the truth of their past to kill his growing affections, and while she hadn't destroyed every vestige of feeling he had for her, he would be hard-pressed to even think the word *love*.

But there were some things they needed to discuss—her house, for one—and he dialed her number and was surprised when she didn't answer. After letting the phone ring eight times, he hung up.

Blythe drove clear around Coeur d'Alene Lake. The weather was changing; fall was imminent. Already the deciduous trees and underbrush were losing the lush green color of summer. The air was different, still warm but with a subtle tang of freshness—the smell of autumn.

A thought suddenly struck her. If she wasn't going back to Connecticut right away she had to let the superintendent of the school she taught at know. She should have phoned him before this. How could she have been so remiss? Well, she would take care of it sometime tomorrow. Surely the appointment with that detective wouldn't take all day. Even with the different time zones between Connecticut and Idaho she should be able to reach Superintendent Harrison.

It was a lovely drive because of the spectacular scenery. Blythe noticed that there were many more homes and cabins around the lake than there used to be. She drove without haste and looked at everything. It kept her mind pretty much occupied, although she couldn't completely get past the unsettling feeling that something had occurred or been said last night that she should have picked up on. She wondered if telling Sierra her story was the problem, but immediately retreated from that conjecture. That couldn't possibly be causing her distress today because she felt so relieved about finally revealing her secret. No, it was something else.

It was a few minutes after four when she returned to the city, feeling rather pleased with herself because she hadn't just sat and worried all day, or puttered over nothing. Whatever was eating at her would eventually come to light, she decided with a slightly uneasy sigh while turning onto Lakeside Avenue. Troublesome things always did.

Approaching the house at a slow speed, she saw Brent's car parked at the curb. Her pulse fluttered. She was glad he was here, and his dropping in like this could mean that he was beginning to forgive her. No, she really didn't believe he would ever be able to do that, but maybe he was reaching the point of accepting what she'd done.

Oh, Lord, dare she hope for so much? With her head high, a smile on her face and her stomach pitching a fit, she used the remote control to raise the garage door, then drove in and parked. While she got out of her car, Brent got out of his. "Hi," he called.

"Hello," she called back. "Were you waiting for me?"

He grinned. "Heck, no. I just decided to park on this street for the hell of it."

Blythe laughed, and the sound of her laughter, so unfamiliar to Brent's ears, spiked his nervous system. He hadn't expected any such onslaught and became a bit wary. A woman's laugh would not physically excite a man unless he was deeply attracted to her, and he didn't want to go around that horn again. He would tell her about his decision not to buy the house and leave. Besides, she didn't seem to be downcast at all, quite the contrary.

She waited for him to enter the garage, then led him into the house through the laundry room, saying the first thing that popped into her mind. "There are so many leftovers from last night that maybe you'd like to stay for dinner and help me eat them."

"Uh...I really can't." Brent searched for a logical explanation as to why he couldn't eat dinner with her and came up blank. He could fabricate a previous engagement, of course, as she'd done the first time he'd asked her out, but lying really went against his grain. He hoped she would merely accept his refusal and let it go at that.

"Oh," she said, thinking that he must already have dinner plans. "Well, if you can't, you can't." She sent him a smile. "Maybe you don't like leftovers, anyway."

"There's nothing wrong with leftovers," he said almost brusquely.

Why was he even here at this hour if he had dinner plans? Her heart sank a little. Why wouldn't he have plans? Probably with a woman. Something tightened into a painful little ball in her stomach. Thus far she had not visualized him with another woman, and she should have. After all, why would an attractive man like Brent go without female companionship?

But the thought of him with another woman hurt. It hurt badly. She forced a smile. "Well, if you're not in a hurry, how about a glass of wine? I'm going to have one."

He surprised her—and himself—by saying, "Thanks, I'd enjoy a glass of wine. A small glass." This would be an appropriate time to talk to her about the house, he thought in defense of his hasty acceptance.

Blythe concentrated very hard on pouring wine into two stemmed glasses. Drawing a nervous breath because she couldn't imagine why he was here when he had dinner plans, she said, "Let's sit in the den." She led the way.

Settled in comfortable chairs, they sipped their wine. Blythe felt on pins and needles waiting for him to explain this unexpected visit. He said nothing, and she became even more nervous.

Finally he asked, "What time did Sierra and Clint leave?"

A nice safe topic, she thought, wondering if he even planned to tell her why he'd dropped in. "Around seven this morning," she replied.

"Then you've been alone all day. I phoned around two."

"You did?" *Why?* She cleared her throat. "I went to church

this morning, then took a drive around the lake. This perfect weather isn't going to hold for much longer. Fall is in the air.''

''I noticed. But maybe we'll have a nice autumn.''

''I hope so. I'm really not ready for gray, rainy days.''

Small talk. When two people didn't know what to say to each other, they talked about the weather. How sad that they had come to this, Blythe thought.

Her gaze fell on the shelf that had held her father's collection of first editions, and she murmured, ''I wish I knew if Mother sold those books.'' She glanced at Brent. ''Sorry. It really doesn't matter what she did with them.'' She deliberately altered her expression with a smile. ''What did *you* do all day?''

''I worked.'' Brent sipped from his glass of wine. ''Then I wondered…well, with your sister going home and all…''

So *that* was why he was here—to see if she'd fallen apart because Sierra and Clint had gone home. It was a kindness that tore at her heartstrings. Maybe he *was* getting past the shock she'd handed him. Well, she could be kind to him, too.

''You really don't have to worry about me,'' she said with a soft smile. ''My well-being is not your responsibility.''

''I didn't say it was, but I still wondered if you were all right.''

Her eyes met his, and she saw things in them that he wasn't saying. He *did* still care for her! How could he? Emotion suddenly overcame her, and she spoke without thinking. ''Brent, how can you even talk to me after what I did?''

''Let's stay away from that subject,'' he said sharply.

It was not a request, it was a command, and not stated at all kindly. It startled her greatly; obviously she'd misread him again.

Shying from her own foolish thoughts about acceptance and understanding, she took a breath. ''Very well, I won't bring it up again. I would like you to know one thing, however. I told Sierra the…the whole story. And I'm going to tell Tamara about it the next time I see her.''

Brent was silent a moment, then said thoughtfully, ''I think it's good that you're no longer keeping the past bottled up, but when you told Sierra about it I hope you didn't represent yourself as some kind of monster.''

Her eyes widened. Was he going to defend what she'd done yet again? How could she possibly read him correctly when he kept confusing her?

''Well, I certainly didn't represent myself as being blameless,'' she replied.

He gave her a piercing look. ''You're never going to forgive yourself, are you? Let me ask you this. Have you forgiven your parents for their misguided influence?''

''I don't know if there's any forgiveness in me for anything or anybody.'' She paused, then added, ''There's none in you, either, Brent,'' wishing he would deny it.

He didn't. He hesitated, then spoke grimly. ''And that's the awful truth.'' They sat there without further conversation for several minutes, each in a private hell. Brent recovered first. ''I didn't come over here to talk about the past. We've done that enough. Now we should be concentrating on the future. We've got some plans, and they just might produce some positive results.''

A bit sick at heart, Blythe managed a wan smile. ''It's what I'm living for.''

''Not the only thing, I hope.''

''What else is there?''

''Don't say things like that,'' Brent said gruffly. ''You've got a lot to live for. Your family, your work, your...'' He couldn't think of anything else, and he became red faced. ''You're, uh, still—still young,'' he stammered.

''I don't feel young.''

''Forty-three is not old, Blythe.''

She could sense an argument heating up, but they didn't see eye-to-eye and probably never would. ''When I was nineteen I felt years younger than that, and now I feel years older than forty-three. Sorry,'' she said abruptly. ''That's just the way it is.''

''Well, it shouldn't be. You have a lot of good years ahead of you.''

"*Good* years?" she scoffed. "What's going to make them any better than the last twenty-four? One thing would help, but we both know that actually finding our child is a very long shot."

"Are you giving up?"

"No, I'll never give up, but facts are facts." She sent him a questioning look. "Aren't they? We don't even know where to begin our search."

"Which is the reason I hired a detective. Blythe, I don't particularly like your mood. You seem to be very argumentative today."

She bristled, because he had no right to judge her mood, whatever it might be. "*I* seem argumentative? Well, put this in your pipe and smoke it. I don't particularly like your mood, either. Let's clear the air, Brent. I do not expect anything from you. I'm glad we're single-minded about finding our child, but that is now and forever will be the extent of our relationship. We both know it, so you never need to feel obligated to drop in and make sure I'm all right." She was breaking her own heart, but couldn't seem to stop the flow of unkind words from her mouth. "My unhappiness today is no worse than it was before you reentered my life. You didn't cause it, and—"

He jumped to his feet. "That's enough, dammit! I *did* cause it. Who got you pregnant? Who didn't always use a condom when we made love? Who knew you weren't on the Pill and was completely aware of the risk he was taking by ignoring protection?" Brent slapped his palm against his chest. "Me, Blythe, me! So don't tell me again how terrible you are and how blameless I am!"

Anger hit her hard, and she, too, jumped up. "You didn't do it alone! I was there! I could have said something! Obviously we made love without protection or I never would have gotten pregnant, but why are you the only one to blame? And did you give our baby away? You didn't even know there was a baby! *Blame me,*" she shrieked. "Damn you, blame me!"

He looked at her. She was quivering and shaking, with red spots of fury in her cheeks and tears misting her eyes.

"It's the only way you'll have it, isn't it?" he said, furious with himself for letting this happen. But since it had gone this far, he had to take it one step further. Maybe what he planned to say next would knock some sense into her head.

"Okay, fine, you win. I blame you for the whole damn thing. I had nothing to do with it. Your parents had nothing to do with it. The home was a wonderful place where happy young girls *happily* gave away their babies. It was where you gave away *our* baby, and the whole thing from beginning to end was your fault. Is that what you wanted to hear? Are you happy now?"

She turned pale before his eyes and sought the chair she'd been sitting on before the explosion. "Go," she whispered. "Just go."

"And leave you on the verge of a total collapse? I don't think so." He lowered himself to his own chair and leaned forward with his forearms on his knees. "That was the most ridiculous argument two people could have. What in hell difference does it make today who was to blame for something that happened twenty-four years ago? Blythe, look at me."

"I don't want to look at you. I don't want to talk to you. I'm not going to collapse, so please go and leave me be."

He was silent a moment. "Do you agree that it doesn't matter who was to blame?"

"Why would I agree when you're blaming yourself?"

"Dammit, didn't anything I said get through to you?"

She finally looked at him. "Oh, yes, quite a few things came through loud and clear."

"But you didn't take them the way I meant them, did you?" Brent raked his fingers through his hair in agitation.

"You meant something different than what you actually said? Well, pardon me, but I'm not a mind reader."

"You're mad as hell right now, aren't you? You know, that could be a good sign. At least you're not crumbling with guilt, as you usually are."

"Don't you dare make fun of my feelings! You're not the one who lived with this thing for over twenty years, I am!"

Brent nodded grimly. "I know what you've lived with, and I'm sorry if I sounded as though I was making fun of your feelings. It's just that the other night I remembered how careless I'd been with protection sometimes, and I couldn't let you go on thinking that you bear all the responsibility for what happened.''

"Fine," she snapped. "Half of the responsibility is yours. Maybe I'll only feel half as guilty now."

"I don't like your feeling guilty at all," Brent said sharply.

"Oh, for crying out loud! What do you expect me to feel? Should I be thrilled that I signed those adoption papers? What's wrong with you?"

Brent sat back and studied her. His eyes played tricks on him, because suddenly she was the radiant Blythe of his youth. The beautiful young girl that he'd loved so much he couldn't keep his hands off her.

He gave his head a shake to clear it and got to his feet. "If you're all right, I'll leave now." He would talk about the house another time.

"Please do," she said coldly.

He walked out and she curled into a ball in her chair and cried her eyes red.

Sierra phoned that evening. "Just wanted to let you know that we're home, safe and sound. I would have called earlier, but Clint and I were busy seeing Tommy off to college. He's one very excited young man." Sierra's voice changed, taking on a personal note. "How are you doing?"

Blythe forced herself to speak normally. "I'm fine, Sierra. I really don't want you worrying about me."

"Let's call it concern instead of worry, okay? I told Clint on the way home."

"How did he take it?"

"He's a hundred percent on your team. I knew he would be—that's the sort of man he is. So, what kind of day did you have?"

"Uh, a pretty good day, actually."

"Did you see Brent?"

"He...came by, yes."

"He's a great guy, Blythe. Clint and I are unanimous in that opinion."

"I suppose he is." What else could she say? Never would she repeat the things he'd said to her today; she could barely let herself think of them.

In bed later, long after that conversation had ended, Blythe clenched her hands into fists. It infuriated her that she could almost smell Brent's scent, and that her pulse had quickened because of it. How could she do this to herself after he'd said such awful things to her? How could she even like him now?

But she did like him. No, it wasn't that simple. She *wanted* him, more right now than she had when he'd swept her into his arms and taken her senses by storm that day in the den. Was she completely crazy? Had she finally gone over the edge? After what happened today she should hate him! Feverishly she kicked her hot feet free of the covers and muttered a coarse word.

What on earth would she hate him for? For saying what *she'd* been saying since the day he'd walked into this house with Bill Harkens?

Blythe had been right about the great weather not holding for long; the next morning she awoke to gray skies and a drizzling rainfall. It matched her mood to a *T,* she thought grimly.

But she was still excited about today's appointment with Ray Grant, P.I. Although she truly dreaded spending time with Brent today, she was ready and waiting when he arrived to pick her up for the drive to Spokane.

The first thing he did when she opened the front door was say, "I apologize for what happened yesterday afternoon. Can you accept my apology and reply, 'Well, hell, Morrison, everybody makes an ass out of himself once in a while'?" He was hoping she would laugh.

She didn't. "You didn't say anything I haven't said to myself a thousand times. Come on, let's go." She started to walk around him.

He caught her arm. "Blythe, let's call a truce. Considering

what we're going to do today, I think we can both be that big, don't you?''

She stared into his eyes and tortured herself by remembering the idiotic feelings she'd suffered last night. Instead of hating him, she had lain in bed wanting him. *I'll never be able to hate him, never!* She tore her gaze from his and said dully, "Yes, I'm sure we can both be that big.''

"Thank you," he said quietly, and released her arm. He pulled the front door shut and made sure it was locked, then they went to his car, hurrying to avoid getting too wet.

"At least it's not pouring," Brent commented when they were underway.

"Not yet, at least," she responded shortly. Regardless of her deliberate coolness, there was something cozy about the pattering rain and the warmth of the car. Even being with Brent was comforting, which she didn't like admitting. It was just that she could so easily let her imagination run away, and envision a commingled future, and she was so terribly afraid of false hopes. Yes, there were moments when she was sure that she felt something from him, but the reality of their relationship now was much like a tinderbox, constantly on the verge of another explosion.

Shying from that subject because it was so unnerving, she took a small piece of paper from her purse. "The list of names Mr. Grant requested that I compile isn't very impressive, I'm afraid,'' she said.

"What do you have?" Brent felt relief because she was talking to him.

"Well, in the first place none of the girls at the home used their last names. I remember a Nona, a Marybeth, an Ellen and a few others, but I never did know their last names. So I think that's pretty much a dead end. The nurses also used first names. I recall a Nurse Emma and a Nurse Ruth, but their name tags did not indicate a surname. In searching my memory, I remember that that was one of the most stringent rules of the house. Everyone's privacy was highly protected.''

"You said there was a doctor. Do you remember anything about him? Or was the doctor a woman?''

"A man, and his name was Redmond. Dr. Elijah Redmond."

Brent nodded. "Good, that should help."

"If he's still living," Blythe murmured uneasily. "He seemed to be…quite elderly. I know that when you're nineteen everyone past thirty looks old, and I keep hoping that he only *seemed* elderly because I was young." Blythe paused a moment, then added with a sigh, "I doubt it, though. I think Dr. Redmond was well into his sixties. Actually, I doubt if any name on this list is going to help Mr. Grant's investigation."

Brent kept his eyes on the watery road. "You did the best you could with that list. That's all anyone can expect."

Blythe felt her body stiffen. "Even you?"

He sent her a glance. "Pardon?"

"If it were the other way around I would expect much more from you."

His lips thinned. "You would not. You're just trying to start another argument. You want me to hate you as much as you hate yourself, and I don't. I know that upsets you, but that's just the way I am."

Stiffly she faced front and said nothing. Her heart ached with old memories and utter misery. He might not hate her, but he certainly didn't love her, and he had…he had. Or he'd been very close to loving her. Why hadn't she looked for her child long before they had met again? Maybe she would have had good news to tell him, rather than the cruel things she'd laid on him.

In the next heartbeat she was glad he didn't hate her, and that he'd been able to say so. She should get down on her knees and thank God that Brent was the kind of man he was. It had been his idea to find their child, and together they had a chance of doing so. She was just so mixed up, she realized, with a ponderous sensation in the pit of her stomach. She loved him and feared she always would. She was forever going to be an unhappy woman, for one reason or another. Even if they did find their child she would never have Brent.

He thought he understood everything about her now, she thought with some bitterness, but how could he? How could any man understand what every woman who'd carried a child under her heart for nine months really felt about that small life? Not that she didn't know men who loved their children as much as any woman could. She'd met many such fathers during her teaching career. But the months before birth seemed to belong so completely to the mother, and that was all she had of her child. She couldn't quite believe that Brent or any other man could fully appreciate that concept.

Blythe continued thinking uneasy, ambiguous thoughts until they reached Spokane and finally pulled into the parking lot of a modest office complex. It was still drizzling, and they hurried from the car to the building. Brent took her arm and led her down a hall to a door with the inscription Raymond Grant, Private Detective.

Blythe's mouth was suddenly dry, and her stomach began churning. A pleasant-looking, middle-aged woman greeted them and showed them into Mr. Grant's office at once.

Ray Grant was a tall, thin, balding man. Blythe estimated his age as being close to her own, a few years past forty. He stood up when they walked in and shook hands with both of them, then gestured to the chairs in front of his desk. "Please sit down."

When they were all seated, they talked about the weather for a few moments, then Ray Grant opened the file folder lying in front of him. "I've made some phone calls, and this is what I've found out so far. The home in Breighton was owned by the LTT Corporation. I have no idea what LTT stands for and neither did the clerk I talked to in Salt Lake City. But shortly after the home closed, LTT filed a dissolution of incorporation with the state of Utah. The clerk gave me the names of the officers while LTT was still doing business in the state, also the name of its registered agent, but so far I haven't been able to run any of them down. I intend to keep trying, because I feel that if I could talk to just one of those people I might learn who actually operated the home." He looked at Blythe. "Unless, of course, you already know."

Her shoulders slumped. "I don't." She passed her sad little list across the desk. "Those are the names I remember, and, as you can see, other than Dr. Redmond, they're all first names.''

Ray Grant picked up the phone and pushed the intercom button. ''Shelley, would you please try and locate a phone number for a Dr. Elijah Redmond in Utah? At one time he lived in Breighton, Utah, or at least he practiced medicine in that town. Thanks, Shelley.''

''How on earth can your secretary get information on every town and rural area in Utah?'' Blythe asked, astonished that Mr. Grant, or anyone else, would even think that was possible.

Ray Grant smiled. ''Shelley's a whiz with a computer, Blythe. If Dr. Redmond is still living in Utah and has a telephone, she'll come up with his number and perhaps even his address.''

''I see,'' Blythe murmured when she didn't see at all. Computers were not her forte, which she had never regretted until now. ''Mr. Grant—Ray—Brent said you mentioned the baby's birth certificate when he was here the first time. Have you learned anything about that?''

The detective shook his head. ''Not yet, Blythe, but I still think it's an important link and I intend to continue pursuing it. Now, I have to ask you and Brent something. I can get all sorts of information by telephone and computer, which is what I've been doing thus far, but I feel certain that a trip to Utah is eventually going to be necessary. For instance, should we come up with Dr. Redmond's address, I would prefer talking to him in person rather than over the phone. My point is that the cost of this investigation could run into thousands of dollars. I guess what I'm asking is, how far do you want me to go? I will be spending your money, after all.''

Brent didn't hesitate a second. ''We want you to do whatever it takes.''

Blythe frowned. ''Ray, the goal of this investigation, as I see it, is to locate the records the home maintained while it was in operation. Dr. Redmond wouldn't have those records, would he? I mean, he was—or he wasn't... Oh, I don't know *what* I mean!''

''Blythe,'' Ray said gently, ''we don't *know* if the home

kept permanent records. At this point we don't even know if the home operated within the law and filed birth certificates with the state. I have to ask myself why it went out of business and why the corporation was dissolved. Now, maybe the answers to those questions are meaningless, as far as your case goes, but I don't like loose ends, and when a question occurs to me during an investigation it drives me batty until I find an answer. Dr. Redmond just might surprise all of us with what he knows about that home.''

Ray smiled. ''Of course, we have to find him before we can ask him anything, don't we?''

Blythe felt slightly sick to her stomach. What had she expected, she asked herself—an instant miracle? Right now all she could visualize was months of waiting and hoping and going through hell while Ray Grant chased down leads. She wanted to find her child *now,* not six months or six years from now.

She fell silent and battled tears while Brent and Ray went over the same ground again. Finally the meeting was over, and everyone stood and shook hands again. She hurried out of the office ahead of Brent, and only stopped running when they were outside and he caught her by the arm.

''Blythe, what's wrong?''

Tears streamed down her face, mingling with the rain. ''I—I had hoped for…so much more.''

''Grant's a good man, Blythe. This isn't going to happen overnight. Come on, let's get in the car. We're both getting wet.'' They hurried to the vehicle and got in.

All but choking on the tears in her throat, Blythe dug tissues from her purse, dabbed at her eyes and asked, ''Are you satisfied with the direction of Ray's investigation?''

''I take it you're not.'' Brent started the motor, then turned in the seat to look at her. ''Would you like me to go back inside and tell Ray we no longer require his services?''

''That doesn't seem sensible. I…don't know what I'd like, other than some answers.''

''So would I, but we're not going to get them immediately.'' She looked so forlorn that Brent unthinkingly reached out to her. Gently he caressed her damp hair. "We have to be patient," he said softly.

A shiver went up Blythe's spine, and in the next instant she slid across the seat and practically threw herself at him. He was completely taken by surprise, but still his arms closed around her while she sobbed into the front of his shirt. He held her, stroked her back, let her cry and nearly cried himself. He felt her emotions so acutely, and he also felt something within himself relent. She'd gone through more misery than anyone deserved, and her load of guilt would bring most people to their knees.

"Tell me what you'd like me to do, Blythe. Do you want me to fire Ray?"

"He…maybe he can help," she whispered huskily as the thrill of being in Brent's arms began sinking in. "We…I shouldn't be so quick to judge his—his methods."

"Then we'll give him a chance, okay?"

"Yes, okay." She tilted her head back to see his face, and realized her lips were but a breath away from his.

Their eyes met and she let her feelings for him show in hers. She saw him swallow and knew he was trying to digest what was happening. Then she saw no more, for his mouth was on hers and she closed her eyes. His kiss at that moment was what she needed more than anything, and she parted her lips for his tongue. She knew they were in a parking lot in broad daylight, but she didn't care who might see them. Besides, the windows were steamed up from the rain outside and a passing stranger would only get a glimpse of the car's interior.

One kiss was not nearly enough, and it led to another, and another. They both began breathing hard, creating more steam for the window glass. Euphoria rippled through her. Brent might not be able to forgive her, but she still affected him physically. She felt his hand slip under her skirt and glide up her thigh, and she adjusted her position just enough for him to touch that part of her that was on fire and aching with need.

She gasped when he reached his goal and began a gentle circular motion with his thumb. She wanted *all* of him, wanted to touch him as he was touching her. But it was much easier to conceal intimacy under a skirt than it would be to unzip his pants. Instead she laid her hand on his fly and kissed him with complete abandonment, all the while panting because of what he was doing between her legs.

"Blythe...this shouldn't be happening," he groaned.

"I can't help myself. Oh, Brent, kiss me again. I need you so much right now."

"You're hot and wet," he whispered raggedly. "You're ready for..."

"I know," she gasped. "Oh, Brent, I know."

"We can't do it here."

"Take me home. We can do anything we want there."

He kissed her again, hungrily, with his heart pounding loudly and so much desire racking his body that he wondered if he could drive safely.

He pulled himself together. "You'd better move over. I'll never make it back to Coeur d'Alene if you're this close."

The drive was torturous, never-ending. Brent turned on the radio in an effort to get his mind off making love with Blythe. It helped a little, but *very* little. He shouldn't be doing this. He shouldn't have kissed her and raised her hopes about the two of them. Nothing could come of it.

But she was so beautiful, and he kept sneaking glances at her. He didn't know what had triggered her intense desire, and the last thing he wanted was to hurt her by saying straight out that their passion in the parking lot could go no further.

He clenched the steering wheel as the battle raged within him. How could he back off now *without* hurting her? A perplexed frown furrowed his brow. Why should he care if he hurt her? Why should it matter?

He set his lips grimly. It *didn't* matter, he told himself. Had she cared about hurting him that day in her den?

What do you want, vengeance? Retribution?

No, never!

He let go of the steering wheel with one hand and passed it wearily over his face. He'd gotten himself into this, and only he could get himself out of it. But he had to come up with a way to let her down easily.

"Brent," Blythe said softly. "Are you all right?"

He tried to smile. "Uh, we got pretty carried away in that parking lot."

"Are...are you regretting it?"

He couldn't say yes, he just couldn't. He'd believed that this part of their relationship was dead, and it wasn't. Not for her, and not for him.

"No," he told her. "I'm not regretting it." In that moment he realized it was true. He wanted her more right now than he'd ever wanted anything. Whatever she had or hadn't done in the past and even the present simply could not compete with the intense ache in his groin.

"I'm so glad," she said, and unlatched her seat belt to again slide over and snuggle against him.

"Hook the center belt," he said gruffly.

"Yes, sir," she whispered, and drove him crazy by wriggling around to find the ends of it.

His goose was cooked and he knew it. No way was he going to call a halt to their passion. If nothing came after it, fine, and if Blythe expected something he couldn't give her because he'd made love with her again, he would deal with it when it happened. Throwing caution to the winds, he wrapped his right arm around her and pressed a kiss to the top of her head, though he kept his eyes on the road. Her sigh of supreme pleasure wreaked havoc with his blood pressure, but he was now resigned to the inevitable. They were going to make love, and he could think of nothing else.

Neither could Blythe. The second Brent pulled into her driveway, she jumped out of the car and ran for the front door with the key in her hand. He was right behind her, and when they were finally alone, shut into her house, she dropped her purse, threw off her jacket, took his hand and whispered, "My bedroom."

Chapter Fifteen

"Hurry!" Blythe was tearing off her clothes and urging Brent along.

He needed no urging; he was already undressing with the speed of light. It was almost impossible for him to believe this was happening in the *way* it was happening, and his mind was spinning from it. He couldn't imagine what it was that had destroyed Blythe's normal inhibitions, but he wasn't going to risk her changing her mind now by asking questions.

The room was filled with a pale, silvery light, caused by the gray day outside. On this floor of the house the sound of the falling rain was pleasantly audible. Down to her bra and panties, Blythe threw back the bedcovers. Her pulse was running wild, and she couldn't slow it down. She felt driven, focused on only one thing, and she knew in the far reaches of her mind that this had never happened to her before. Not in the same way. Not with screamingly raw nerves and what felt like an inferno in the pit of her stomach.

She looked at Brent just as he shed his final garment, his briefs, and she quickly undid her bra and dropped it and her panties to the floor. They lay on the bed at the same moment. Brent drew the covers up over them and they each slid to the middle of the bed, to embrace and kiss and moan at the wonder of holding each other without the barrier of clothing.

"You have a wonderful body," she whispered, stroking his chest.

"You're so beautiful you take my breath away."

She couldn't quite believe that, but it was a delight to hear and she didn't deny his flattery. Besides, she thought vaguely, if he didn't mind that her breasts weren't as firm and upright as they'd once been, why should she? In fact, he seemed totally mesmerized by her breasts, lavishing kisses and caresses on them, and his adulation not only felt incredible, it made her feel better—even proud—about her body.

Actually, she realized with an emotional start, in Brent's arms today she felt as young as she'd been in college. It was a marvelous sensation, and she clung to it while her hands roamed his hot skin with wondrous abandonment.

They turned this way and that, moving against each other, touching and kissing until they were both breathing in short, quick gasps. Their foreplay was delicious, but it was so arousing neither could sustain it for long.

"Now," Blythe said hoarsely. "Now, Brent."

He moved on top of her, kissed her mouth with unbridled passion and slid into her. The pleasure was earthshaking, and he groaned deep in his throat while she dug her fingertips into his back. There was no serenity in their movements, and very little gentleness. It was rough and earthy, with each of them taking from the other what they needed so badly, and in the taking, giving as much or more than they got. It was spontaneous combustion, an explosion of lust and passion.

Blythe felt tears streaming down her temples, but they were tears without sorrow or guilt and she let them flow. In minutes she was hot and sweaty and writhing, meeting Brent's every thrust with one of her own. She started moaning and whimpering as the final bliss came closer and closer, and when it began, she cried out and clutched at Brent as though he was about to desert her.

Recognizing the signs of her greatest pleasure, Brent gave his body free rein, and in seconds he came to a roaring climax and shouted her name. "Blythe!"

It was over. Neither could move so much as a finger, and they lay there with their eyes closed, gradually catching their breaths.

Blythe opened her eyes and felt a mild shock because she was not on cloud nine at all, but in her own bedroom. She wasn't sure that she wanted to face reality so soon again, but what choice did she have?

Brent was also thinking about reality, *their* reality. What was it now? Why was he here? Why did *she* think he was here? He hadn't yet told her that he no longer wanted to buy the house. She had to be counting on it, and maybe now she was also counting on him. It was so damn confusing, all of it, and he couldn't sort out his feelings.

And then he felt the sting of tears in his eyes and couldn't believe this was happening to him. Where had this emotional eruption come from? Embarrassed, he left her, shoved the covers aside and sat on the edge of the bed with his back to her and his feet on the floor.

Blythe stretched lazily, then noticed that he was just sitting there. "Brent?"

He didn't move, not even to wipe away the moisture that had seeped from his eyes. His emotions were in shambles—he at least recognized that—but why was he crying? He had no answers to give Blythe should she catch on to his turmoil; it was best that he leave quickly.

Blythe frowned. "Brent?" she said again.

He reached down to the floor for his pants, shoved his feet in the legs and stood to pull them up without ever turning around. Clearing his throat, he mumbled, "I've got a pile of work waiting at the motel."

Blythe sat up. "You're leaving?"

He heard the bewilderment in her voice, but had no words to assuage it. He, too, was bewildered. "Sorry, but I have to."

"But…" *Why aren't you looking at me?* She drew a breath. "Is—is something wrong?"

He kept his back turned while he put on his shirt and buttoned it. "Nothing but a mountain of work."

She realized his voice sounded strange, abnormally husky. The life went out of her. He was regretting what they'd done, was possibly even angry with himself for letting it happen. Nothing had changed between them because they'd made love today, nothing at all.

She sank back to her pillow and pulled the covers up to her chin. He sat on the bed again to put on his shoes and socks, and she watched his broad back, the stiff, unyielding set of his head, and felt her heart breaking into a million pieces.

He got up, turned just a little and smiled briefly. "Talk to you later, okay?"

"Yes," she whispered. "Later." He walked out and her fingers uneasily plucked at the blankets. She wished she had seen his face better, but it had been heavily shadowed because of the rain outside and the approach of nightfall.

Faintly she heard him downstairs, the slam of the front door and finally the sound of his car starting. Then there was no sound at all, except for the rain on the roof and her own skittering heartbeat.

She suddenly felt like a fool, and she buried her face in her pillow. She had behaved like a sex-starved tart, and what man would say no to a woman who had draped herself all over him? *She* had caused this, not Brent.

Finally she sat up, switched on the lamp and grabbed a handful of tissues from the box on the nightstand. Blowing her nose, she made a vow. Brent would never need to worry about her coming on to him again. She would never again humiliate herself like she'd done today. There was only one reason that she would even speak to him again—finding their child—and that would only last until they either attained their goal or decided to give up because it just wasn't possible.

Blythe tensed. She knew in her soul that she would never be able to accept "impossible." Maybe Brent would give up if their search dragged on ad infinitum, but she never would. Never!

* * *

Brent didn't even attempt to get any work done. But he looked at his computer equipment and the stacks of papers that covered the dresser and table in his motel room and felt a rising antipathy. He hated this damn room. If he had followed through on his intentions instead of getting bogged down with the Benning house, he would be living in a nice little home with space and ample lighting and he wouldn't have this mess to contend with. Obviously his normal good sense had taken flight the minute he'd seen Blythe again.

He sat on the bed with his head down and realized that he still felt like bawling. He rubbed his eyes with the heels of his hands, a weary gesture accompanied by a feeling of helplessness. It was a shock to his system to face what he really felt for Blythe. He didn't just care for her, he was in love with her. For a while after she'd hit him with the truth about their child he'd been able to ignore what had begun at their first meeting, but he knew that today's startling events had knocked the pretense out of him.

Not that he planned to tell her how he felt. There were too many baffling feelings still churning within him to just blurt out, "I love you, Blythe." Why in hell hadn't she come to him when she'd realized she was pregnant? There was no acceptable excuse for her running home to her parents instead of coming to him, and then she'd compounded her first mistake by obediently and undoubtedly meekly doing everything Myra and Harry Benning had told her to do. It was all so senseless.

Regardless, he was in love with her, he thought darkly, the emotion all but choking him. He didn't want to be, but all the arguments against loving Blythe didn't seem to affect his feelings an iota. How could a man both resent and love a woman?

He finally went to bed, but then his mind took up almost exactly where it had left off before he'd undressed and showered. He suspected that what he felt for Blythe was a permanent condition. He knew he was going to have to see her again. He knew that he would make love with her at any and every opportunity. He also knew that he wasn't going to get boyishly romantic over being in love. He and Blythe were mature adults. They had both been married; they both knew the score. Today she had wanted sex and had unabashedly let him know. He could certainly do the same with her.

All that aside, however, he had to talk to her about her house. He had let her believe he still wanted to buy it for too long already. He would take care of that tomorrow.

Blythe slept restlessly and woke up in the morning feeling dull witted. A shower helped, and when she was able to think clearly she made another decision: she was not going to phone the superintendent of her school at all. She was going home, and this time nothing was going to stop her. She would stay in touch with Ray Grant and maybe even with Brent. But her and Brent's long-distance telephone conversations would consist solely of what each of them was doing to find their child. Once in Connecticut she would start writing letters to the state of Utah. If her child's birth certificate had been properly recorded, then someone should be able to find it.

But before she left Coeur d'Alene, she had to do something about those miserable file cabinets in the basement.

She was hurt and angry over yesterday, and she forcefully grabbed up the phone book and began calling office suppliers. Her voice was hard and unfriendly when she asked, "Do you have a commercial-size paper shredder in stock?"

Her third call produced results. "Yes, we have one, but only one."

"Fine," she snapped without asking the price. "I'll be right down to buy it. Put my name on it. It's Blythe Benning. Be sure and hold it!"

She was in her car with the garage door rising when she spotted Brent's car at the curb. Why was he here this morning? How did he have the nerve? Every cell in her body tightened, and she deliberately, furiously ignored him getting out of his vehicle and began backing her own car from the garage.

"Where are you going?" he called, bending down to see through her side window.

She had a notion to keep on going, but she slammed on the

brakes and rolled down her window. Her voice and expression were as hard and cold as chipped ice.

"I'm on my way to pick up a paper shredder."

"Oh." Brent thought a moment. "Would you like some help?"

A scathing refusal was on the tip of her tongue, but that was when his good looks hit her. He was a beautiful man, muscular and long legged. And so vital. He exuded good health and intelligence, everything any woman could want in a man. He'd been, she recalled with painful distinction, exactly the same in college—dedicated, ambitious and sexy enough to have lured her into bed on their third date. Her virginity had surprised him; her responsiveness had surprised *her*. He'd hurt her terribly yesterday, but he had also lifted her to the stars. Her left hand made a fist as confusion beset her. She should despise the ground Brent Morrison walked on, and instead she loved him as she'd never loved another man. It wasn't fair.

"Are you sure you have the time to help?" she asked coldly. "What about those mountains of work?" She had tinged the word *mountains* with sarcasm, and she saw streaks of red appear in his face.

"I'll make the time." Damn, she was an irritating woman. How could he care for someone this annoying?

"I plan to work all day on those medical files," she warned. "Are you offering that much of your precious time?"

He clenched his jaw. "I said I would help and I will."

"Then fine," she snapped. "I'll be back in twenty minutes." She finished backing out of the driveway and drove away.

Brent stood there with his mouth open, hardly believing her rudeness. Shaking his head in disgust, he returned to his car and got in. He shouldn't have offered to help her with that damn paper shredding, but he'd instantly seen it as an opportunity to ease into a discussion about the house. He sure hadn't expected her to leave him standing in the driveway. She could at least have given him the key to the house so he could wait inside.

He heaved a sigh and settled himself for a twenty-minute wait.

* * *

Blythe learned when she got to the office supply store that she didn't have to buy the paper shredder, she could rent it. But the man waiting on her was slower than molasses, and there was an extensive rental form to be filled in. She gave him her Connecticut driver's license as ID, and then had to explain why she didn't have an Idaho license. Then he asked for a cash deposit or a credit card. Impatiently she slapped a credit card on the counter and tapped her toe while he laboriously wrote down the information and made a copy of the card.

"Honestly," she muttered. It would have been easier and probably much faster just to buy the damn shredder. But it was expensive and would have been one more possession to do something with before she left.

Finally the shredder was loaded into her car. She checked her watch. She'd been gone for forty minutes. Brent probably hadn't waited.

She thought about him as she drove home. He had overcome the tragedy of losing his wife and daughter, which bespoke of a strong constitution. Why was she so different?

The answer to that question was immediate and soul shaking. He was not to blame for his own terrible loss, but she was to blame for hers. However hard he'd tried to make her see otherwise, it was an immutable fact. He couldn't or wouldn't face that truth, and she would never be able to do anything else. Even if they became the very best of friends, or more—an unlikely prospect, considering yesterday's fiasco—it was something they would never agree on.

The resentment Blythe felt when she saw that Brent's car was still parked at her curb unnerved her. She did *not* need his help, and she certainly didn't want to spend the day with him. Instead of letting anger get the better of her, she should have calmly told him so.

And then, as she drove into the garage, remorse struck her. When had she become so heartless and unforgiving? She turned off the ignition and laid her head on the steering wheel.

Brent walked into the garage and saw how she was sitting. She looked defenseless and defeated, and his heart went out to her. He opened the driver's door of her car and peered in. "Blythe?"

She lifted her head. She wasn't even going to try to explain her distress to Brent. He had to know that it had something to do with yesterday, and was there any point to talking in circles about it? Neither of them would be honest about it, so it was a subject better left alone.

"The shredder's in the trunk. If you still want to help, here's the key." She held out her car keys.

Their eyes met when he took the keys from her hand, but it seemed that neither of them could go beyond a brief peek into the other's eyes, and without a word he hurried to the back of the car. She drew a long, uneven breath and wondered again why he was here this morning. Her next question was how she was going to deal with his "help." How could they possibly work together all day when they could barely look at each other? He was every bit as uncomfortable as she was, which again raised the question about why he was here at all.

Her eyes narrowed speculatively. Something was on his mind, something he must feel needed saying. Her stomach roiled. If it was some lame explanation of why he'd left so abruptly yesterday, he could shove it up his nose because she didn't want to hear it.

She finally picked up the box of trash bags that fit the bin and would receive the shredded paper, got out of the car and pushed the door closed. Brent had the shredder and bin in his arms, and she opened the laundry room door ahead of him.

"The trunk is still open," he told her in passing.

Almost militantly she marched back to the car and slammed it shut. When she went inside, Brent was waiting at the door to the basement stairs.

"You do want this thing downstairs, don't you?" he asked.

"Well, where else would I want it?" She grabbed the doorknob, twisted it viciously to open the door and then stepped back so he could go down the stairs first. She followed him down and then ducked around him to open the door to the room with the file cabinets. "Set it anywhere," she told him.

He lowered the shredder and bin to the floor. "It's a lot heavier than it looks," he said. "You would have had trouble carrying it in by yourself."

"I've carried bigger burdens," she retorted.

He knew she wasn't talking about physical pounds, but made no comment on her remark. He was not going to be drawn into another argument, no matter what she said today.

"Well, where do we start?" he said, looking at the many file cabinets.

The shredder really didn't look much different to Blythe than the one she used at her school in Connecticut, which only could accept one or two sheets of paper at a time, and then they had to be inserted carefully or the unit would shut down.

"Is this really a commercial shredder?" she asked with a frown of uncertainty.

"There are bigger units, but I'm sure this one will do the job just fine."

"Then we might as well get started. Or *I* might as well. You really don't have to do this, you know."

The expression in her green eyes was challenging, daring him to back out of his offer to help. Was she hoping he *would* back off so that she could further justify her anger toward him? He felt something he rarely felt—stubbornness. It stiffened his spine and took over his system. If his very life depended on leaving this house this very minute, he would look death in the eye and stay.

"I don't *have* to do anything I don't want to do," he barked at her. "Does that give you a clue to my intentions? I said I would help and I meant it."

"Oh, well pardon me all to hell," she drawled sarcastically. "I certainly didn't mean to step on your massive ego." Internally she winced. In her entire life she had never talked to another person the way she just had with Brent. And what she'd said was an abominable lie. She had never once seen signs of him having a massive ego, not twenty years ago and certainly not since they'd met again. She couldn't even blame his ego for what he'd done to her yesterday. She could blame it on regret, yes, and an ardent wish that he hadn't made love with her again, but those things had nothing to do with his ego.

It was *her* ego that had taken a beating yesterday, and it was her ego that was making her behave like a shrew today. She drew a breath. It was time she acted her age.

"All right," she said quietly. "If you really do want to help, let's get started."

They worked with their conversation confined strictly to the job they were doing, and after a few hours Blythe began thinking about lunch. Thinking *uneasily* about it. She would prefer not to sit across the table from Brent, but if he was going to stay and help with this boring, tiresome job all day, then she couldn't let him go hungry.

Shortly after twelve she said, "I'm going upstairs to make some sandwiches. If you'd like to wash up…?"

"Yeah, I would, thanks." Brent stretched his back. He'd been doing the actual shredding, with Blythe going through the folders for staples and paper clips before handing the papers to him. They had gotten a good rhythm going and had already cleaned out three of the cabinets. He believed they could empty every cabinet in the room today, if they were willing to work late.

But he would leave that up to Blythe. He followed her up the stairs and headed for one of the bathrooms. When he walked into the kitchen ten minutes later, she was standing at the counter, making sandwiches. He sat at the table.

She felt his eyes on her back and sighed silently. Eating together carried its own brand of intimacy. She would not be able to sit at the table with him and act as though he wasn't there. But what on earth would they talk about? Not yesterday, she thought with her teeth clenched. If he dared to bring up yesterday she would not be able to hold her tongue. Ray Grant

came to mind. Yes, they could talk about Ray and his inves
tigation.

Bringing a plate of sandwiches and a pitcher of iced tea t
the table, she sat down. "Help yourself," she said.

"Thanks."

Before Brent could start a conversation she might not like
she started one she could live with. "I've been thinking abou
Ray Grant."

"Well, there's really not much to think about there, Blythe
Either Ray will come up with some pertinent information o
he won't. My opinion is that if there's any information to find
he'll do it."

Something occurred to her that had thus far passed her by
"I'm going to pay half his fee, you know," she said rathe
belligerently.

"Do I look worried about that?"

"No, but I have a feeling that when it's time to pay th
bills, you're going to get all macho and insist on paying fo
everything. For my own peace of mind I have to pay my share
and you are going to have to let me."

"Fine," Brent said curtly. "Since we've exhausted tha
subject, let me bring up another. Did you find the key to th
fireproof cabinet?"

Blythe frowned. "No. I'm probably going to have to call
locksmith."

"How about letting me try to pick the lock?"

She cocked a suspicious eyebrow. "Do you know *how* t
pick a lock?"

He couldn't help laughing. "Don't start thinking I'm some
kind of cat burglar, but I've picked a few locks in my time.
might not have any luck with this one, but it's worth a shot
don't you think?"

"Yes, I guess it is," she said slowly.

Brent realized that this was a good opportunity to talk t
her about the house. He even opened his mouth to get started
but then closed it again. For some damn reason he could no
tell her that he no longer wanted to buy the house!

Annoyed with himself, he brought up the fireproof cabine

again. "Do you have any idea what your mother might have felt needed to be kept in a fireproof, locked cabinet?"

"None at all. Especially since her important papers were in a strongbox in her bedroom. I mean, if the deed to the house wasn't significant enough for Mother to keep it in a fireproof cabinet, what would be?"

"You know, the key to that cabinet could have been lost for years. Maybe there's nothing significant in it."

"That's entirely possible, but the darn thing's got me too curious to just forget it. Besides, it's totally useless without a key, and maybe you'd like to have it."

Her reminder that the house and its contents were going to be his rocketed through Brent. There would probably never be a better opportunity to tell her that he no longer wanted to buy the house than the opening she'd just given him.

He still couldn't do it. This time he was more than annoyed with himself, he was downright disgusted.

"Well," he said casually. "That cabinet's no good to anyone the way it is, and I can't see throwing it out without finding out if it does contain something."

"That's exactly the way I feel about it," Blythe said. "Maybe you *can* pick the lock."

"I'll give it a try."

"Good." They were through eating, and she got up and took their used dishes to the sink. Together they returned to the basement room.

Brent immediately walked over to the fireproof cabinet. After studying the lock, he dug out some of the paper clips she'd found in the file folders. He fiddled around with the clips and lock for a while, then shook his head.

"I'm afraid it's going to have to be drilled open," he said. "That's what a locksmith would have to do, Blythe. Do you have an electric drill with a very thin bit?"

"No. The only tools in the garage are rakes and things for the yard."

"Too bad." Brent chewed on his bottom lip for a moment. Strange as it seemed, he was becoming as curious about what this cabinet contained as Blythe was. "Tell you what. I'll bring a drill over tomorrow and we'll get this cabinet opened."

"You don't have to do that. I'll just call a locksmith." Darn it, she didn't want him coming back tomorrow!

He ignored the reluctance in her voice and insisted, "No need for that. I'll take care of it. Let's go back to work."

Even though she was fuming, she carried on with the shredding. She thought of telling him that she was going home to Connecticut as soon as this job was completed, but she didn't want any kind of a discussion about her decision. She would be gone before he realized it, and there was something satisfying in imagining how he would take it.

But, oh, she would miss him!

No, no! Don't even think it! You stupid, stupid woman. You couldn't possibly still be in love with him after the way he walked out on you yesterday.

She became very quiet and remained so through the rest of the day. She made soup for dinner, then they worked until nine. All of the cabinets were empty, they had filled a mountain of trash bags with shredded paper and they were both tired.

She walked him to the front door. "Thank you and good night."

"You're done in. Go straight to bed."

She rolled her eyes. "Don't tell me what to do, Brent. I'm not a child."

He looked off into the night. "I might know that better than you do. See you in the morning."

"You do *not* have to come back tomorrow!"

"Yes, I do. Good night."

Blythe was wearily getting ready for bed when the telephone rang. It was Tamara, and her youngest sister's voice in her ear diminished some of Blythe's fatigue.

"I'm so glad you called," Blythe said warmly. "How are the babies?"

"Finally asleep. They are such a handful, Blythe. Mind you, I'm not complaining. I love them so much it scares me."

"Of course you're not complaining," Blythe said reassuringly. "Three babies at one time is a miracle, but I can well imagine how busy they keep you."

"They do, but that's not why I called. Sierra phoned this morning, and I told myself all day that I was going to call you as soon as the babies were down for the night. Sierra said that it was wonderful seeing you, and that the two of you talked about coming here for Christmas."

"Yes, we did talk about it."

"It would be so great for the three of us to be together at Christmas. You know, it wasn't that long ago that we barely knew each other, and now I think of you and Sierra at least once every day."

"I think of you and Sierra very often, too, Tamara." Blythe was beginning to feel a churning in her stomach. She had been planning to tell Tamara the truth of her past the next time they were together, but the impulse to tell her now, on the phone, was too strong to ignore. "Tamara, I know you didn't call tonight to hear a long, sad story, but there's something I'd like you to know."

"Is something wrong?" Tamara instantly sounded worried.

"Something has been wrong since my first year of college."

"Something terrible? Blythe, you sound so bitter."

"I'm sorry, I didn't mean to speak in that vein. This has nothing to do with you, and it's not my intention to cause you any concern. But I've concealed this secret for too many years and I can't do it anymore. I told Sierra about it when she and Clint were here this weekend. I'd like you to know about it, as well."

"I'm listening, Blythe. I want you, Sierra and myself to be sisters in the true sense of the word."

"I feel exactly the same." Blythe took a deep breath. "Tamara, when I was in my first year of college, I became pregnant." She heard Tamara's startled gasp. Wincing only slightly, Blythe started relating the rest of her story. After a few minutes she heard Tamara crying softly in her ear, and her own eyes misted over. But she fought emotion and kept talking, finally reaching the present. "And so Brent and I are determined to find our child. We know he or she is grown, but that's all we know and it's not enough.''

''Of course it's not. You'll do it, Blythe, I know you will. Oh, my dear sister, if there's anything I can do to help, you must let me know.''

''Thank you, I will.''

They talked for another ten minutes, each weeping quietly. Blythe finally cleared her throat. ''I don't want you to be unhappy about this, Tamara. Perhaps unloading one's burdens on someone else is a selfish act, but I cannot live with secrets ever again.''

''You must never think of yourself as selfish because you told your sisters, Blythe. If one's family doesn't stand by a person, who will?'' Tamara almost choked on a sob. ''How you must have suffered these many years.''

''I can't deny it.'' Blythe noticed the time. ''I'm keeping you on the phone much too long. I'll call you if and when Ray Grant comes up with anything.''

''Please do, Blythe. Promise.''

''I promise. Good night, little sister. I love you.''

''Oh, Blythe, I love you, too. Good night.''

As tired as she was, Blythe lay awake a long time that night. Her life was changing. She no longer had a secret and it was almost possible to think that she might be a happy woman someday.

''Oh, Brent,'' she whispered as she envisioned the *im*possible—her and Brent together, forever united and deeply in love.

It would never happen. Why was she torturing herself with foolish fantasy?

Chapter Sixteen

The first thing Blythe did the next morning was to contact a dealer of used office equipment. The man brought a truck, a dolly and a helper with a strong back to the house within the hour. He looked the cabinets over and made an offer that Blythe accepted without haggling. The dealer offered to buy the fireproof cabinet, too, but Blythe told him it wasn't for sale at the present. "Maybe later on," she added. "I'll let you know."

Brent arrived shortly after noon with an electric drill and a few other tools, but didn't immediately head for the basement. He had something to tell her.

"I heard from Ray Grant," Brent said. "He hasn't yet been able to locate Dr. Elijah Redmond, but he thinks the doctor is our best bet and he's concentrating his efforts on finding him."

The news only slightly disappointed Blythe, mostly because she never had had a whole lot of faith in Mr. Grant's investigation. Still, would another detective be able to do any better with so few facts to go on?

She couldn't bear to think that they had already found out

as much as they ever would, but the signs seemed to point i
that direction. If only the home hadn't shut its doors so lon,
ago, if only she knew some last names. If, if, if...

Well, she had plans—one, at least—and as soon as she wa
resettled in her home in Connecticut she would start her letter
writing campaign. Maybe she should tell Brent of her inten
tions, but that would bring about a discussion of when she wa
going, and why she was leaving before escrow closed on th
house, and it was just too complicated to talk about. Coul
she say, "I'm leaving because of you"? It was more true tha
not, but her system had calmed since Monday, and she reall
had no desire to hurt Brent, however deeply he had hurt he
that day.

She still didn't understand his giving up his whole day yes
terday to help her shred those records, nor was she completel
comfortable about his being here again today. But here he wa
and armed with the necessary tools to unlock that fireproo
cabinet, to boot.

Unquestionably, emotions of all sorts swirled within her jus
from looking at him. She would be taking memories to Con
necticut that she would be better off not having, but she woul
live with them, just as she'd lived with all the others for s
many years.

"Well, I guess you're ready to tackle that lock," she said
There was something in his eyes—a sadness—and it disturbe
her because his eyes had been so alive before she'd told hin
about their child. It was, she realized with a sinking sensation
one more reason to feel guilty.

But her guilt had already been so complex and burdensom
that this addition to its weight, while not trivial, really couldn'
make her feel any worse than she had before her confession

"Yes, I'm ready," Brent said quietly. "Shall we get to it?'
She nodded. "Might as well."

They went to the basement room, which looked stark an
bare with only one cabinet in it. A startling chill went up
Blythe's spine; she was suddenly afraid of what that fireproo
cabinet might contain. *You ninny! You don't have a clue to it
contents, so calm down.*

"What happened to the others?" Brent asked.

"I sold them this morning."

"That was fast work."

"Yes, well, there was little point in letting them just sit here."

Brent set to work, plugging in the electric drill and choosing a bit from several he had with him.

It was then that Blythe noticed that the drill was brand-new. "You had to *buy* this drill? I was under the impression you owned one."

"I do, but it's in Seattle. I don't carry tools like this in my car."

"And what did it cost?"

He sent her a dark look. "Since it's my drill, that's really none of your business."

Anger darted through her. "You bought it solely for this job! Dammit, why didn't you just let me call a locksmith?"

"And why don't you stop looking for reasons to argue?" Turning his back on her, he switched on the drill and applied the bit to the cabinet lock.

Well, she thought caustically, *he* certainly wasn't in the best of moods today. Feeling unduly chastised, she stood there with her arms folded and glared at him while he worked. The high-pitched humming of the drill grated on her nerves, and she left the room and waited in the larger one. Her thoughts naturally drifted to what might be in the cabinet. Again she felt a peculiar onslaught of fear. This time she couldn't get rid of it, and she nervously paced the room, waiting for Brent to finish.

The drill stopped running, and she thought that Brent would call out for her. But then she heard other noises, metal against metal, and realized he was still working on the lock.

Sighing, she continued to pace and to worry about what might be in the cabinet. Then the worry and dread in her system made her angry with herself, because she and Brent were probably going through this folderol for nothing. Why would there be anything in a file cabinet without a key? Probably all four drawers were empty.

"Blythe?"

Even though she'd been waiting for Brent to call her name she jumped.

"I'm done, Blythe. You can open the drawers now." Brent appeared in the doorway between the two rooms. "Did you hear me?"

She cleared her throat. "Yes."

"What's wrong?"

"Uh, nothing." She could tell he was puzzled about her not rushing to open those drawers, but she was too ashamed of her strange reluctance to explain it. Besides, she couldn't explain something she didn't comprehend herself.

Lifting her chin, she walked toward Brent and the doorway. He didn't move aside to let her pass, and she stopped and gave him a questioning look.

"You've been wanting to see what that cabinet contains and now you don't," he said. "How come?"

"That's absurd," she scoffed. "Of course I want to see what's in it. If you'll let me get to it, that is."

Wearing a seriously thoughtful expression, Brent stepped back. She whisked past him and approached the cabinet. Her mouth was suddenly dry and her palms sweaty; fear and dread were upon her again.

But it was so silly, and unexplainable, and she forced herself to take the handle of the top drawer and pull it open.

"Well, for goodness' sake," she exclaimed, deeply shaken.

"What?" Brent asked, and moved to stand next to her.

"It's full of...of childhood mementos."

She began taking things from the drawer and handing them to Brent. Bound together with string were her old report cards and Sierra's and Tamara's. And scribbly little drawings they had done as children, and achievement and attendance awards they had received in school—everything they had ever brought home from school, it looked like, as the drawer was crammed full. When Brent's arms could hold no more, he set the things on the floor.

Blythe's eyes misted over. "I never saw my mother as sentimental, but she must have been,'' she said unevenly. She looked at the pile on the floor. "I—I don't understand this.''

Brent could see how unnerved she was, and he felt the strongest urge to pull her into his arms and comfort her. But he decided to reserve any comfort he might offer—and she might not accept—until after she had gone through the other three drawers.

"Check the next one,'' he said gently.

Blythe drew a shaky breath. Her hands weren't steady, either, as she slowly slid the second drawer open.

It contained baby clothes. "Oh, my Lord,'' Blythe moaned. Booties, tiny sweaters, blankets, dresses, all packaged separately in plastic wrapping, nearly filled that drawer. "Mother, couldn't you ever tell us anything?'' she said in a choked voice.

"Were these things worn by you and your sisters?'' Brent asked.

"I—I'm sure they were.'' She looked at Brent through tear-filled eyes. Forgotten was any hurt he had caused her. Forgotten was the hurt she had caused him. She was so glad he was here with her and that she hadn't had to see these things by herself that everything else seemed to have vanished from her mind. "Thank you for being here,'' she said tremulously.

He touched her hand, a small gesture that meant the world to Blythe. She gave him a watery smile, then opened the third drawer.

It contained Harry Benning's beloved first editions. Each book was stored in a specially designed box. "At least this makes sense,'' Blythe said with a long sigh.

Brent nodded. "Very good sense.''

Unable to imagine what she might find in the fourth and final drawer, Blythe sank to the floor to open it.

She saw a small stack of letter-size manila envelopes and nothing else. "What on earth?'' she mumbled, taking the first envelope to examine it.

Her eyes widened. In her mother's handwriting was her own name! Quickly she thumbed through the other envelopes and saw one addressed to Sierra and another to Tamara. There was a fourth envelope with nothing written on it.

Brent had his arm on the top of the cabinet and was leaning against it, watching her. "What are those?"

"I'm…almost afraid to find out." She looked up at Brent. "Three of them are addressed to my sisters and me. Individually addressed. They're…something from my mother."

Brent inhaled slowly. A message from a mother to her daughters was a kindly gesture, he felt. If the items in this cabinet were any measure, Myra Benning hadn't been as self-centered and uncaring as he'd been thinking.

"I wouldn't be too alarmed about them, Blythe. At least take a look at what's in your envelope. You might even be pleasantly surprised."

Brent's attempt at reassurance couldn't quite dispel the uneasy premonition Blythe was feeling. She had to check the envelope's contents, of course, but she wasn't at all eager to do so. Looking at it in her hand, she felt the seconds tick by.

Brent remained silent, though he, too, was becoming uneasy. He was, he realized, picking up very discomfiting vibes from Blythe, and they were altering his previous opinion of a mother's message.

Finally Blythe slowly pulled out a sheaf of handwritten pages. "It's a letter," she said with a noticeable catch in her voice. "Oh, God, Brent, I'm not sure I can read it."

He could no longer remain distanced from Blythe's pain. He'd tried everything imaginable to hang on to anger, and now he felt that he'd been cruel and coldhearted. He sat next to her on the floor and took the letter from her trembling hand.

"If you don't want to read it, then don't do it," he said gently.

Her teary eyes rose to his. He was back to being nice to her, and this time she had no wish to disenchant him. Instead she absorbed his concern as thirstily as a sponge takes on water.

"I'm so sorry," she whispered. "I've hurt you so badly."

"We've hurt each other, and I'm sorry, too."

"You were happy before we met again. Your life was good."

"It will be good again. I'll get through this, Blythe, and so will you."

"I...wish I were as confident about that as you seem to be." Despair brought tears to her eyes; she'd been "getting through" for so many years, and the thought of living that way for the rest of her days was disheartening.

Brent glanced down at the letter in his hand and noticed the greeting: "My dearest Blythe." What had prompted Myra Benning to write letters to her daughters that would not be read until after her death? Was it possible...? The idea was stunning and he was almost afraid of it. At the same time he realized that it made a certain amount of sense. Certainly Myra had died with secrets. Perhaps all of her secrets were in these letters. His pulse quickened.

"Blythe," he said, forcing himself to speak calmly, "maybe you should read this letter."

She looked confused. "I know I said differently not five minutes ago, but I've heard you say that your mother was a secretive woman. Maybe when she learned of her illness she, uh, she decided to reveal..." Brent was struck by despair himself and stopped talking. If he got Blythe's hopes up and there was nothing in this letter about the past, then the drop in her spirits could be devastating. "I'm sorry," he murmured. "I shouldn't be talking you into anything."

Blythe was staring at the letter. Her heart had started pounding. "What if Mother wrote something about my child? Is that what you're suggesting?"

"I shouldn't have brought it up."

"Yes, you most certainly should have!" She grabbed the letter from his hand and began reading. It was a long letter, and halfway through it, Blythe reached for the fourth envelope and pulled out some papers. Her heart nearly stopped beating. "This can't be true—it can't!"

Brent all but came unglued. He'd been watching her closely, nervously, and her exclamation was like a stab in the heart. *What* couldn't be true? What had Myra Benning put in her letter and that fourth envelope? He wanted to grab everything away from Blythe and ease her pain. He was so sorry he'd suggested that she read the letter that he felt sick to his stomach. But he couldn't grab anything; she was voraciously reading again.

Blythe finished the letter, then shoved it and the papers at Brent. "Read them," she said, and drew her knees up to lay her head on them. The sobs shaking her shoulders hit Brent hard, and he was torn between reading the letter and attempting to soothe her. "Read them!" she said again. "Read them now!"

With his stomach doing somersaults, he started reading. "No," he said hoarsely when the story began unfolding.

Blythe's sobs grew louder, more agonized. Then, without warning, she got up and ran from the room. "Blythe!" Brent called, and stumbled to his feet. He followed her upstairs, but was stopped by the bathroom door being closed in his face. "Blythe," he said helplessly. He stood there for several minutes, worrying about her. But who had a better right to bawl her eyes out?

Backing away from the door, he went to the kitchen and sat at the table, where he finished reading the letter, examined the documents and wept himself.

Never in his wildest dreams would he ever have guessed the truth. Never!

When Blythe finally came to the kitchen, she looked ravaged. She looked, in fact, as though she'd been to hell and back.

Brent felt as though a steel band was binding his chest. He drew in a labored breath, got to his feet and pulled her into his arms for a hug he needed as much as he'd ever needed anything.

She stood still and let him hold her, but she couldn't act as though she hadn't received the worst blow of her life. In her heart she felt sorry for Brent, who was an innocent party in all of this.

He finally leaned back enough to see her face. "You can't let this destroy you," he said in an odd, strained voice.

She saw his red eyes and knew he'd been in the same hell that she'd been in. "Neither can you."

"We need to talk about it."

"What is there to say?"

The defeat and listlessness in her voice concerned Brent. Somehow he had to pull her out of this frightening mood. "Why don't I make a pot of coffee?" He tenderly tucked her disheveled hair behind her ears.

She knew her rolling stomach would not tolerate coffee. "I'd like some herbal tea."

He led her to the table and sat her on a chair. "I'll make both. Where do you keep the tea?"

"It's in the same cabinet as the coffee." She knew she should help him, but she couldn't garner the strength, and she sat immobile and lifeless while he put the teakettle on the stove and prepared a pot of coffee.

Her eyes began burning again, and she moaned and covered her face with her hands.

He hurried over and knelt beside her, and though his own heart felt as splintered as hers must, he said softly, "Blythe, it's not the end of the world."

"No, it's worse," she said dully. But she dropped her hands and wiped her eyes with a tissue she'd pulled from her pocket.

"You can't look at it that way."

"How *should* I look at it? Do you think I should be happy over something so…so repugnant?"

"Maybe not happy, but aren't you a little bit relieved? At least you know the truth now."

"The truth," she said bitterly. "It makes me furious."

"I know, honey, I know."

His endearment snagged her attention, and she looked into his eyes. "You're trying to make me feel better when you feel like hell yourself. Oh, Brent." Gently she laid her hand on his cheek. "You don't deserve this."

He laid his hand on hers to keep it on his face. "Neith[e] do you."

For the first time in twenty-four years she felt the same. N[o] one deserved what she'd discovered today, not even a woma[n] who had given her baby away.

"I—I'm glad you were with me when I found the letters," she said in an emotional whisper.

"If I hadn't been, would you have told me about them?"

"I...think so. Yes, I know I would have."

Any doubts he'd had about loving her vanished so com[-] pletely in that moment it was as though they had never existe[d]. Should he tell her how he felt about her? Would knowing h[e] loved her with all his heart make her feel better? Or would [it] just make her feel worse?

"I would have told you," she continued. "I wouldn't hav[e] been able to let you go on searching for our child when [I] knew...everything." Tears filled her eyes again.

He wiped them away with a gentle finger. "If you cry, s[o] will I."

She tried hard to smile and said again, "I'm so glad you'[re] here."

"So am I." He attempted to smile, as well. "The water['s] boiling. I'm going to make you a nice hot cup of tea." Kissin[g] her palm, he laid her hand in her lap. "It's going to be a[ll] right, Blythe, I promise."

He stayed with her that night, holding her when she crie[d] aware of her every movement and sound because his own eye[s] would not close. Even though she had said there was nothin[g] to say, they had talked and talked before going to bed, seekin[g] solutions, and trading and discarding ideas.

He had urged her to read Sierra's and Tamara's letters, an[d] after she had, she'd told him, "They're almost exactly lik[e] the one Mother wrote to me. Would you like to read them?"

"No," he had replied, adding uneasily, "Once they rea[d] their letters they will know it all, too, won't they?"

"Yes," Blythe had whispered. "Brent, do I dare send them? Do I dare *not* send them?"

Those particular questions plagued Brent for hours that night, going around and around in his mind until he thought his head would burst.

About two in the morning Blythe whimpered, sobbed and snuggled closer against him. He hadn't been thinking of sex, but he was suddenly almost painfully aroused. He couldn't stop himself from caressing the woman he loved, and although he wasn't sure she ever came completely awake, they made wildly passionate love.

After that he slept.

Blythe opened her eyes and looked at the clock on the bed stand. She had slept until 8:00 a.m. In the next instant she realized that her pajamas were gone and that she was stark naked. So was Brent.

Then she remembered what they had done in the night, and a strange sort of peace settled upon her. She lay there thinking—there was so much to think about—until Brent woke up and said, "Blythe?"

She turned her head on the pillow to look at him, and said softly, "I love you. You don't have to love me back. I could never expect so much from you, but I had to say it at least once. I'm not looking, or even hoping, for your forgiveness. What I did will always be between us, I know that, but—"

He placed his fingertips on her lips. "Please don't do this to yourself. We both have to forgive and forget."

"How can we?"

"It will come, if we let it."

She looked into his eyes for a long time. He hadn't said that he loved her, too, but that was all right. At least he knew now she felt about him.

"Brent, what are we going to do?"

"Mail those letters to Sierra and Tamara."

Blythe's breath caught. "I have to, don't I?"

"I think so, yes. I would also make copies of those docu
ments to send with the letters."

Tears filled her eyes.

Blythe kept putting off mailing the letters, and Brent nev
once hinted that she should not procrastinate. He felt s
would do it when she was ready, and he wasn't going to pus
her into anything.

The days passed, and they saw each other often. When l
wasn't with Blythe, Brent was in his motel room working o
the Sunrise project, which he couldn't ignore even though l
wished he had nothing to do but be with Blythe right now.

Still, he sincerely believed that Blythe needed some spac
and time to work through what she must. She would som
times fall silent, and Brent knew that she was thinking of tho
letters and the fact that there were no longer any unanswere
questions about the past and their child.

He phoned Ray Grant from the motel and explained th
situation without discussing details. "So, we really don't nee
a detective now, Ray. But I'd like to thank you for everythin
Send your bill, and I'll put a check in the mail when I get it.

"This is an interesting case, Brent. I'm sorry I wasn't mo
help," Ray said.

"You did what you could."

To Blythe, Brent never mentioned Ray Grant, and sh
seemed to have forgotten they had even hired a detective.

But then there was so much on her mind it was a wonde
she remembered to get dressed in the morning. For one thing
even though Myra's letters were still a shock, Blythe reco
nized relief in her system. The worry and stress of unanswere
questions that had all but eaten her alive for so many yea
were gone.

Still, every time she saw the manila envelopes, which wa
often, as she had stacked them on the kitchen counter near th
telephone, a shiver went through her. Was she going to ma
them or wasn't she? Unquestionably, those letters would caus

Sierra and Tamara pain, and was it important enough for them to know the whole truth?

Blythe's biggest problem, she realized after a week of procrastination, was that there was no closure to the situation. For her it was still an open wound that she feared would never heal until everyone involved knew the truth. She brought up the subject with Brent one afternoon.

"Am I being selfish because I want...*need*...an ending to my story?" she asked. "Tell me honestly, Brent."

"You're feeling as though the whole thing just stopped without an ending?"

"Didn't it?"

"Well, yes, I suppose it did. But you know the ending, if you pursue it."

"No, I really don't. It could go any number of ways." Her heart skipped a beat. "It could go badly, couldn't it?"

Brent realized she was asking for solace, revealing to him her greatest fear, and even though he hadn't yet told her, he loved her too much to say anything that might hurt her.

"This is my honest opinion," he said. "There's nothing selfish about your needing closure on a twenty-three-year-old mystery." He gently touched her cheek. "You're not a selfish woman, Blythe. I believe with all my heart that you never have been. I believe that you've given to everyone much more than you ever got. May I cite an example? Who volunteered to stay thousands of miles from her own home to take care of her mother's estate?"

Blythe smiled wanly. "I think you might be a bit biased in my favor." Daily they were becoming closer; daily her love for him was expanding. Was the same thing happening to him? Dare she even think he might come to love her again? He was so kind to her now, so considerate. Was he forgiving and forgetting, as he'd told her they must?

"I probably am, but have you ever wondered how many people would even speak to a parent who had done to them what your mother did to you? Blythe, you will never convince me that you have a selfish cell in your body. If you need an ending, go for it. And count on your sisters' intelligence and love. You're not dealing with morons, you know.''

"I...never thought of it that way. You're right, Sierra and Tamara are exceptionally intelligent women.''

She made her decision. She would mail the letters, but not without first making a phone call to each sister. The arrival of those letters without some kind of warning could be devastating, and she couldn't do that to either Sierra or Tamara.

Chapter Seventeen

The phone calls were traumatic for Blythe. To each sister she said, "I found some letters Mother wrote to us, and I'm putting yours in the mail." Immediately Sierra and Tamara began asking questions, and Blythe couldn't hold back the tears that dribbled down her cheeks. "I'm sorry," she said huskily, "but I can't talk about it until you read your letter."

When she hung up after the second call, Brent pulled her trembling body into his arms. "Don't feel bad, Blythe. You did the only thing you could have done, the right thing."

"But it's so awful," she sobbed into his shirt.

"It's going to be all right, honey. We have to believe that." It was small comfort, but the only thing he could think of to say. He kept saying it until she stopped crying.

The wait was excruciating. Once those letters were posted, Blythe became edgy, anxious and so nervous she couldn't sit still for more than a few minutes at a time. Brent knew what she was going through and did everything but stand on his

head to try to get her to think about something else. Nothing
worked. She wouldn't leave the house, except for doing a little
yard work, and even then she carried the cordless telephone
around like an extension of herself.

"If Sierra or Tamara should call, I have to be here to talk
to them," she insisted.

"I know, honey, but those letters aren't going to be delivered the day after you mailed them."

Blythe looked pained. "I should have sent them one-day
service," she worried aloud. "Why on earth didn't I think of
that? I don't know if they'll be delivered in two days or five.
Sometimes the postal service is incredibly efficient, and sometimes it seems to take forever for regular mail delivery."

"I know," Brent said again. He used those words a lot these
days, mostly because he had no reason to disagree with anything Blythe said. But even if there was room for argument in
some of her comments, he couldn't bring himself to cause
even minor discord in their relationship. It was going well for
them and he wanted to keep it that way. Once this Benning
family crisis was over, he was going to tell Blythe that he
loved her, and to ask her to marry him. He would have already
done so if she wasn't so distraught. Since she was, he felt he
should bide his time.

Still, he worried about her. *She* was half-crazy worrying
about how Sierra and Tamara would take those letters, and
while that wasn't a trivial matter to him, either, it was Blythe
that concerned him most. The strain on her emotions affected
her appetite and she wasn't eating much. Nor was she sleeping
well. On the nights he stayed with her he often awoke to find
her downstairs drinking tea or walking the floor.

His biggest hope was that once Sierra and Tamara read their
letters, everyone involved would get on with their lives. Oh,
it wasn't going to be the same life they had all been living to
this point—he didn't try to kid himself about that—and he
definitely felt some of the same anxiety that Blythe did. But
it was different for him than it was for her, and he knew that
she understood that because of their many emotional conversations.

Blythe was aware of Brent's deeply rooted concern for her, which only made her feel worse than she already did. She hated causing him further distress, but she didn't know any way around it. She loved him with all her heart and tried very hard when he was in the house to act as though everything was fine. But since she could hardly force food into her mouth, and was suffering the worst case of insomnia of her life, her little act was pretty much ineffective.

Three days after she mailed the letters, her telephone rang in the late afternoon. Not that it hadn't rung during those three days. She'd had quite a few calls, in fact. But this was the third day, and intuition told her it was either Sierra or Tamara on the line.

With her pulse nervously jumping, Blythe stumbled over to the kitchen phone and picked it up. "Hello?" All she heard was sobs. Blythe's throat constricted so tightly she could hardly speak. "Sierra, please don't cry."

"Blythe…how can you…bear it?"

"It…it's almost a relief," Blythe said in a choked whisper. She cleared her throat. "Now, please stop crying and let's talk about it."

When Brent walked in an hour later, he found Blythe sitting in the den, pale, silent and still. "One of them called," he said intuitively. "Which one?"

"Sierra."

"How did she take it?" He sat next to Blythe on the small sofa and held her hand.

"At first she was…in shock. We talked about it, and I think she was feeling better when we finally said goodbye."

Brent put his arm around her and brought her head to his chest. They sat there for a long time, drawing solace from each other.

Another day passed, and another, and Blythe's spirits reached an all-time low. "Tamara's not going to call," she said with tears in her eyes.

"Honey, she could have written a letter instead. She'll contact you, I'm sure of it."

"I wish *I* were," Blythe said sadly.

On Monday, a full week after the letters had been mailed, Blythe got up early and went down to the kitchen to put on the kettle for tea.

Brent hadn't stayed with her last night and the house was very quiet. Too quiet, she decided. She knew he was trying to give her some space, and he also had his work to keep up on. But their relationship had changed drastically, and even though nothing had been said about a future together—he hadn't even said that he loved her—she felt in her heart that he did. He couldn't be so kind and caring if he didn't, and she needed him here with her, holding her during the night and sitting at the breakfast table together.

The doorbell pealed, startling her. It wasn't Brent ringing the bell, because she had given him a key to the house. But who else would be at her front door at six in the morning?

Tightening the sash of her robe, she hurried to the foyer to peer through the peephole. "My Lord," she whispered, and fumbled clumsily with the dead bolt. She yanked the door open and said weakly, "Tamara."

There were tears in Tamara's beautiful hazel eyes. "Hello, Blythe."

"What...how...? Oh, do come in." Blythe stepped back from the threshold, and as Tamara came in, Blythe saw the strange car in the driveway. "You didn't drive all that way, did you?"

"I flew to Spokane and rented a car."

Blythe shut the door. "You must have traveled all night. Come to the kitchen. I've got water heating for tea. Would you rather have coffee? Give me your coat. I'll hang it in the closet." She was flustered and couldn't help it. It hadn't occurred to her that Tamara might show up like this.

Tamara took off her dark blue coat and hung it in the foyer closet herself. "You look beautiful, Tamara," Blythe said, taking in her stylish dress and pumps.

Tamara tried to smile. "You look like you just got up."

Blythe's laugh was feeble, but it was better than tears, which were stinging her nose and eyes something awful. "I did."

They went to the kitchen. "Sit down," Blythe said. "Tea or coffee?"

"Tea, please."

"I only have herbal tea," Blythe warned.

"That's what I drink at home. I developed a fondness for it when I was...pregnant."

"The babies! Who's looking after your babies?"

"Their father."

"Oh, my goodness, really? Can he manage to take care of three babies?"

"Well, Stubby is there, too. I told you about Stubby, didn't I? He's more friend than employee, but Sam hired him years ago to help out with the ranch. Anyway, he loves the babies and is wonderful with them. Sam will manage very well with Stubby's help. Besides, I'm only going to be here for today. My flight home leaves at five this afternoon."

"And you'll be traveling most of the night again," Blythe said quietly.

Tamara wiped her eyes. "I...I had to talk to you...in person." She sank to a chair at the table and covered her face with her hands. "Now I don't know...what to say," she said with a sob.

Blythe moved around the table and laid her hand on Tamara's shoulder. "If it's any consolation, neither do I," she said as the tears she'd been fighting finally got the better of her and ran down her cheeks. "But I'm so glad you're here," she said huskily. "So very glad."

Tamara dropped her hands from her face and looked up at Blythe. "I always thought you were so beautiful," she said in a choked voice. "I always felt something special for you."

"I...I've been so afraid you would hate me."

"Why would I hate *you*? My God, if I were going to hate anyone... No, I don't mean that. I still love Moth... Blythe,

I don't know what to call her now! I don't know what to call you! My whole life was a lie!''

The teakettle began whistling, and, crying quietly, Blythe prepared a pot of tea. She brought cups and saucers to the table, along with the teapot, and then sat down.

"I knew this was going to be hard on you," she said sadly. "I debated for days about whether I should mail those letters. They were in a fireproof cabinet.... Oh, that's neither here nor there. Tamara, before I told Sierra and you about my past, I had decided that I could never live with a secret again. I think that's the real reason I had to mail Mother's letters.

"I have this picture in my mind of Mother putting those letters in the cabinet and thinking that we would find them together. I've asked myself a million times why she felt it necessary that we know the truth after she was gone, and I have no answer."

"I think she did it for you. She owed you, Blythe."

"Didn't she also owe you?"

"I don't know. Did she? She raised me as her daughter, and she had some strange ways. But she was good to me and I never doubted that she loved me. But I would imagine that you've had a lot of doubts about her having loved you."

"Some," Blythe admitted. "During the bad times I doubted everything and everybody. During the bad times I *blamed* everything and everybody, when I had only myself to blame. I wasn't a child when I got pregnant, Tamara. No one forced me to run home and let Mother take over my life."

"I'm looking at you and trying to grasp the fact that you are my mother. Blythe, it's—it's…" Tamara broke down and sobbed into her hands.

"I know," Blythe said gently. This beautiful young woman that she'd believed to be her sister was the child she had given birth to twenty-three years ago. "They didn't let me see you," she said raggedly. "After you were born I heard you crying, and they wouldn't let me see you. They wouldn't even tell me if my baby was a boy or a girl."

Tamara got up and walked to the counter to take a handful of tissues from the box sitting there. She wiped her eyes and blew her nose. "How did she pull it off, Blythe? How did she fool everyone so easily?"

"I've thought about that a lot. It was quite simple, actually. She set up a disagreement between herself and Dad that never happened, and she went to Colorado. The home I stayed in during my pregnancy was just across the state line in Utah. She visited me every so often, and she appeared to be pregnant, an easily created disguise. She was there when I delivered, and the adoption was obviously prearranged, because she took you with her when she left. Then she stayed in Colorado for another few months to make it all look completely logical, and finally came home."

"And she altered my birth certificate to indicate that I was born in Colorado. The copy you sent of the original proves that. And the copy of the adoption papers you also sent..." Tamara's voice trailed off. "She always acted so properly," she said bitterly. "And she wasn't proper at all. She was deceitful, and cruel, and—"

Blythe broke in. "I believe she suffered over it, Tamara."

Tamara's eyes widened. "How can you be so kind?"

"Let me show you something." Blythe got up. "It's in the basement."

Tamara followed her downstairs to the small basement room, empty except for that one large fireproof cabinet. Blythe pulled open the top drawer. "Take a look."

Tamara complied, and her astonishment mirrored Blythe's the day she'd finally seen what the cabinet contained. "I can't believe she kept all this stuff," Tamara exclaimed.

"Now look in this drawer," Blythe said, pulling open the second drawer.

"Baby clothes! Ours?"

"I believe so. Tamara, in her own way she loved all of us. We cannot drive ourselves crazy thinking anything else."

"You've forgiven her!"

"More every day. Dad, too. And it feels good, Tamara, so damn good to finally let go of it all."

Tamara's eyes got teary again, and she stepped close to Blythe and put her arms around her. Blythe bit down on her lip, but she couldn't stop the tears that filled her own eyes, and the two women—mother and daughter—stood there with their arms around each other for a very long time.

"Would you like to meet your father?" They were upstairs in the kitchen again, this time eating some breakfast.

Tamara almost stopped breathing.

"You don't have to if it would make you uncomfortable," Blythe hastened to say.

"I think I do have to," Tamara said, although she was obviously uneasy over the idea. "Yes," she said after a moment. "I would like to meet him."

"I'll call him."

"She's *there?*" Brent was suddenly as jumpy as a drop of water on a hot skillet. "When did she come?"

"This morning. Brent, she wants to meet you."

"Uh, I'll be right over." Hanging up, he sucked in a huge breath. He was scared to death.

"Tamara, this is Brent Morrison. Brent, this is Tamara." The introduction was as simple as Blythe could make it. She had deliberately avoided the words *sister, father* and *daughter*.

Tamara held out her hand and smiled, albeit wanly. "It's very nice meeting you."

Brent suddenly felt like bawling. This beautiful young woman was his daughter. His daughter! He took Tamara's hand and pulled her forward in a hug.

"I don't think we need to stand on ceremony, do you?" he said huskily, stepping back to look into Tamara's eyes. "You're as beautiful as your mother."

Tamara's smile got warmer. "Thank you."

In a few minutes she was showing Brent pictures of her triplets. "They're wonderful," he told her. He grinned at Blythe. "Do you know what these babies make us, Grandma?"

Blythe laughed. "Yes, Grandpa, isn't it fabulous?"

They spent Tamara's remaining hours in Coeur d'Alene together, and by the time she had to leave they were all talking at once and having a wonderful time.

Tamara hugged each of them at the door. "Now, I insist you both come to Texas for Christmas. Sierra and Clint are coming, and it's going to be the very first Christmas that all of us will be together."

"We'll be there," Brent said.

When Tamara drove away with a toot of the car horn, Brent put his arm around Blythe and they stood on the sidewalk and watched until her car was out of sight.

"She's incredible," he said softly.

"Yes, she is," Blythe said with an emotional catch in her voice. "Now I know what was bothering me after Sierra and Clint's visit. Sierra and I stayed up the night they were here. It was when I told her about our past. She asked how old our child would be now, and I said twenty-three. Her first reaction was to say that was how old Tamara was. It went completely over my head at the time, but the next day something started nagging at me and I couldn't figure out what it was." Blythe sighed. "How could I have been so stupid? I should have been able to put it all together years ago."

"You're weren't stupid, you were trusting. Come on, let's go inside."

They walked into the house holding hands, and Blythe poured two glasses of wine, which they brought to the den and sat down to drink.

"Are you happy now?" Brent asked hopefully.

"I should be, shouldn't I?" After a hesitation she said, "Yes, of course I'm happy. It's over. I can hardly believe it. It must be even harder for you to believe."

"Well, I never would have guessed the truth, that much is certain."

"I do feel stupid, you know. There were signs that would have led to the truth, and I overlooked every one of them."

"Don't do that to yourself, Blythe. You trust people, and the ability to trust is a God-given gift."

She looked at him for a long time. He was so very, very

special to her, the father of her daughter, the man she would love for the rest of her life. And all along, when he should have been hating her, he'd tried to make her feel better about herself. If nothing else, she owed it to him to try.

She smiled. "Maybe I'm just looking for something else to worry about. I'm so used to living with a knot in my stomach, I'm apt to fall apart without it."

Brent sat back in his chair and chuckled. "I think I know what you mean."

"Oh, I just thought of something I can worry about."

"What is it?"

"Whether or not you're going to ask me to marry you," she said teasingly.

"Well, let's do something about that right now," Brent exclaimed. And he slid off his chair and got on his knees in front of her.

She became flustered. "Brent, I was only kidding!"

He was no longer chuckling, laughing or even smiling. "But I'm not." He took her hand. "Blythe, I love you with all my heart. Would you do me the honor of becoming my wife?"

It was what she had been praying to hear, but she could not give him an immediate answer. "Brent, are you positive? I'm sorry, but I have to know. Have you been able to forgive me?"

He answered quietly. "I've thought so much about forgiveness, Blythe. I think now that your confessing what you believed to be a great sin was harder to forgive than what you'd actually told me. I was knocked out by it because it was so obvious you'd told me about it to stop me from loving you. But you know what I believe now? I think the real reason you told me was because you couldn't let me love you *without* my knowing that we'd had a child."

"That's…an exceptionally kind perspective," she murmured. "I'm not sure it's true, or that I deserve such consideration."

"What *do* you deserve, Blythe? Eternal condemnation? Ostracism? Maybe you should be exiled from everyone who loves you."

She fell silent and thought of all the years she had lived with self-condemnation, and of how she had almost completely cut herself off from her family. Self-imposed exile. Maybe if she hadn't withdrawn into herself the way she had she would have unearthed the truth long before this.

"I've paid the piper long enough, haven't I?" she asked huskily.

"I'd say so." Brent relaxed and smiled. "So, are you going to marry me?"

"Yes, my darling, yes." She leaned forward and pressed her lips to his.

They were married two days later.

Brent decided that they needed a honeymoon. He felt that Blythe, especially, needed a change of scene, and he presented her with his plans shortly after the ceremony. She readily agreed, and a few days later they boarded a plane bound for Seattle. They stayed in Seattle for two days so Brent could show his wife the sights, and while he was there he put his house up for sale. They hadn't yet decided where their permanent residence would be, but he knew it wouldn't be Seattle.

Blythe enjoyed seeing the Seattle area. She had never been happier, nor more beautiful, because her inner tranquility created a radiance about her that astounded and pleased Brent. This was the way he'd wanted her to be since their reunion, and he, too, radiated utter and complete joy.

Their next journey was a flight to Hawaii, and for two weeks they relaxed in a gorgeous condo on Maui. They ate in marvelous restaurants, played in the swimming pools and on the beaches, went to luaus and several times danced until dawn at a fabulous night club that overlooked the rolling surf. One day they shopped, and Brent bought anything and everything that Blythe even hinted at liking.

"Stop!" she finally said with an adoring laugh. "Brent, this honeymoon is already costing a small fortune. You can't buy me everything we look at."

He kissed her right where they were, in a delightful little

shop filled with very expensive items. "My love, the one thing you are never to worry about is money."

She arched an eyebrow. "Did I marry a rich man without knowing it?"

Brent laughed. "Rich enough so that you'll never need to worry about finances."

Blythe laughed, too. "Well, maybe I should tell you about *my* money."

"Did I marry a rich woman without knowing it?" he asked teasingly.

"I think that well-off is a better description than rich." Blythe took her husband's arm. "Let's talk outside."

They slowly strolled down the street. "I told you about my first marriage," Blythe said quietly. "And about Richard's death." Because Brent had been curious, one evening she had told him everything she could remember of her short-lived first marriage. She realized now that she'd omitted a few things, not deliberately but simply because they hadn't seemed important at the time.

"What I didn't tell you was that Richard had inherited a nice sum of money on his twenty-first birthday, and he left it to me. There were also two large insurance policies on his life. I was the beneficiary."

Brent was silent a moment, then he grinned devilishly. "In that case, sweetheart, *you* can pay for the honeymoon."

She playfully socked him on the arm, and they giggled like two kids all the way back to their condo.

They'd been back in Coeur d'Alene a week when Blythe noticed Brent's restlessness. "Darling," she said "You don't have to keep me company every minute of the day. I know you have work to do."

"It isn't that, sweetheart. It's…something else."

She could tell he had something serious on his mind. "Come on," she said. "Let's take our coffee to the den and talk."

They sat in facing chairs, and Blythe sensed an unusual nervousness in her husband. She sipped her coffee and set the up on the table next to her chair. "All right, out with it," he said. "If something's bothering you, I want to know what it is."

Brent sat back and looked at his wife. She was especially beautiful this morning in a royal blue robe, and he loved her so much that he wondered how he had ever thought himself happy before meeting her again. He knew in his soul that she loved him in the same enduring way, but he couldn't help worrying about how she would take this conversation. He had, after all, been putting it off far too long.

He cleared his throat. "Well, it's this. I don't want us living in this house."

Blythe became quite still. "The house makes you uneasy?"

"I don't feel at home here. I knew I wouldn't, and I should have told you how I felt about it before this. But you were counting on my buying it, and I hated disappointing you." He waited for her response.

She drew a breath. "All right, I can accept that. We don't have to live here. Do you have somewhere else in mind? Connecticut, perhaps? My home there is quite nice. I think you would like it."

"I don't want us living in Connecticut, either," Brent said evenly.

"Really. Well, I guess I can accept that, too. Are you thinking of moving back to Seattle?"

"No." Again Brent cleared his throat. "I'm thinking about..." He leaned forward. "Blythe, I'd like to design and build a house that will be strictly ours. Do you understand what I'm saying?"

"Yes," she said. "You'd like a house that doesn't trigger any bad memories for either of us."

"That's it, exactly. Of course, what we have to decide now is where we want our new house to be built."

She became thoughtful. "I would like to continue teaching, but I'm sure I could get accredited in any state, so that's not a problem. What about your work?"

"I can set up a home base for my work anywhere. The new house I'd like us to have isn't about my work or yours. It's

about us. Now, I'm going to have to be in Coeur d'Alene until
the Sunrise project is completed, at least a year, and I like
Coeur d'Alene. But how do you feel about it? You grew up
here. Maybe you're anxious to get away from it.''

"No...not at all," she said slowly. "Not anymore, at any
rate." She looked at her handsome husband. "Brent, if you're
thinking of building our new home in Coeur d'Alene, it's fine
with me."

"You're absolutely positive? Blythe, if you have the
slightest doubt, I want to hear it."

"I don't. I've always liked Coeur d'Alene and—" She
stopped talking because he had sprung from his chair and was
pulling her up for a fervent hug.

"Oh, how I love you," he exclaimed. "Blythe, we are going to have the best marriage ever!"

"Yes, we are." She snuggled against her beloved husband
with a sigh of pure contentment.

It was that night in bed that Blythe began thinking about
the house. She nudged Brent. "Are you awake?"

He chuckled. "I am now." He wrapped his arms around
her and started to kiss her.

"Darling, I need to talk to you about something," she said
a second before his lips touched hers.

"Oh. I thought you wanted my bod."

She laughed. "I do. I always will. But I've been thinking
about this house. Sierra and Tamara each own a third of it
and...and we have to do something so they receive their
share."

"An easily solved problem, sweetheart. We'll put the house
on the market again."

Blythe frowned. "What if it doesn't sell?"

"It will. Honey, it's no more your responsibility than
theirs."

"But I feel it is."

"Okay, how about this? If it doesn't sell by Christmas, I'll
pay Sierra and Tamara for their share of the house's value.
We'll get the money back when it does sell."

Of course, she thought with enormous relief. She should have thought of that herself. Only she would never permit Brent to write those checks, *she* would do it.

She snuggled against her wonderfully generous husband and sighed happily. Then she yawned. "I'm getting sleepy. Do you know something? I really *don't* have anything to worry about anymore."

He laughed. "Wait until you have to start choosing colors for our new house. And cabinets and appliances and lighting fixtures. You'll have lots to worry about, believe me."

She laughed, too. "But those will be fun worries." After a moment she asked, "Won't they?"

"Yes, my love, those will be fun worries. And we'll share every one of them."

He kissed her tenderly, then passionately.

It was a long time before they slept.

Epilogue

Christmas Eve had been a joyous occasion. Blythe had adoringly watched Brent holding their grandbabies, loving them as she did, and her heart had overflowed with warmth and happiness. Now the babies were asleep and the husbands had gone to bed. Blythe, Sierra and Tamara were alone, wearing their nightclothes and sipping wine in Tamara's living room.

There was such peace in the house that Blythe felt emotional. She was with her family. It didn't matter if they were sisters or mother and daughter. The three of them were family and they loved each other.

"Dinner was delicious," Blythe said to Tamara. "You're a wonderful cook."

"Well, I didn't used to be," she said with a laugh. Her smile became a bit poignant. "My life is so different than what I'd planned."

"Do you miss your job?" Sierra asked. "Your career?"

"At times, but usually I'm so busy with the babies I don't have time to think of anything else. And, of course, I'm so happy with Sam that I would never change a thing."

"I know what you mean," Sierra said softly. "I never dreamed marriage could be so wonderful."

"I feel the same about Brent," Blythe said. "We're very fortunate women, aren't we?"

"Yes, we are," Tamara agreed.

They chatted on while they sipped their wine, and then Blythe got up. "I have something for each of you, and Brent and I agreed that I should give it to you tonight." She pulled from the pocket of her robe two envelopes and gave one to Sierra and the other to Tamara, then resumed her seat.

"Well, for heaven's sake," Sierra exclaimed while staring at the check in her hand. "Blythe, did you sell the house?"

"Yes," Blythe said. It was true; the house had finally sold. "I had started thinking it would never sell, and then out of the blue came a cash buyer. That sum includes your share of the life insurance, the sale of the car and furniture and the cash in the bank. Mother's estate is now officially closed."

Tamara was looking at her check. "Sam and I can do a lot with this money. Blythe, thank you."

"You're very welcome. Well, I could use one more small glass of wine, and then it's bedtime for me. What about you two?"

"Sure, why not?" Sierra said.

"I want more wine because I have a toast to make," Tamara said. When their glasses were filled again, she stood up. "This isn't going to be a speech, so don't panic and run," she said. "But there's something that needs saying." She paused a second, then blurted, "I'm glad my parents finally got married!"

Blythe and Sierra broke up, and the three of them laughed until tears ran down their cheeks.

"Okay, that was a joke," Tamara said while wiping her eyes. "But this isn't. There was a time when the three of us hardly knew each other. Now we do, I couldn't be happier and my toast is to us." She held up her glass. "To the Benning women!"

"Hear, hear," Sierra said, with her glass in the air.

"To the Benning women," Blythe echoed. They each took a swallow of wine, and Tamara sat again.

"I'd like to say something, too," Blythe added. "It's abo
Mother and Dad." She looked at Sierra, then at Tamara. "M
I?" They both nodded.

"No one is perfect, although Myra and Harry Benning tri
very hard to make people see them that way. Mother w
especially conscientious about the appearance of perfectio
We all grew up knowing that, although I didn't really reali
it until I was older.

"But I think we have to face the fact that they didn't d
everything wrong. It's very strange that they could have bee
so deceitful and still have instilled in us the virtues of hones
and decency, but they did it. Perhaps it was their secrecy th
makes me despise secrets. Perhaps it was their deceit th
makes me despise deception, trickery and lies."

"You really have forgiven them," Tamara said quietly.

"Completely," Blythe said softly. "Can't you?"

"I've been trying to. Sam and I have talked about it man
times. His own family...well, he had no love at all as a chil
and his opinion is that any child who is loved really has noth
ing to complain about. Not that he doesn't understand ho
traumatic it was to learn that the woman I believed my who
life to be my sister is really my mother." Tamara suddenl
covered her mouth with her hand, but she couldn't cover th
sound of giggles. "It...it just...struck me...as funny," sh
gasped.

Blythe and Sierra looked at each other, and they starte
giggling, too.

"I...I'm sorry," Tamara gasped between giggles.

"Don't be," Blythe managed to gasp between her own gig
gles. "It *is* funny."

"It...it's like...a soap...opera," Sierra gasped.

They laughed until they were weak, and then they sat ther
with silly grins on their faces. "Well, *this* has been an expe
rience," Blythe finally said breathlessly. "Maybe we shoul
sell our story to the movies and make a million dollars. W
could include Sierra's amnesia, and Tamara having triplet
and...and..."

They were off again, laughing so hard they couldn't speak at all.

"Okay," Blythe said, taking in a big breath. "It's funny now, but it wasn't funny before. Not for any of us. But, damn, I'm glad we can laugh about it!"

She looked at Tamara. "There's one more thing I'd like to say. Mother could have let you be adopted by strangers, and instead she devised that elaborate scheme so you would remain in the family. I think it's something we should remember and be thankful for."

Tamara's mouth fell open. It was a moment before she could speak. "I never thought of it that way. Oh, you're right, Blythe. It *is* something to remember and be thankful for. The Benning legacy is love."

"So," Blythe said softly, "maybe you can forgive her, after all."

"Yes," Tamara said with tears in her eyes. "Maybe I can."

Blythe got to her feet. "I am now going to go to my room and crawl into bed with my handsome husband. I would suggest you two do the same."

"Crawl into bed with your handsome husband?" Sierra said innocently. "Is there room in your bed for the four of us?"

Laughing again, Blythe went to each woman and hugged her. "You're bad, both of you. Good night."

In her assigned bedroom, Blythe tossed her robe aside and crawled into bed. She tried not to jostle it so she wouldn't wake Brent, but she always slept next to him and she slid over so they would be close.

"Did you have a good time with Sierra and Tamara?"

"You're awake. Oh, Brent, I'm so happy I could explode, or something."

He turned over and put his arms around her. "I opt for the 'or something,'" he whispered in her ear.

She smiled. "Have you been lying here thinking naughty thoughts?"

"You'd better believe it." He worked up her nightgown and began playing between her legs. "How does this feel?"

She spread her legs farther apart. "Like heaven on earth," she whispered throatily. "Oh, do that some more."

"This?"

"Yes, that." In seconds she couldn't lie still. "I'm going to…" she moaned, and she did. But she knew it was far from over.

She was right. They made love until she was weak and trembling. Then, sated and tired, husband and wife lay in each other's arms. "Merry Christmas, my love," Brent said in a drowsy voice.

She glanced at the clock. It was after midnight. "Merry Christmas, darling."

Sighing happily, she closed her eyes. Her last lucid thought before sleep took her was about perfection. She had attained it without deceiving anyone, without hurting anyone.

And she never had those awful dreams anymore. "Thank you, God," she whispered.

* * * * *

Silhouette® SPECIAL EDITION®

AND BABY MAKES THREE:
THE NEXT GENERATION:

The Adams men and women of Texas all find love—and parenthood—in the most unexpected ways!

Bestselling author Sherryl Woods continues to captivate with her popular series about the headstrong heroes and independent-minded ladies of charming Los Pinos, Texas:

November 1998: THE COWGIRL & THE UNEXPECTED WEDDING (SE #1208)

Could fit-to-be-tied cowboy Hank Robbins convince mule-headed mother-to-be Lizzie Adams to march down the aisle?

December 1998: NATURAL BORN LAWMAN (SE #1216)

Justin Adams was a strictly by-the-book lawman—until he fell in love with a desperate, devoted single mom on the run!

February 1999: THE UNCLAIMED BABY
(Silhouette Single Title)

The family saga continues with a passionate, longer-length romance about a fateful stormy night that changes Sharon Adams's life—forever!

March 1999: THE COWBOY AND HIS WAYWARD BRIDE (SE #1234)

Rancher Harlan Patrick Adams would do just about anything to claim stubborn Laurie Jensen—mother of his infant daughter—as his own!

Available at your favorite retail outlet.

FOLLOW THAT BABY...

the fabulous cross-line series featuring the infamously wealthy Wentworth family...continues with:

THE MILLIONAIRE AND THE PREGNANT PAUPER
by Christie Ridgway
(Yours Truly, 1/99)

When a very expectant mom-to-be from Sabrina Jensen's Lamaze class visits the Wentworth estate with information about the missing heir, her baby is delivered by the youngest millionaire Wentworth, who proposes a marriage of convenience....

Available at your favorite retail outlet, only from

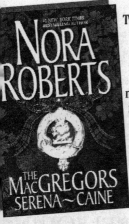

COMING NEXT MONTH

#1219 A FAMILY KIND OF WEDDING—Lisa Jackson
That Special Woman!/Forever Family
When rancher Luke Gates arrived in town on a mysterious mission,
he had everything under control—until he lost his heart to hardworking
ace reporter Katie Kincaid and her ten-year-old son. Would Katie still
trust in him once she learned a shocking secret that would forever alter
her family?

#1220 THE MILLIONAIRE BACHELOR—Susan Mallery
During their late-night phone chats, Cathy Eldridge couldn't resist
entertaining a pained Stone Ward with tall tales about "her" life as a
globe-trotting goddess. Then a twist of fate brought the self-conscious
answering-service operator face-to-face with the reclusive millionaire
of her dreams....

#1221 MEANT FOR EACH OTHER—Ginna Gray
The Blaines and the McCalls of Crockett, Texas
Good-natured Dr. Mike McCall was only too happy to save
Dr. Leah Albright's ailing kid brother. And, as an added bonus, the
alluring, ultrareserved lady doc finally allowed Mike to sweep her off
her feet. But would their once-in-a-lifetime love survive the ultimate
betrayal?

#1222 I TAKE THIS MAN—AGAIN!—Carole Halston
Six years ago, Mac McDaniel had foolishly let the love of his life go.
Now he vowed to do anything—and *everything*—to make irresistibly
sweet Ginger Honeycutt his again. For better, for worse, he knew they
were destined to become husband and wife—for keeps!

#1223 JUST WHAT THE DOCTOR ORDERED—Leigh Greenwood
A hard-knock life had taught Dr. Matt Dennis to steer clear of emotiona
intimacy at all costs. But when he took a job at a rural clinic, struggling
single mom Liz Rawlins welcomed him into her warm, embracing
family. Would Liz's tender lovin' care convince the jaded doctor he
truly belonged?

#1224 PRENUPTIAL AGREEMENT—Doris Rangel
It was meant to be when China Smith blissfully wed the only man she
would *ever* love. Though Yance had proposed marriage for the sake of
his son, an enamored China planned to cherish her husband forever and
always. And she wasn't about to let a pesky prenuptial agreement stand
in her way!